I0575535

DAUGHTERS OF HESTIA

MARCELLA STRANG BIXLER

To my father, Norman T Strang,
whose unrealized dream I am now completing

To my mother, Patricia,
for her love and support

CHAPTER ONE

Sweet Goddess, I'm finally back.

Not home, but the closest I come to it these days. After three weeks in the backcountry of Eremos, I'll finally get a shower, a hot meal, and a bed, even if it's just a company bunk.

At this distance, the entrance to the base is barely visible. It looks like a small crack in the sandstone cliff face, surrounded by an expanse of orange-yellow desert. But it's big enough inside to house a few hundred workers—not to mention the dining halls, the equipment bays, and the ships that transport all this ore off-planet.

I transmit my identity codes to the base, then set the glider on autopilot, settling into the cracked leather of the pilot chair. It's hot in the cockpit, even with the tinted windows. My hair is sticking to the back of my neck, even though it's pulled into a ponytail, and I can feel the stickiness of dried sweat underneath my bra. The cooling unit broke down a few days ago. That's typical of these freeworker companies since they're always skimping on maintenance of their equipment. It was the same with the solar suit they'd issued me, the one with the worn-out seams. There was no way it could handle the levels of radiation that Eremos emits during the daytime, so I'd decided to work at night on this field run. I'd slept in the desert caverns during the day and gathered specimens once the sun went down.

Anyway, I hadn't minded working at night on this expedition. The view had been beautiful, with Eremos's two big purple moons rising over the starlit mountains and the empty desert glowing in the moonlight. My only companions had been the wind and the small desert creatures out foraging. I've always liked the quiet. But, even for me, it had been too much after a while.

I never would have pictured myself living this way, back when I first left home. But there weren't too many ways to make a living once I left the Legion, at least not legal ones. And I couldn't go back home to Hestia. I'd picked up a few useful skills, but most of them weren't transferable to the civilian market. So I've just cobbled together jobs like this one. They don't require much skill, but they don't pay much either.

The speaker crackles, signaling an incoming transmission. "Codes received. You're cleared for arrival to bay C." The station agent sounds like he's from the Eastern District. After all this time working with other freeworkers, I've gotten to know the accent. "Welcome back, by the way."

I don't recognize his voice, but I smile back anyway. It's nice to talk to someone, anyone, after all this time. "Thanks. So, what's for dinner in the chow hall tonight?"

"Let me see. Hmm... It looks like lizard stew."

That wouldn't be my first choice. But I guess that eating from the local supply is cheaper for the company. "My first hot meal in three weeks, and I get lizard stew?"

He chuckles. "Sorry, I guess you're out of luck."

"Ah well, maybe tomorrow night. Thanks anyway..."

"There's tequila, though."

"Ah, thank the Goddess for small mercies."

I've never been much of a drinker, but every little pleasure counts.

The glider seems to take forever to reach the base entrance, but finally the gate opens, and my glider eases into the entrance bay.

I open the cockpit doors, letting in the cool, damp air, luxuriating in the chill. A few other landers are parked nearby, but there's no one else around. I'd like to hit the showers, but I'll need to log in all the equipment and specimens before I can relax.

I'm bending over a specimen bin sometime later when I hear a familiar voice behind me.

"Hey there, Vesta!"

Not the first person I wanted to see. I straighten up, arrange my face, then turn around. "Varnon, how's it going?"

He flashes me a smarmy grin, his teeth white against tanned skin. He's a good-looking guy, with thick blond hair and a nice build. Friendly. A little too friendly, actually. He'd tried to flirt with me before I headed out, but I'd brushed him off. Something about him bothers me. I get the sense that any warm female body that's available is good enough for him, which isn't exactly flattering. But then, I never have gotten used to the casual hookups that are part of the freeworker lifestyle. Too much a contrast to how I was raised on Hestia, I guess.

I force a smile. "I just have to get finished here, then hit the showers. You know how it is." I go back to stowing the samples in the collection units, hoping he'll take the hint.

"You want to get some dinner once you get cleaned up?" I hesitate, and his grin slips. He clears his throat. "A bunch of us are getting together."

Maybe he isn't trying to hook up after all, just being friendly. I certainly can't look too alluring, covered in the residue of three weeks' worth of dirt and sweat.

"Sure, that sounds great."

"See you after your shower." His grin is back—a leer, really—as he looks me up and down, then saunters away.

I roll my eyes, then turn back to checking in my equipment.

*　　*　　*

My assigned dorm is a single sleeper unit, so it's cramped, but at least it's private. That's better than most of the barracks I've bunked in over the last few years. The bed is furnished with the green-blue scratchy blanket and flat pillow that for some reason every company barrack is equipped with. But it's also got a shower with real water. You can't always count on that in a barracks situation, especially on a desert environment like this one.

The shower nozzle will only give out a warm trickle, but it feels good to finally get clean. I only get three minutes, barely enough time to rinse away the soap, before the water shuts off.

I wrap myself in a towel and pad over to the mirror next to the bunk. It's been a while since I've seen my own reflection.

My face looks thinner than I remember. I've always thought my face was too pointy, with a sharp chin on a wide face. But now it looks almost gaunt. My skin used to be a rich olive, but the color has faded from too many night shifts. I never used to like my figure back when I was younger, with my narrow hips and small chest, but I've gotten used to it over the years. I like my hair though. I haven't bothered to cut it since I left the Legion. Now it hangs, thick and dark, past my shoulders.

Everyone back home used to say that I looked like a twin of my brother Simon—a female version anyway. He's only a year older than me. And we have the same green eyes, the same olive skin, the same tall, narrow build. I wonder what Simon looks like now.

Don't think about home, I remind myself. That's an essential part of the freeworkers' code. Well, it's more like a survival strategy. It's better not to think about what you've left behind.

I dig through my dresser to grab a fresh jumpsuit and sandals, then brush my hair and weave it into a loose braid. I'm a bit leery now about joining Varnon in the dining hall, but I'm suddenly starving, and it will be nice to have some company when I eat for a change.

The dining hall turns out to have a friendly ambience. Music is playing in the background and there's a pleasant hum of conversation. Workers are gathered at tables, a few at the bar, some lounging on couches. I spot Varnon, sitting at a table with some other workers I don't recognize.

I call up the meal of the day from the automat. The station agent was right about the menu—lizard stew. But a hot meal is still better than field rations.

Varnon summons me to his table with a lazy wave. He pulls out the chair next to him, his arm draped over the backrest, as he introduces me around.

I forget the workers' names as soon as they say them. I wish that wasn't true, but it's an effect of the freeworker lifestyle. Peoples' names tend to lose their importance when you know that you'll never see them again. The only reason I remember Varnon's is that he's made such a pest of himself.

The woman across from me has wild, frizzy hair and a low-cut blouse. Her thigh is pressed up against Varnon's. She lifts her glass in greeting and drains her shot of liquor.

The man next to her has dark skin, short gray hair, and a general impression of being old and tired. "How long were you out for?" he asks me.

"Three weeks," I answer around bites of my stew.

They seem friendly enough. But that might be due to the tequila bottle on the table that's nearly empty. They've been drinking awhile, if their glassy eyes are any indication.

"Oh, I hate the long ones," the frizzy woman says. "I did three months once, back on Vitrea. Longest dry spell I ever had." She nudges Varnon with her thigh, but he just looks annoyed.

"I did longer than that on a border outpost once…" Varnon says. *This will take a while.*

It's always the same when you meet other freeworkers. We always talk about the planets we've been posted to, the strange things we've seen. It's less painful than talking about the homeworlds we've left.

"What do you think? Is the GRIP going to crack down on Nexia?" the gray man asks.

The GRIP is shorthand for the Republic. Their full name is the Galactic Republic in Perpetuity. That's some legal term, "in perpetuity." It means "forever." The GRIP loves its contracts, its authority. And I guess that forever is how long they plan to be around.

The frizzy woman shrugs. "I hope they don't send in those Enforcers. I can't stand those Legion thugs!"

Varnon and other guy murmur their agreement.

I haven't told anyone on this posting that I used to be an Enforcer in the Legion. It's not something that makes you popular. Most freeworkers either hate them or fear them, usually both.

"It was just a contract violation." Varnon waves his hand in dismissal. "The GRIP sent its warning. I'm sure they'll back down."

The conversation shifts to talking about contracts, complaining about the company rules, the typical stuff that temps grumble about.

"What about you?" I realize they're all looking at me expectantly. "Are you re-upping your contract?"

I wipe my mouth with my napkin. "I'm not sure." This company was better than most. But ever since I'd left Hestia, I hadn't found anywhere I'd wanted to stay for too long.

"You should re-up, Vesta. Stick around." Varnon's arm slides over my shoulders as he leans in closer. His breath smells of tequila.

It's been a long while since I've had any physical companionship. My body might crave the release, but it's not worth it, especially not with a guy like Varnon. Anyway, I learned my lesson back in the Legion—don't get involved with men you work with. Since then, the

6

few times that I've hooked up with someone have always been between postings, somewhere I'd never have to see him again. It's easier that way.

I pull away and Varnon lets his arm drop. I hope he got the message. But it's probably better to get out of here and into bed before he forgets.

The frizzy woman pours a shot of tequila and pushes the glass my way. "Come on, it's time to have some fun."

"Thanks." I take the offered shot and down it. It burns on the way down. I feel an immediate craving for more, but one drink is my limit. That's probably another vestige of my upbringing on Hestia. Drunkenness was frowned upon there.

I push my chair back and stand up. "Thanks, but I'm beat. I've got to get some rack time."

"Aw, come on," Varnon says. "Let's keep the party going." But the frizzy woman looks happy that I'm leaving. She's probably hoping to get Varnon for herself. I head out before he tries again to convince me to stay.

I'm at the door to my quarters when I hear Varnon's voice behind me. "How about some company?" He jogs up to me, standing too close. His eyes are glassy.

"Go home, Varnon." I use my forceful voice, the tone that says not to mess with me. He backs away for a second, and I turn away to open my door and slip inside.

When his hand grips my shoulder, I act on instinct. Pull him forward, use the momentum to spin him around, pin his body against the wall with his arm twisted behind his back. I haven't forgotten my Legion training. At least, my body hasn't.

"What the hell, Vesta." Varnon's voice is muffled from his face being mashed against the wall.

I hadn't meant to pin him, just make him leave me alone, but my training kicked in before I could think. I back up a few steps, releasing him from the hold. Still, I stay alert just in case he tries something.

7

He turns around slowly, rubbing his elbow. He doesn't look drunk anymore. The adrenaline rush must have sobered him up.

"What'd you do that for? I'd have left you alone if you'd asked me to."

"Sorry, Varnon." I choke on the words, but I don't want him holding a grudge. He knows a lot of people on base. I don't want him smearing my name. "I just reacted. No hard feelings, right?"

He just stands there rubbing his arm, looking confused. "Where'd you learn to do that, anyway?" I can tell when he puts it together, a look of dawning horror on his face. "You were an Enforcer, weren't you?"

Just what I don't need. If he tells the others, no one will want to work with me. He might as well just say that I'm a spy for the GRIP. That's what they'll all assume anyway.

He backs away, holding his hands out before him in a gesture of supplication. "Look, I don't want any trouble with the Legion..." Then he darts away around the corner.

So that's it then. The whole base will know about my Enforcer history by morning. There goes my contract. There's no way the company will keep me on if no one will work with me.

I cover my face with my hands and rub my eyes. Goddess, I'm so tired. So many postings, so many temp gigs, and for what? So I can just leave again.

But I can't let that kind of thinking set in. If there's one thing I've learned since I left home, it's that I have to keep going, just take one day at a time.

I take a deep breath and let it out in a long sigh. OK, so I can just get a good night's sleep, then figure out my next steps in the morning.

I punch the entrance button to the dorm room, then settle down on the bunk. Goddess, it will feel so good to finally get some decent sleep.

Then I notice the blinking indicator light on the comm unit next to the bed.

What now? I put the message through.

Legionnaire Vesta. Report to District Command Headquarters with all haste.

No, no, no.

Legionnaire was my rank in the Legion. I've always known they could call me back, of course. It was part of the agreement when I'd enlisted. At the time, I'd been too desperate to care. I'd been eighteen years old, a naïve kid, full of dreams about how I could serve in the Legion and finally get the status I'd never had on Hestia. I thought I would get education, training, travel, glory. Needless to say, that's not how it turned out. The Legion doesn't want outworlders in its higher ranks. They want auxiliary troops, ones who know their place and who follow orders.

They were probably calling me up for that Enforcement Action, the one those other freeworkers had been talking about. The Legion must need some extra troops for an offensive. It won't matter that I'm still under contract to this surveying company; the authority of the Republic supersedes any other contracts. I have to go. There's no getting out of it.

I reluctantly key in my acceptance, then settle back on the pillow. At least I can finally get some sleep. Maybe things won't seem so bad in the morning. I close my eyes, am just starting to drift off, when the comm tweets again. Bleary-eyed, I sit up to squint at the message.

Summons confirmed. Transport in route to current location. ETA 2000 hours.

Someone's in a hurry for my arrival. I try to make sense of it with my tired brain. If I was being called to re-enlist, I'd expect an order to rendezvous with a general troop carrier, not a fast transport to District Command headquarters. That place was for high-ranking officers, not ex-enlisted Enforcers like me.

I'm starting to get a bad feeling in the pit of my stomach. I don't know what this summons is about, but I have a feeling that it isn't good. Legion Command doesn't pay any notice to outworlders like me. If I've come to their attention for some reason, I'm most likely going to end up regretting it.

*   *   *

I'm waiting in the loading bay for the shuttle when I start to notice the stares. There's a crowd of freeworkers nearby, most of them waiting to ship out on the local freighters that will bring them to their next assignment. At first, I think it's just my own paranoia, jittery nerves from my confrontation with Varnon. But then I see people whispering to each other, looking back at me with increasingly hostile glares.

Varnon must have talked. It doesn't take long for gossip to travel on a base this small. I glance nervously at the chronometer, hoping my shuttle gets here soon.

A big guy walks over, a few others trailing behind. I stand up to face him.

"I hear you're an Enforcer." His eyes are narrowed in hate. The other freeworkers are all watching, waiting for a fight.

I know enough not to appear weak. I cross my arms, my eyes scanning the watching crowd. "Not now. Not for years. That's in the past."

He doesn't look reassured by that, not that I blame him. All of us freeworkers have a past we'd rather forget but being a Legion soldier… that's not an easy one to forgive.

"Who sent you?" A tall, bulky woman walks up from behind the big guy. She looks even more ready to do some damage. The other freeworkers are moving closer. Soon I'll be surrounded.

"That shuttle coming in," someone yells. "It's a Legion cruiser. She's lying."

I move back to get a better view, dropping into a fighting stance. There's no way I can take them all.

The bulky woman lunges toward me. I pivot and throw her to the ground, turning back just in time to deflect the big guy's punch. I strike him on the jaw, dropping him. The others are surging forward, a mass of anger.

A whoosh of air blows them back. I sag in relief.

I know that sound. A Legion shuttle, moving into the landing bay.

"Clear the area," a tinny voice commands over the bay loud-speaker. "Authorized passengers only."

That pilot just saved my ass.

The freeworkers back away to make room for the shuttle. The big guy and bulky woman get to their feet, but they keep their distance. They wouldn't dare challenge the Legion directly.

"Watch your back, traitor," the big guy growls. Then he's gone, filing out of the landing bay with the rest.

I take a shaky breath, facing the ship as the ramp for the Legion crafts unfurls. A crewman, dressed in the distinctive blue and silver of the Legion, posts at the entrance. I've never been happier to see that uniform.

"Legionnaire Vesta?" the soldier asks, looking askance at my plain jumpsuit and worn boots. "Time to board."

I grab my duffel and follow him quickly up the ramp. I settle down in the nearest empty seat, slumping with sudden exhaustion as the doors shut behind me.

This is it. Three years of struggle as a freeworker, wiped out in one day. By morning, the onlookers here will have spread the story all through the freeworker network. I'll be branded a Legion spy, unwelcome anywhere.

Whatever the Legion is summoning me for, I hope it's worth it, because there's no going back now.

CHAPTER TWO

A day later, I'm touching down on the surface of Medina, the planet where Legion Command operates its district headquarters.

I'd been the only civilian on the vessel that brought me here, surrounded by the silver and blue of Legion uniforms. They'd kept to themselves, looking askance at my plain jumpsuit and worn boots. But I'd appreciated the chance to rest in a comfy bunk and enjoy the good food. Whatever my complaints about the Legion, the physical perks weren't one of them.

The Legion troops push past me down the landing ramp, until I'm left standing alone in bright sunlight, squinting against the glare. The Legion installation sprawls out in front of me, blending artfully into the landscape of meadowlands with mature oak trees and a creek. I'd heard that the GRIP liked to show off its nicest terraforming environments here. This must be one of their showpieces.

I walk up to the entrance of the facility, a massive archway of white stone. The words "In Defense of the Republic"—the motto of the Legion—are carved into the stone. Underneath are idealized depictions of Legion soldiers, enforcing order and fighting against the covenant-breakers. I used to believe in that once.

When I joined up, they'd promised me that I could earn a commission. I'd been naïve and desperate enough then to believe that false promise, had sweated and strived for it. But I'd soon discovered that outworlders don't earn commissions, nor do they get training at the officer academies or the right to travel to the Core Worlds. My options in the Legion were just as limited as back on Hestia, although for different reasons.

The elaborate archway leads into an enormous foyer, the ceiling rising up higher than any building I've ever seen. The whole place is built from pure white stone, with little flecks of pink and gray that shimmer in the light. I stand there for a minute, gawking like a tourist until my wrist unit pings, directing me to whatever rendezvous point I'm being summoned to. I wish I could linger here, just pretend I belong. But I can't keep Legion Command waiting.

I follow the route on my comm, slowing to take it all in. There are windows everywhere along the route, opening to views of beautiful landscapes, a showcase of the GRIP's world-building options. All the main templates are here—desert, agricultural, ocean worlds, all the main areas needed for resource extraction. Some pleasure models are on display too, the kind for the ultra-rich to enjoy in their leisure time. I've heard about those, but it's nothing like seeing them in person. This must be a taste of what the Core Worlds are like.

When I reach the rendezvous spot, I'm confused because there's no one else here except a woman in uniform. She has a pinched expression on her face.

"Legionnaire Vesta, I presume? Your shuttle was late." She smiles tightly. "Admiral Sennon will see you now."

I get a sick feeling in my stomach. "Wait, I'm supposed to meet with an admiral?"

The door behind her slides open, and she returns to her console, dismissing me.

My heart is pounding, but I march forward with as much authority as I can muster. The admiral's office is a smaller version of the main entrance, large and high-ceilinged, ringed with windows. My footsteps echo in the open chamber as I walk toward him. He's bent over a console, ignoring me. I stand silently, waiting to be acknowledged.

He's older, maybe late-middle age. His hair and beard have gone silver, but he still looks stout and strong. The uniform insignia shows three stripes, the highest rank.

Finally, the admiral looks up, studying me with keen blue eyes. "Legionnaire Vesta."

I'm not actually a legionnaire anymore, but I'm not going to correct him.

"Admiral, sir." I bow to the waist, as required by his rank. My heart pounds harder, wondering what he'll say next. This whole situation doesn't make sense.

The doors open behind me with a whoosh of air. I hear booted footsteps approaching from behind at a steady, fast clip.

"Ah, Commander Joren."

The other man walks past me to join the admiral at his side.

Commander Joren looks younger than I'd expect for an officer of his rank, maybe in his early thirties. He has brown eyes under thick brows, and a wide, stern mouth. My first thought is that he looks like one of those images that you see on a Legion recruitment advertisement, the kind that show the ideal soldier. With his square jaw, broad shoulders, and impeccable posture, he certainly looks the part. The only flaw in his image is the length of his dark brown hair, which curls over his neck—not regulation.

I offer him the required bow, then focus my eyes just above the admiral's head, imitating a respectful soldier standing at attention. It's better to play it safe until I know why I'm here.

The admiral clears his throat. "You have been summoned here to be considered for a contract, Legionnaire. One that is important to the welfare of the Republic at this time."

The welfare of the Republic. During my time in the Legion, I had heard that justification given for all kinds of actions, most of them hurtful to the vassal worlds.

"I wouldn't have chosen you for this mission, but Commander Joren asked me to recruit you."

My eyes dart over to Commander Joren, looking for any clue as to why he would do such a thing. I don't know him. And, as far as I know, no one should know much about me, especially the Legion. I've done a good job in the last few years of staying anonymous.

Joren's mouth and jaw are stiff, like he's irritated at something. I can't imagine what I could have done to piss him off.

"You enlisted during the Consortium conflict, did you not?" The admiral adjusts something on the console, projecting a stream of images into the air. The largest hologram is an image of me from my Legion training, back when I first enlisted. My head is freshly shaved, my eyes wide and innocent.

The admiral squints at the text beneath my picture, reciting the details of my service record. "You fulfilled the standard seven-year contract. Basic combat and weapons training. Some limited experience in communication and data collection. Failed to re-enlist." The admiral looks away from the display, pinning me with his sharp blue gaze. "Most troops in the auxiliary units choose to stay on after their initial enlistment. So, why *did* you leave the Legion?"

There's no way I'm answering that honestly. "It wasn't what I expected, sir."

The admiral's upper lip curls in a faint sneer. "No, I can't imagine that a life in the Provinces could have adequately prepared you for the Legion."

I set my jaw at the contempt in his voice but say nothing.

"Her training should be helpful on this mission, sir," Joren's voice, a warm baritone, lacks the tone of contempt that I would expect of an officer of his rank. Not that I've ever met anyone of that high of a rank before. "She has some experience in the science sector and planetary exploration. Some facility for languages."

This Commander Joren knows too much about me. That should bother me. But it almost sounds like he's taking my side against the admiral.

The admiral straightens, tugging on his uniform jacket. "The Legion has a proposal to make, one you would be wise to value. Your services are required for a mission that will be in service of the Republic. In return, your status in the Republic will be upgraded from temporary worker to permanent resident. You'll receive permission to access the central districts. You will become eligible for the training academies and the higher tiers of employment. Something more than an outworlder such as yourself should ever deserve under normal circumstances."

I can't believe what he's offering me. The admiral is dangling in my face all that I've been dreaming of since I left Hestia—status, permanency, belonging, respect, freedom. But they don't offer privileges like that to people like me... not without a price. And, from what I know of the Legion, it's not going to be a price that I'm willing to pay.

"And what is the nature of this mission, sir?"

The admiral smiles, a small, tight movement that doesn't reach his eyes. "This mission is in need of a local guide."

The images hovering above the console change, transforming into a display of a planet—a beautiful world of blue oceans, white clouds, and two large landmasses to the north and south.

Hestia. My home planet.

A feeling of frozen horror settles into my body.

This is bad, very bad. Worse than I thought. There must be a conflict brewing between Hestia and the GRIP.

"Commander Joren will be leading this mission." Joren studies me closely, his brown eyes too perceptive. He can sense my fear, my hatred. "It won't be necessary for you to rejoin the Legion for this mission, but you will show the same conduct as if you are. Is that clear?"

I haven't agreed to anything yet, and the admiral is already demanding that I lick Joren's boots. But I won't do it. I won't do the GRIP's dirty work, not against my own homeworld.

"Before you answer, there are some details about the situation on Hestia you should be aware of." Joren steps over to the console and brings up some images on the data display. The images zoom in on the Northern Continent, focusing on the Caldera Mountain range in the far north. "The northern region of Hestia is exhibiting signs of a problem with its environmental systems."

I've never even seen a map of that region before, much less traveled there. I'd grown up in the South, like most Hestians. That's where we farmed, where the Capitol had been built. The North was for the herdsmen. We traded with them, but they'd always kept to themselves.

"I don't understand. If there's a problem with the environmental systems, why not just contact the Patriarchs?"

"Is that what the local authorities call themselves?" Admiral Sennon's voice holds a tone of contempt, as if amused by the pretensions of such commoners.

Joren's face tightens. "We did contact them... but they're not allowing access."

It couldn't be true. No one denies access to the GRIP. It's a breach of contract, grounds for an Enforcement Action. Everyone knows that.

"They're refusing?!" Oh Goddess, what if the Patriarchs really are hiding something on purpose, and the GRIP knows about it?

"They haven't directly refused," Joren answers, "but there have been delays in access. Enough to be grounds for an incident."

An incident. Such a polite word for the devastation that an Enforcement Action could bring to a vassal world like Hestia.

"We need a local guide, for discretion. To avoid a confrontation with the Hestian authorities."

So that's what they want. They want me to help the Legion infiltrate Hestia, to act as a spy against my own people.

I'll refuse. What can they do to me? The cold spear of dread down my spine is my answer. They are citizens, and I'm a freeworker. They can do whatever they want with me. But I won't spy against my own people, no matter what the price.

I face the admiral, trying my best to hide the fury and fear inside. "With all due respect, sir, I must decline this contract."

His face is a mask of shock. Then his eyes narrow, his lips thin. "Who are you to refuse the Legion?"

I look over at Joren, expecting the same look of disapproval. He's holding a tension in his shoulders and jaw, but he's looking at the admiral, not at me.

"I've given my answer." I offer a quick ceremonial bow to the admiral, then turn my back on them, walking quickly away, my heart beating wildly.

Footsteps follow me, then stop. Joren's voice calls out, "Are you sure about that?"

I stumble for a moment. Something in his tone of voice throws me off, like he knows something I don't.

"You still have family on Hestia."

At those words, I come to a dead halt. I turn to face him.

His expression is unreadable, his hands tightened into fists at his side. "I wouldn't want what happened on Telos to happen to them."

Telos. The memories implode inside me... the smell of burning flesh from the laser cannons, the roar of the war machines, the cries of the dying.

He knows that I was posted there. He knows that Hestia could be next.

I charge toward him, driven by a desperate fury. Goddess, how I hate him! How dare he threaten my home!

He stands his ground, imperious in his pristine Legion posture as I advance upon him, his eyes fixed on mine.

His eyes! I stop abruptly, my words forgotten. His eyes are not calm at all, but dark, and drowned in pain. His eyes seem to plead with me to listen.

The admiral steps forward, challenging. "Who do you think you are, acting like that to an officer? You should be jailed for such an offense."

In an instant, the warning in Joren's eyes is gone. He holds up his hand, stalling the admiral's tirade. "No matter, admiral. It's not important."

The admiral looks between us, seeming reluctant to let it go. Then he composes himself, settling back into his aura of authority. "Very well, commander. It's your mission. You can handle the discipline as you see fit."

"So," Joren holds his arms stiffly at his sides, his tone neutral. "Do we have an agreement?"

Damn him for doing this to me, for trying to make this my fault, for this whole impossible situation.

A painful pressure constricts my throat, a knot of unshed tears. I don't trust myself to speak. The sobs might come out instead. I nod my agreement.

"The voice program needs a verbal response to endorse the contract," the admiral goads.

I clear my throat. "Yes, I agree to the terms of the contract."

"Excellent. The terms are set." The admiral speaks the words with satisfaction, almost baring his teeth.

"You'll be staying here on base tonight." Joren's voice is careful, almost disinterested. "Your comm unit will direct you to your bunk. The mission begins in the morning. That is all."

I turn and walk out, subdued. I can feel Joren's eyes on my back the whole way, until the doors close behind me.

CHAPTER THREE

I sit on the dormitory bunk, dressed in a pair of thin pajama pants and an undershirt, drying my hair with a towel. The shower has relaxed my body, but my mind can't stop spinning.

It won't be long until I see Hestia again. So often I'd dreamed of going back, of seeing my family. I knew it would never happen, so I'd put such hopes out of my mind. Of all the circumstances to return, this has to be the worst.

The voices of off-duty enlisted personnel echo from down the hall. I'd passed them when I'd checked in to the barracks area. They were gathered together in the common area, playing games and drinking, relaxing in their off-duty time. That used to be me, once upon a time.

The door chime sounds, alerting me to a visitor. I look up at the display screen. It's Commander Joren, of course.

My stomach tightens in anticipation as I walk to the door.

He stands just outside the entrance, backlit from the dim lights in the corridor. He's not wearing his uniform jacket. His white dress shirt hangs open at the neck. His eyes move over my body, noting my undershirt and sleep pants, my damp hair. I feel a strange warmth in my stomach.

"I didn't mean to wake you." That warm baritone again.

A low roar of laughter comes from down the hall. He turns toward the sound for a moment, then back to me. He looks uneasy, as if he's doesn't want to be recognized. Interesting.

"I thought we were meeting in the morning?" I challenge.

"I wanted to talk to you first." He gestures to the room behind me. "Can I come in?"

I hesitate for a moment, then back up, reluctantly giving way. He walks slowly into the room, stopping several feet from me.

If only I'd put on my coat and my boots before I answered the door. I'm only wearing my night clothes, and I'm barefoot, so he's even taller than before. Although, with the mussed hair, the shadows under his eyes, and only half in uniform, he looks less intimidating, almost human.

I wave my hand in invitation. "So, talk."

His eyes study my face, as if searching for something. "Look, we're going to be working together for a while. We need to be on the same team."

Oh, that's rich, coming from him.

"But we're not. I'm only here because you threatened Hestia."

He runs his hand through his hair, lets out a frustrated breath. "I think you may have misunderstood my intention."

"I think your intention was pretty clear."

His eyes narrow, assessing. "My intention is to prevent war on Hestia. Would you have agreed if I hadn't?"

I snort, indignant. "You don't think the bribe was enough? The admiral seemed to think that I was for sale to the highest bidder." It stung to be seen that way, as if money and status was all I cared about. But then, everything is business to the GRIP.

"I could have told the admiral that a bribe wouldn't convince you."

"And how would you know that?" I challenge. But he's read my personnel file, studied up on my background. He knows too much about me already.

"I've been in a position of command for a long time. I've learned to read people." He leans forward, too close. "I can see that you want to help your home world. More than you care about yourself."

I hate that he presumes to know me. Even worse, so far he's been right.

"There's something more you need to know about Hestia." He shifts uncertainly. "I didn't get the chance to tell you before."

It's something bad. I knew it.

"A recon drone was sent out when the Patriarchs denied us access."

Of course. There's no way the GRIP would let their disobedience stand.

"The anomalies on Hestia are more serious than we thought. The weather has been showing disruptions. The crops may be affected."

On Hestia, the harvest is already underway. Somehow, no matter how long I've been away, I still keep track of the seasons there. If our family farm has been impacted, Papa must be struggling now. The familiar pang of worry and dread hits, the emotional reminder of home. But it's not just Hestia that will suffer if the crops fail. So would all the worlds that depend on its exports. That would mean famine on a large scale.

"If we can't get access with your help…" Joren hesitates, watching me carefully, seeming to weigh his words. "…then the Legion *would* be called in. That wasn't a threat, just a fact."

The GRIP would have to act, especially if the Patriarchs were involved in covering it up. Damn him for sounding reasonable. He acts like he would actually care about that.

I need to know if that anguish I saw in his eyes was for real.

"You still didn't answer my question," I challenge. "Why would you care about the Legion marching on Hestia?"

There's that look in his eyes again, just a hint of what I saw before. "Let's just say I've seen enough of what happened on Telos. I'd prefer a peaceful solution here. With your help, we can do that."

My resolve to stay detached is weakening, a desperate hope flaring up its place. "A peaceful solution. So... how exactly can we do that?" Oops, I'd said "we."

His voice quickens as he leans forward. "We've secured a small team of scientists—not Legion. They'll be coming on the mission to determine the source of whatever's happening environmentally down there. Figure out how to fix it."

"You think they can?" I want to believe him. Sweet Goddess, I do. But what if he's wrong?

"I'm sure of it. I've enlisted a terraforming scientist and a planetary engineer. They're from the Institute."

I've heard of the Institute, of course. Who hasn't? It's renowned as the center for all knowledge on the secrets of terraforming. The GRIP owns the process, and it controls the Institute. And only Citizens—the hereditary residents of the oldest settled worlds—are qualified to be there.

"And they're coming to *Hestia*?!" He may have been trying to reassure me, but the idea of the Institute coming to Hestia makes me even more uneasy. It doesn't make sense that an isolated settlement like Hestia could draw attention like that. "And what about the Patriarchs? What's going to happen to them?"

There's still the matter of their attempt to hide evidence. I don't want the ruling fathers of our government to bring any harm to Hestia, but I wouldn't mind if they were punished, either.

Joren's mouth tightens. "It's local politics. The Republic is feeling... forgiving... at the moment."

"Huh, I haven't known the GRIP to be forgiving."

His lips twitch. "That's fair. But it's only been a few years since the last Conflict. It's in everyone's best interest to avoid a military solution. Sanctions will be imposed. I can't say for sure until we know more, but it won't involve an attack."

I have no real reason to trust him. But something inside me, something from my gut, tells me that I should.

Joren's face softens. "Look, I'm not asking you to trust me, but I want you to know that we're not enemies. We don't have to be."

This must be the strangest situation I've found myself in since I left Hestia. Who would believe that a Legion officer would be talking to me—an outworlder—like this, as if my opinion or cooperation mattered? It seems too good to be true. But he's offering me an alliance. If it will help to save Hestia, I have to do it.

"OK. Allies, then." I reach out my hand to grasp his. Joren's hand, big and warm, covers mine, and I feel that curious feeling in my stomach again before I let his hand drop.

He takes a step back, clears his throat. "Well, then. I'll let you get some rest."

He turns to go, but then stops, turning back to me for a moment. "You know, you surprised me back there. I've never seen anyone stand up to Admiral Sennon like that."

Despite myself, I feel a smile pulling at my lips. "Yeah well, I've always wanted to put an officer in his place."

He grins, and a dimple appears in his cheek, his heavy brows lifting to show a warmth in his brown eyes. "I'm sure you have."

The door slides closed behind him. I settle back onto my bunk, curling up around my bent knees.

If what Joren is telling me is true, then Hestia is in more trouble than I thought. No matter how much anger I have toward Papa for what he did, I still love them. My brother Lucas may be hard-hearted like Papa, but not Simon. And not Britta or Agatha.

Mama would never forgive me for not helping however I can, even though she's gone.

No matter what my personal feeling are about Hestia, it's still my home. I've never found anywhere else that matters as much. And a whole lot of innocent people will pay the price if this problem isn't fixed, and quietly. I have to do my best for this mission, for Hestia's sake.

I know enough not to trust the admiral to follow through on everything he promised me, but I can certainly count on the danger to Hestia if this mission doesn't succeed. If there's one lesson I've learned from my time in the Legion it's this: The GRIP may not follow through on its promises, but it always follows through on its threats.

CHAPTER FOUR

The appointed meeting room is in the scientific wing, a long walk from the military barracks where I'd spent the night.

Joren stands by the window of the meeting room, deep in conversation with an elegant, dark-skinned woman. She has the look of a Core World Citizen with her shimmery, silken pantsuit and headful of shiny black curls. The woman moves closer to him, smiling flirtatiously, holding a long-stemmed glass of some exotic drink.

She calls out to an older man who is sitting alone at the meeting table. He looks up, an answering smile lightening his somber expression. The man has a lean, ascetic face, and a narrow, almost fragile, build. His short hair and neat beard is an unusual color—a rusty orange that matches his ruddy complexion.

Joren spots me standing outside. He excuses himself and starts walking over.

I hurry into the room. As I cross the threshold, I notice a woman leaning against the far wall. She wears a Legion uniform—a Security Officer rank, from her insignia. Her steely-gray hair is shorn close to the skull. Her wiry body holds a coiled tension, her weathered face regarding me with suspicion. I look away, trying not to show my unease. She's testing me, I can tell.

"Vesta," Joren calls out. His tone sounds different than last night, more impersonal. He's dressed in civilian clothes—a pair of loose trousers and a fitted short-sleeved shirt. Even without the uniform, though, he would be difficult to mistake as a civilian. He holds himself like a soldier—tough, disciplined—with a stance that I've never seen outside the Legion. His jaw shows the beginnings of a beard, the dark stubble just growing in.

I blurt out the first words that come into my mind. "Does the Legion know you haven't shaved?"

He looks taken aback, then rubs his jaw. "I'm getting ready for the mission. Don't Hestian men wear beards?"

"Most of them." My father and uncles always wore beards, thick and black. My brother Simon, though, had never sprouted enough facial hair to grow one.

Joren puts his hand on my shoulder, guiding me toward the others. "These are the scientists I told you about."

The elegant woman extends her hand in a graceful gesture. "Welcome, Vesta. I'm Dr. Kya, the energy scientist of this mission." Her voice is unexpectedly warm and her intelligent gold eyes have a teasing humor in them.

Joren gestures toward the red-haired man at the table. "And this is Dr. Sion, our terraforming specialist."

Dr. Sion rises from his seat, studying me carefully as he shakes my hand in the Imperial style. His eyes are keen, like those of a crow. "Ah, our Hestian guide." His words are clipped, a strange accent I don't recognize. "Welcome."

Joren indicates the uniformed woman standing stiffly by the wall. "And this is Lieutenant Darla, our security officer."

Darla approaches slowly, studying me with suspicion. "So, you're our Hestian, then?" From the tone of her voice, I assume that isn't a compliment. "The commander tells me you were an Enforcer." She emphasizes the word "were," highlighting the fact that I had left the Legion. "Most Legion soldiers are honored to serve the Republic. I suppose that outworlder recruits don't hold the same values."

I'd met too many mid-level officers like Darla back in my Enforcer days. They usually envied the officers above them and bullied the soldiers beneath.

Joren interrupts, his voice brusque. "Let's get started."

Darla smirks, then marches over to the meeting table, claiming a seat at the far end. Kya sits next to Sion, darting an amused glance at Darla. I wish that I could find Darla's attitude as entertaining. She's clearly going to be a problem for me.

"Before we get started," Joren begins, "I'm going to need you, Sion, to give Vesta some background information."

"Of course." Sion studies me curiously. "How much do you know about the terraforming process?"

Suddenly everyone's eyes are focused on me.

"Just explain the basics," Joren answers, saving me from having to admit my ignorance. My school on Hestia covered basic reading and writing, some math, a bit of history, but nothing more.

"Well," Sion sits up straighter in his seat, as if he's about to give a lecture to his students. "When a world is terraformed, the process happens in stages. All of these stages are accelerated when compared to natural processes. What would take millions or even billions of years to develop, we can create in decades." I had heard that much before. The details of worldbuilding are a trade secret, of course, but it's common knowledge that the Institute has some way of terraforming worlds in a short period of time.

"The first stage is the seeding of the atmosphere. That creates the water and the necessary conditions for life." The holo display changes, showing the image of a planet in the process of being terraformed, the atmosphere thickening, the rapid accumulation of water on the surface.

"The next stage is the formation of the land and shaping of the planetary crust. This relies on a process of advanced volcanism." I follow along, fascinated, as volcanic peaks spew forth lava, cracks in the planet's crust shifting.

"In the third stage, we introduce the life forms, plants, animals, and so on." The planet rapidly fills with green plants, trees, and flowers, a rich profusion too rapid to follow. And then animals, so many varieties of animals, are spreading out too, filling every niche. "When that process is complete, the planet is suitable for human habitation."

The displays fades away. "Which brings us to the anomalies on Hestia." Kya brings up a holo image of Hestia's surface. "The energetic disturbances are centered in this region here, in the northern mountains." She aims her light pen, pointing out the boundaries of the Caldera Range in the far North. "The energy readings are four times the intensity we should be seeing in this region. This is the epicenter, here. If you look at the topo map, it's coming from the interior of the largest peak in the mountain range."

These mountains are in the farthest reaches of the northern landmass. I've never even been much farther north than my family's farm. For how familiar I am with that region, it might as well be another planet.

"Let's move on to strategy." Joren pulls out a light pen, approaching the holo map display. He points to a small area on the Southern Continent, situated on the shore of the eastern ocean. This place is familiar, at least. "This is the Capitol of Hestia. It's also the location of the only space port on the planet." It was only after I left Hestia and joined the Legion that I realized how rare that was. I had taken the remoteness of our world for granted back then. "It's a small port. Mostly merchant ships dealing in raw goods. That will be our cover when we arrive."

That was a good cover story. There were a lot of inter-system trade ships that did business in the Capitol. Most of them were small operators, buying up grain, meat, produce, and other raw materials to re-sell on nearby systems. We'd likely arrive unnoticed.

"From there, we'll be traveling north, up through the farmlands, through this isthmus of land, and up to the Northern Continent." He traces the path north, following the Great Northern Road, which leads up to where the herdsmen live in the North. The Capitol is in the Southern Continent, on the eastern sea. A journey of that length will take about a week, maybe more.

Sion squints at the map. "How far is the Capitol from the mountains?"

Joren sighs. "It will be quite a journey, well over five hundred kilometers. We'll need some inside intel to blend in. That's why we have our local guide." He glances over at me, and so does everyone else.

Darla speaks up, her gravelly voice as rough as the rest of her. "I don't understand, commander. That's a rough journey. Why aren't we just putting down at the base of the mountains and trekking it from there, sir?"

Joren shifts uncomfortably, and so do I. I've never seen a lesser-ranking officer interrupt a superior like that. "We have information that access to the local airspace is being monitored. This operation is covert, so we travel overland."

Darla doesn't seem happy at the idea of the Legion deferring to an outworlder government. And I'm surprised by it myself. Joren had said the GRIP wanted to avoid hostilities, if possible, but that does seem out of character.

"Vesta, we could use your input to tell us about the Traders' District."

I clear my throat, stand up. I grab a light pen, bringing up a more detailed image of the Capitol. "OK, here's the port." The space port is located at the eastern edge of town, near the ocean. On the topo map, it shows the ring of the port walls, the blue of the bay, and the hodgepodge of streets in the Capitol laid out in a random order. "Just outside the walls of the port is the Traders' District. That's where we'll get lodgings." I remember that district well. I'd stayed there ten years ago, just before I left Hestia. "The off-world traders all stay in those few blocks. The rest of the city is just for locals…"

My voice trails off. This doesn't make sense. There's no way that off-world traders would ever travel outside the Capitol and into the interior of Hestia. So how would posing as traders help us in our mission? Unless…

Joren has already read my mind. "I've heard that some local traders travel up to the northern region?"

How does he know that? But yes, a small number of itinerant traders do travel up north on the Imperial road. They passed by our farm every summer when I was a child, trading tech and trinkets for food and drink.

"Wait, so you're saying that we disguise ourselves as Hestian traders in the Capitol? Then we can travel north until we reach the mountains?"

It just might work.

"Exactly," he grins. "What would we need to outfit ourselves for that cover?"

I scramble to come up with an inventory of what we'd need. A solar wagon. Maybe two. Mounts. Tents and sleep sacks. Food. Local clothing.

Sion studies the topo map, his eyes squinting at the geography over which we'll be traveling. "Mixed agricultural plains, then grasslands up north. We won't need to climb until we reach the mountains." He looks to me. "What kind of transport would we be using over that terrain?"

This is what Simon and me always used to talk about when we were teenagers, what an adventure it would be to go up north where the herders lived. I'd never met anyone who'd been up there. "The traders always use standard solar hover wagons. It's always better to have a couple of horses too, just in case."

Kya's dark eyes are wide. "We'll be traveling by wagon and horses?" She sounds mildly horrified. It's hard to imagine this refined woman riding in a solar wagon or sleeping in a tent.

Sion looks amused at her dismay. He steeples his fingers. "Horses are one of humanity's perfect ancestral animals. Although, I agree, I don't plan on riding one."

I look dubiously at them. "The hard part will be getting there undetected." Sion and Kya, with their more distinctive coloring— Sion fair, and Kya dark—would be noticeable outside of the Capitol. "It would be best if you both stayed out of sight in the wagons, at least once we leave the Capitol. Joren and Darla, you could both pass as Hestian." Joren's complexion is a little lighter than mine, but not too much that it would attract notice.

Kya rolls her eyes. "Are you telling me that we'll be hiding in this little hover wagon for five hundred kilometers?!"

"At least you don't have to ride," Sion says, amused.

"I'll have to do all the talking. Joren and Darla's accents will be too noticeable on Hestia. None of you know anything about Hestian culture."

"Agreed," Joren says. "So, let's decide on the route."

I turn back to the display, tracing a path through the Farm District. "This route will follow along the trade routes where the merchants usually travel. That way we can avoid the main roads and not attract attention." And there is another reason I am choosing this route—it avoids my family's land. We will be about thirty klicks east of the boundary of my family's property. That should give enough of a cushion so that we won't risk being seen by anyone my family knows. "The agricultural region spreads over the plains from here to here, over most of the settled areas. When we reach here," I indicate the narrower segment of land that is the gateway to the Northern Continent, "we'll be entering the Northern grasslands. Only the herders live there. There's not too many of them compared to the farmers in the South—at least that's what I've heard. We won't be likely to run into anyone once we get that far."

"You've heard? You don't know?!" It's Darla again.

"I've never traveled that far north. I grew up on a farm."

Joren gives Darla a warning look. "No intel is complete. We're lucky to have a native guide to get us this far."

Darla doesn't look convinced, but she stops talking. It makes me wonder about her lack of respect toward Joren's command, though. I expect her contempt toward me and toward Hestia, but a junior officer like Darla shouldn't have to be corrected in front of civilians.

"From there, it should be a clear shot across the Northern plains to the mountains. And that's when Kya and Sion will take over."

I settle back in my seat, letting out a breath.

So we just have to travel undetected for over five hundred klicks while we smuggle two Institute scientists and their equipment in a hover wagon.

Great. No problem.

"Hopefully it gets there in one piece," Kya says, looking concerned. "I won't be much good to you if my equipment is damaged."

"That reminds me," Joren says. "Vesta, I need you in the loading bay to help Kya and Sion with the gear."

That's a job I've done before, but I wouldn't expect these scientists to be doing something as basic as loading equipment. That's usually done by junior staff. But on a small mission like this, it looks like rank and status will matter less than it usually does in the Imperial system.

Joren looks around the table, focusing on each of us in turn. "I don't have to remind you how important this mission is. It's going to need every one of us to work together as a team." He seems to be focusing on Darla as he says that last part.

A team. I haven't been part of a team since I left the Legion. And before that, when I left Hestia and my family. If this mission is going to succeed, we're going to have to learn to rely on each other. From the glare that Darla gives me as she strides away, that isn't going to be easy.

CHAPTER FIVE

By the time I get to the loading bay, Sion and Kya are already securing the gear. Sion is carefully lashing down a large metallic object—it looks like a specimen container unit—while Kya looks on.

"I can help with that," I offer, jogging over.

Sion doesn't look up. "This research gear is quite delicate. We'd rather handle it ourselves."

Kya smiles kindly, as if to apologize for Sion. "We could use some help with the rest of it." She points at a cluster of boxes near the wall. "You could bring those over."

"Sure, no problem." I use the hover lifts to move the boxes into place.

"Remember Palius?" I look up, but Kya is talking to Sion. "I hope this gear holds up better than that."

"These models are sturdier." He pats the crate. "They should travel well enough."

She smiles, her cheek dimpling. "Better than me?"

"Well, my dear Kya, you do love your creature comforts."

She rolls her eyes. "It's only for a few weeks." Her tone is breezy, light, but I detect a note of nervousness underneath.

"This will be less time in the field than Cassia." But Sion, too, sounds tense. "We'll have the mobile sanitation module, solar cookers. Not very rough."

"Have you two worked together before?" I ask.

They both stop abruptly, a strange look on their faces, as if I've caught them out.

Kya recovers, smiles winningly. "A few times. I don't like to be away from home too often, though. My mates always miss me if I'm gone too long."

When she says "mates," I realize she must be from Cava. That world is well-known for their unusual kinship system, with families made from marriages of multiple partners with many shared children. I'd been shocked when I'd first heard of it, back when I'd just left Hestia, but I've realized since that most of the GRIP's worlds are nothing like Hestia. The GRIP doesn't much care about how people live, so long as they sent in their tithes and kept the trade flowing.

"So you're from the Core Worlds?" I ask, hoping to learn more.

"I'm from Cava," she answers easily. "And Sion here is from Vinici."

All of the Core Worlds are well-known, even legendary, to the rest of us. From what I can remember, Vinici was one of the original three colonies, second only to Patria. This is certainly esteemed company I'm keeping, especially in such an obscure region as this.

"We are not as infamous as Cava, I'm afraid," Sion answers in his patrician voice. "More traditional."

"Only one wife for Sion." Kya's voice is teasing, a dimple in her cheek. "But a son and daughter back home." She looks over at me. "What about you, Vesta?"

I feel awkward suddenly, as Kya waits for my answer. It must be this return to Hestia, bringing up the old feelings and expectations of home. On Hestia, I would have been married by now, and a mother many times over.

37

Before I can answer, I hear crisp bootsteps behind me. I turn, expecting Joren, but it's Darla, striding up aggressively, frowning at the crate of supplies I stowed.

"Are those the medical supplies?" she demands.

Kya points at the bins waiting to be loaded, looking amused. "They're over there."

Darla scowls in my direction. "I'm the medic on this mission. I'll expect those supplies to be intact when we land."

Darla is the medic? I can only hope that I don't get injured on this mission. I can't imagine that she has a gentle touch.

"What regiment did you serve in?"

This isn't an idle question. Darla must know I was in an out-worlder unit, the least valued in the Legion, fair or not.

"The fifty-seventh," I admit.

"Hmm," she sniffs. "Then you'll be used to low standards. But that won't be acceptable on this mission."

I grind my teeth to avoid answering her in kind. "I'll do fine, thanks."

"Still, you haven't served under a battalion commander before. An officer of the commander's rank will expect more of a soldier."

Then she strides off onto the ship.

Kya shakes her head, a smirk on her face. "I hate it when they give us a security stiff. She'll be difficult."

Sion asks for my help in moving the last of the gear onto the ship. As we're finishing up, I realize what's bothering me about what Darla said.

"What did she mean, about serving under a battalion commander?"

Kya and Sion exchange a look.

"Commander Joren, he *was* a battalion commander," Kya answers, uneasy. "During the Conflict."

That doesn't make sense. Battalion commanders oversee massive troop divisions, the kind that invade planets. There's no way an officer of that rank would be assigned to a small mission like this. And why would he not be of that rank anymore?

Sion puts down his tools, giving Kya a scolding look. "I would not mention any of this to Joren, if I were you."

I nod slowly. "Sure. Of course." During my time in the Legion, I'd learned how to follow orders and keep my mouth shut. I know better than to ask Joren any awkward questions about his past.

Kya and Sion start talking about their vacation plans, an obvious change of subject. Sion, at least, doesn't want to talk about Joren's past.

But I can't let go of my worries.

First, high ranking scientists like Kya and Sion are assigned to this mission, and now a disgraced battalion commander. This mission just keeps getting more complicated. I try to shrug off the feeling of foreboding settling in my chest.

*   *   *

It's just like it was in the Legion—hurry up and wait.

Joren and Darla haven't shown back up yet, so we're stuck on the landing craft. Sion and Kya are tucked away inside in the ship. I'm posted by the landing ramp, trying not to pace.

The landing craft is a K30—commercial, not military—but it's not too different from the troop ships used by the Legion. I'd made planetfall on those vessels enough times to remember. Back then, I would have been waiting around with the rest of my squadron-mates. We'd be joking around, telling stories—anything to get our minds off the coming mission. This time, though, I'll have to face it alone.

Joren and Darla finally arrive, Joren looking distracted as he walks past me onto the ship, disappearing into the cockpit to talk with the pilot. Darla comes up the ramp behind him, her face wearing a scowl that seems to be her customary expression. I wait awkwardly in the main compartment, trying not bounce or fidget.

Joren emerges a few minutes later, signaling everyone to circle up. Kya is dressed in the plain jumpsuit of a space trader. But somehow it still can't disguise her highborn manners, her graceful style. Sion looks mostly the same. He doesn't seem focused on appearance—too much in his head. He could easily pass as a ship's engineer.

Joren crosses his arms over his chest, his face held tight. "OK, so this is what will happen when we reach the port. You'll all stay on board as I liaison with the port authorities. I'll get the permits for our visit to the Capitol. That's when Vesta will be taking lead." I feel my tension ramp up. A lot is riding on me, especially at the beginning. "Once we clear the gate, Vesta will guide us through the trader's quarter. Any questions?" We all shake our heads. "OK, gear is ready. Let's get strapped in for planetfall."

We break apart, heading down to the transport area where our jump seats are waiting. I can't count the number of times I've done planetfall like this in the Legion. But this is different—this is Hestia. I'm glad to see my hands aren't shaking.

"Please don't tell me this the only thing holding me in place!" Kya holds up her harness straps, looking skeptical.

"You must be used to those luxury shuttles," I tease as I fit her harness down tight. "The kind that don't need jump seats."

I head over to Sion and check his harness as well. This was all part of the pre-flight routine, back in the Legion. We always checked our comrades' equipment before a drop. I head to my seat and get secured.

Joren is seated in the row behind me, giving orders to the pilot to get the craft underway. The ship begins to hum as the engines engage.

Outside the porthole window, I watch as the sun peeks out over the horizon of the planet, a corona of light signaling the arrival of dawn. The Southern Continent is visible through a scattering of clouds.

My eyes trace the contours of the continent, following the landmarks. There's the Capitol, next to the Bay of Ralda, with its familiar crescent shape. I follow that line northward, all the way to the border between the agricultural lands of the South and the narrow isthmus that connects to the Northern Continent. My parents' farm lies about fifty kilometers from there, just south of Lake Nume.

What are they doing right now, I wonder?

Papa will be out in the fields. Probably not doing the work himself now, not at his age, but he'll be directing the workers. And Lucas and Simon will both be working the land too. Britta and Agatha must be married by now. They will have moved away to join their husbands' farms. I must have nieces and nephews by now. I've missed it all, ten years' worth of living. I'll be passing so close to them on our way north. Close, but not close enough to see them again.

This is really happening. I'm actually going back home.

Lightning-fast, the memories flash. My mother dying, her hands cold and stiff as we prepare her body for burial. My father, his face stern and disapproving, as the Patriarchs take me away. Me hiding at the spaceport, searching frantically for a ship to take me off-world. Then, looking back at Hestia from the window of the shuttle as I'm leaving, knowing I would never see my home world again.

I can't do it. I can't go back there, only to lose my home all over again.

My hands claw frantically at the straps of my harness, my breath ragged.

"Whoa, whoa!" Joren's voice sounds far away. I hear the clicks of a harness being unfastened. And then he's crouching in front of me, his hands gripping my shoulders, looking steadily into my eyes.

"I can't go back!" I can barely get the words out. I don't have enough air.

"Breathe." His voice is soft, firm. "Don't think. Just breathe."

Joren's eyes focus on mine, his steady gaze like an anchor to my churning thoughts. My attention collapses to the rhythm of my breath as it fills my belly, to the beat of my heart as it gradually slows.

I use the sensations to ground my thoughts, feeling the warmth of Joren's hands on my arms, the pressure of my fingers as I grip the hard curve of his bicep. I watch the dark brown stubble lining his jaw, his eyes fixed on mine—brown, with a gold ring around the irises.

Within a minute or so, my heart rate slows down. I can think clearly again. Joren's eyes search mine, looking for confirmation that I'm all right.

We both seem to realize the awkwardness of the situation at the same moment. I pull back, a wave of horrified humiliation rushing through me. I try to refasten the straps of the harness, but my hands are shaking.

He crouches back on his haunches, those intriguing brown eyes of his studying me closely. But he doesn't look at me with pity or contempt. Just assessing, making sure I'm OK.

"Are you ready, Legionnaire?"

He's treating me like a soldier again. That means he still sees me as competent, still trusts me to do my job.

"I'm ready." I hope I sounded convincing.

He nods, then walks back to his jump seat and straps himself in. He calls out to the pilot on his comm, "Alright, we're all secure. Let's go."

The engines power up as the shuttle prepares to enter Hestia's atmosphere. I close my eyes, turning away from the view of Hestia below.

I have to keep my mind on the here and now, not on what might happen when we get to Hestia. Not on the past. And not on Joren and what he thinks of me.

The shuttle hits the atmosphere with a heavy thump, the gravity of Hestia grabbing hold of us. I keep my eyes closed, staying calm by focusing on my breath.

And, unbidden, the image arises of Joren's steady brown eyes looking into mine. For some reason, that helps to calm me too.

CHAPTER SIX

I watch through the window as we descend below the cloud layer, revealing a first glimpse of the Capitol. The small city sprawls westward onto open land, its eastern border hugging the shore of the eastern ocean. As we get closer, I can make out more details of the city. The space port runs along the eastern shore, marked by the walls that separate it from the rest of the city. Just west of that is the City Center, with its civic buildings and temples. South of that district is the vast central marketplace, where the raw materials of Hestia are bought and sold and then shipped off-world.

The landing gear emerges from the ship chassis with an abrupt thump. We settle into our landing spot in the port, and the ship sets down gently on the tarmac.

The others are already unbuckling. I scramble up, nervous to meet Joren's eyes after my recent meltdown, but his eyes slide past me. He's going to act like it didn't happen, so I am too.

Kya laughs, her voice unsteady. "That was rougher than I expected. But we made it." Sion is already heading out to the cargo area to check on the gear. Darla stands sentry at the door.

Joren calls us to gather in the cramped center vestibule. "OK, this is it. From here on out, we're going to need to work together as a team." He glances over at Darla, singling her out. "Vesta, you'll be walking up front with me." I move to stand beside him. He reaches up to open the hatch.

The air, hot and humid, carries the smells of food and spices from the Traders' District. I close my eyes for a moment, taking it all in. For the first time in years, I'm breathing Hestian air, feeling Hestian sunlight on my skin.

We step out into the bright sunlight of midsummer. The tarmac is a flat expanse of gray, enclosed by the high walls of white stone that enclose the port. In the distance are the massive trade freighters, bound for the inner worlds after stocking up on Hestia's natural resources.

"This port is so small," Kya says, looking around. "I've never been to one this size before."

It does look smaller, now that I'm accustomed to the sprawling hubs of the Commercial District. The freighters berthed nearby are all older, bulky models, built for moving the raw materials from Hestia to the processing centers farther in at the central districts. Our ship is one of the few smaller crafts berthed nearby.

The others fall in behind Joren and me as we head toward the port entrance. We pass by other traders along the way, most of them the middleman and scavengers who make their living on the fringes of interstellar trade. They don't seem to take any special notice of us, which is a relief, since I can clearly see the difference between the citizens I'm traveling with and the outworlder traders we're trying to impersonate. I just hope it's not that obvious to everyone else, not if we want to stay covert.

"No one does any talking but me," Joren orders, as we approach the main gate, a massive structure of metal and wood. It's a symbol, I think, of how much Hestians want a barrier between Hestia and the outside world. Joren presents his credentials to the sentries at the gate, and the gate opens, releasing us into the crowded streets of the Traders' District.

The buildings are a random collection of mismatched styles—inns, storefronts, street booths, and bars made of whitewashed stone or painted wood. Most spacers won't travel past these few blocks. And why would they? Hestia doesn't have much to offer off-world visitors.

Most of the people we pass are locals, all men. Many of them wear the jumpsuits or synthetic leisurewear of traders, others dressed in the cotton and linens of farmers. There are a smaller number of traders, some of them female. Even so close to the port, though, the number of off-worlders is limited.

"Where are all the women?" Kya asks.

"There aren't many women in the city," I answer, embarrassed for my home world. "Not Hestians anyway."

"Where do we go from here?" Joren asks, preventing Kya from asking me any more questions.

I lead them around the next corner, seeking out the inn I remembered from when I was last in the city.

How exotic the Capitol had seemed to me then! How astonished I'd been at the ornate stone buildings and the open plazas in the City Center, so different from the quiet simplicity of the farm. How I'd gawked at the city's traders and their wares. Now, I see only a dusty border town, filled with people of no particular significance to the larger Republic, a place I've outgrown.

I trace the route by memory, following the trail of familiar landmarks. There is the bakery with the savory pies, its blue paint peeling in the summer heat. Around the next corner, we pass the row of pricier hotels that service the Imperial crews, their rooms opening to covered balconies.

We turn the final corner, and there's the old inn. It has two stories and a back stairway that leads out to the alley, like most of the old buildings in the district. I had stayed there, in disguise as a young man, just before I left Hestia—not that anyone would possibly remember me. Spacers were interchangeable to the innkeepers, and no one would connect a young Hestian boy to a space merchant woman, not ten years later.

We're greeted at the front entrance by the innkeeper's wife, a portly woman of late-middle age who looks at us with disinterest. Hestians don't care much for outsiders. All spacers would be the same to her.

"How long you staying?" She wipes her hands on her embroidered apron. From the smells of cumin and coriander coming from the kitchen, she's cooking a pot of bello stew.

"Only one night," Joren answers, affecting the bored look of a spacer on a routine stopover. "Two rooms, next to each other."

The woman looks us over, sparing a look of disapproval at us being mixed company and having adjoining rooms. "Five hundred credits." She sniffs as if to say that there's no way of accounting for the sinful ways of foreigners.

Joren pays with Imperial currency. Hestia is one of the few worlds that still uses physical currency, yet another reason we're considered primitive.

"Supper will be ready presently in the dining room," she mutters, then hands Joren the room keys and heads back into the kitchen.

"What are these?" Joren whispers.

"Keys. They open the locks on the rooms," I answer.

We follow him up the staircase to the second floor. Our rooms adjoin each other, with a door in between. Each face the street, offering a view of the marketplace beyond.

The room that Kya and I share is decorated in quintessential Hestian style. The two simple beds both have brass bed frames, with plump pillows stuffed with goose feathers. The blankets are made of white homespun cotton, with embroidered accents of sky-blue, the curtains made to match. All the simplicity of Hestian craft is on display, even down to the small marble statue of my planet's namesake tending her hearth, placed on a table by the window.

Kya throws her bag down on the bed nearest her, claiming it. She sits on the bed, gently bouncing as she looks around the small room.

I walk over and pick up the statue. It's carved of traditional white marble, like most statues of Hestia are. The figure of Hestia is bent over her hearth, which has a candle wick protruding from it, waiting to be lit.

"What's that statue for?" Kya asks.

I light the candle with the matches set next to the statue, strangely moved by the simple ritual. "That's right, you don't recognize her." It's easy to forget that not everyone knows about Hestia, since she's been a part of my every childhood memory. I hold the statue in my palm, displaying it. "This is Hestia, the goddess of home and hearth."

She stops bouncing. "Wait, the planet is named after a goddess?"

I set the statue carefully back in place. "It seems strange, I know. But the hearth is important here. They say that as long as the women tend to the hearth fires, our world will always endure."

She snorts derisively. "Why is it the women's job? On Cava, we all share in the work."

"That's what I always used to ask when I was a kid. I'd ask, 'Why doesn't Simon—that's my brother—have to do it?' That was usually when there was something fun I wanted to do, and my mother told me I had to do my chores."

Kya laughs. "I was *always* in trouble. My mothers and fathers were very strict. But I still managed to get away with things."

She opens up her bag and takes out a brush, a cloth, and a small jar, setting them on the bed. She brings it over to the where the ewer and basin are set before the mirror and sits down, setting out her supplies.

47

"So, you have a brother," she says. "Are you from the same mother or the same father?"

I'm confused by her question. "Well, both. My mother and father were married for thirty years, at least. And then I have my oldest brother Lucas. And my two sisters, Britta and Agatha. I was the baby, the youngest of five."

She looks wistful. "What a world, in which one woman and one man can five children! You're lucky, you know."

She must be joking. "But you're from Cava," I sputter. "Surely, you're luckier than me."

"You would think that, wouldn't you?" Her voice is soft, almost sad. "I suppose I am, in a way. But you have things here that we don't on Cava... resources, space. We can't have big families on Cava. That's why we've learned to share."

"But you're from the Core Worlds," I protest. "They're rich and powerful."

She splashes her face, washing away the cleanser and drying her face with a cloth. "Have you ever been to the Core Worlds?" she asks, her eyes searching mine.

I'm taken aback. Doesn't she know that I'm not eligible? "Well, no. I'm not a citizen."

"Oh, of course. I forgot." She looks embarrassed. "Not every Core World is the same, Vesta. You'll see that when you get your citizenship. Some worlds are richer than others. And some are more equal than others."

"Which kind is Cava?"

She starts gathering up her supplies. "Cava is one of the older worlds. But we were a... test project, I suppose you'd call it." Kya hovers over her bed, pulling her clothes out of her bag and putting them away as she talks. "A lot of mistakes were made in its development. We don't have the same resources that later worlds do. We've had to use our engineering skills to make it livable." Kya sits back on the bed, facing me. "We have to share our space, share our children, even share our husbands and wives." She grins wickedly. "Not that I'm complaining about that part."

I can't help but laugh at Kya's audacity.

She stretches languidly. "So where's the lav? I need a shower. With *lots* of hot water."

"This is a rooming house, so there's no private lav. There's a common one, down the hall."

She pretends to sulk, pulling a sad face.

"What, I thought you liked to share?" I tease.

She groans, but then grabs a towel and heads down the hall.

Before I can settle in, I hear a crisp knock on the door connecting our rooms, and Joren walks through. He looks around at our room, then back at me.

"Where's the marketplace?" he asks. "I'd like to get started on our supplies."

"It closes at dusk. I'll have to go in the morning."

He looks irritated at the delay, but nods, turning to go.

"Wait," I call after him. "I'm going to need some clothes from the marketplace." He looks confused for a moment. "I'll need to disguise myself to buy the supplies. A woman would attract too much notice here."

Joren looks me up and down, as if trying to picture me as boy. Inexplicably, I blush.

"You think you can pull it off?" He sounds doubtful.

"Of course. I used to do it all the time when I was younger."

His eyebrows lift.

"My brother Simon and me. We used to take off sometimes to have some fun. You know, ride out to see the herders when they drove their herds south to the Capitol. Learning to fight. Stuff like that. I couldn't do that as a girl."

"So, you got in trouble a lot." His lips twist, his dark eyes warm. "Why does that not surprise me?"

Is he teasing me? I wish my body would stop responding with that curious warm feeling when he looks at me like that.

"I can go get the clothes," he offers. "Just tell me what you need."

CHAPTER SEVEN

I stand by the open window, looking down at the boulevard below. The light has almost faded away, illuminating the street but leaving the room in darkness. Traders and merchants walk by leisurely in search of a meal or a night's entertainment. A man in a trader's jumpsuit cuts through the alley toward the night bazaar, the path marked by paper lanterns.

Ten years ago, I had stood on this very street, desperate to find a way off-world. I'd been terrified, yes, but also excited, daring to hope that this would be my chance to finally live free. I thought that I'd outgrown those foolish hopes. And yet, here I am again. Only, this time, I'm going in the opposite direction.

I hear footsteps behind me. Joren stands at the threshold, the door between our suites open. In the low light, I sense rather than see him, just the outline of his body. As he walks over to me, I can make out the details of his face. His brown eyes look almost black in the low light.

He holds out the cloth bag he's carrying, offering it to me. "Here, I hope it fits."

I dig through the bag. Inside are men's clothes and a wide-brimmed hat. I hold out the clothing in front of my body to judge the size. He's chosen well. The man's shirt, woven of a light blue linen, is cut blocky and thick, loose enough to hide my curves. The same goes for the khaki trousers. They should be big enough to disguise my slight hips. Now I just have to put them on, go back to disguising myself as a man in order to move freely about the city. I can't believe I have to go through this again. When I left, I'd promised myself that I would never be controlled in this way again.

I offer a tense smile. "Thanks. These should fit." I stuff the clothing back into the bag and shove it down on the bed.

Joren tilts his head, his brows drawn together. "Is something wrong?"

"No. Nothing." He just stands there, waiting. "It just reminds me of what it was like before," I admit. "As a woman on Hestia. I'd forgotten what that's like."

Simon and Lucas had always been able to do what they wanted, to be free. But I had to hide my identity if I wanted to do anything that didn't fit the rules for girls.

"Is that why you left?"

I don't know why I tell him. Maybe it's the curiosity in his eyes. Or the strange intimacy of the situation, standing here in the half-light. Maybe it's that I've never told anyone about it before, and I need to tell someone.

"My mother..." My throat tightens, threatens to close. She... died." I haven't talked about her since I left Hestia. The grief has been packed away, just like all my other memories.

Something flickers in his eyes. There's that look again, the anguish I saw in him before. He has known a similar pain, something like mine.

I swallow, lick my dry lips. "Things changed after that. I couldn't be on Hestia anymore." I don't want to tell him about the rest, about

Papa sending me away. That would be too much to trust to a stranger. "So, I went to the port. Tried to bribe my way onto a ship. But I only had Imperial currency." The traders had laughed at me, at my ignorance. I must have seemed so naïve with my farmer's clothes and my coins.

He shrugs. "You couldn't have known."

"One woman, a captain, she took pity on me." I can still picture her dark curls and purple coveralls, her stern face. "She's the one who suggested that I join the Legion. When we reached Malbien, I went to the recruiting center and enlisted."

"That was a good call. The Legion was taking on a lot of new recruits then, during the Conflict."

I snort. "They would take any able body, you mean. So, they took me, even though I wasn't the best candidate."

"Maybe. But I read your service record. You did well." Of course, he knows too much about me. Now, even more. "And you were the best candidate for this mission."

It's embarrassing, the way my chest warms with his praise. He's trying to build me up for some reason.

"The *only* candidate, you mean. I don't expect there are too many ex-Hestians in the Republic, ready to be recruited."

He shrugs, his grin crooked. "*Best… only…* same difference."

I can't help but grin back. This feels too close, too easy.

The lock turns in the outer door, startling us apart. Kya pushes her way in, holding a tray of food. Her eyes widen, moving back and forth between us. I feel like I've been caught doing something I shouldn't.

"Hope you're hungry, Vesta." Kya sets the tray down on the table next to me—a bowl of stew and freshly baked bread. "It's not as good as the goulash on my world. But it fills your belly."

"I should be going." Joren steps away, heading to his adjoining room, then turns back around. "I'll be shadowing you tomorrow in the marketplace. If you need help, signal with your comm."

"I'll be fine. I don't need back up."

His lip twitches. "Humor me."

When the door closes behind him, Kya frowns quizzically at me. "What was that about?"

"Nothing, just talking about the mission."

"Hmm. It looked like something."

"Kya!" I protest.

"Oh, I was just teasing. Here, eat."

She sits with me as I eat my dinner, telling me about the Hestians from the dining hall. It feels good to have someone to talk with again, and Kya never seems to run out of things to say, stories to tell. She *is* kind, not what I expected at all from an Institute scientist. But then, nothing about this mission has made any sense.

When my belly is full, we settle in for the night. Soon, I hear Kya's light breathing shift into the rhythms of sleep. I close my eyes, trying to let go of any thoughts of the past or worries about the future. Tomorrow, I will be alone in the dusty streets and markets of the Capitol, the weight of this mission resting on my shoulders.

CHAPTER EIGHT

I lean back against the battered wood of the stable, sweltering under the late-afternoon sun. Even the cool juice I bought in the market-place can't cool me down. The air holds a cloying, damp heat, unusual for this late in the summer. My head is itching under the straw hat, and the strip of cloth that cinches down my breasts has started to chafe. I was careful to flatten my chest as much as I could this morning, and it's been hard to take a full breath.

I was worried at first that someone would find me out. Despite what I told Joren, I still had worries about passing as a young man after all these years. I had pitched my voice low and plumped up my Hestian accent. But no one had seemed to notice anything strange at all. After a while I had relaxed, just focusing on buying the supplies, all of them piled up on the rented hover trolley beside me. All except for the wagons, which should be waiting for us back at the warehouse. All I need to do now is buy the horses and then I can finally head back.

I look around for Joren, searching through the colorful stalls of the bazaar. He'd been good to his word, watching over me from afar all day, my invisible shadow. I'd catch glimpses of him from time to time as he browsed at a nearby booth, playing the part of an off-world trader.

"Those herdsmen," a booming male voice carries from behind me, "they've been causing trouble."

I turn to look, but the wall blocks my view.

"They haven't been bringing their beasts to market." A different man this time, with a Capitol accent. "I think they're holding something back."

The men sound Hestian, likely local merchants.

"Think they can do what they want," the first man answers. "Loyal only to themselves. And their women, they're a disgrace."

The second man grumbles in response. Then their voices fade as the men walk away, leaving me with a sick dread in my belly.

Could it be true? Have the herdsmen not arrived in the city, so late in the season?

Every year the herdsmen drove their beasts south from their grazing lands in the North, a ritual as reliable as the harvest. The herds were then sold in the city, or else slaughtered, and the meat loaded for tribute or trade off-world. For them not to have arrived would be unthinkable.

And the men's attitudes toward the herders were strange too. The herders had always been outsiders in the South, yes, but never treated with contempt. Those men were speaking of the herdsmen with contempt.

"Hey there, boy!" A horse dealer calls out to me, his stained teeth showing through a bushy black beard. "Are you here to buy?"

I clamber up, wiping my mouth. "Yes, uncle," I answer, in deference to his age. "I'm here to buy some mounts for our farm."

"I have some quality horseflesh for you then, son." He throws his arm over my shoulders, guiding me toward the stables.

I've missed this. The smell of horses and hay, the talk of the farm. He leads me through the stables, showing off his stock of suitable mounts.

"The corrals seem a bit empty this year," I say, hoping the man will volunteer some information.

"Ay, son. A bit late this year, I reckon. No sign of the herdsmen yet. If they're holding out for a higher price, they'll be sorely disappointed. The GRIP doesn't like being kept waiting, that's for sure."

So it's true, then. They haven't come.

"You don't need any of those beasts. Look at these stallions over here."

I settle on two horses, one a speckled tan and white, and the other a solid deep brown. I'll be the only one riding, but it can't hurt to have a spare mount, just in case.

"You sell good stock, uncle. My father said I should pay you a fair price."

I offer just less than what he's asking. It must have been more than he expected, judging from his wide eyes.

"Blessings for your family," he calls out as I lead the horses away, the hover trolley following behind us.

I'm exhausted by the time we reach the rental warehouse. It's situated a fair distance from the marketplace, one among many in an anonymous row of gray buildings. Luckily, there aren't many people around at this hour, not with the marketplace still in full swing, so no one should be paying much attention to us.

I loop the horses' reins over the metal bar outside the door, then slip inside, desperate to free myself from this itchy disguise. I tear off the hat and hurl it to the ground, pulling out some hair pins in the process. Then I reach under my shirt to unwind the cloth from my breasts, freeing them from constriction. I tear open the top two buttons of my shirt, pulling on the fabric to let the air cool my skin while I run my hand through my hair.

"You're back."

I spin around, heart pounding. Joren steps out from the rear of the warehouse.

"Goddess bless it, Joren! You scared me!"

He has a strange expression on his face—not quite embarrassed, something else. He clears his throat. "Did you get everything?"

"Weren't you watching the whole time?" I ask, an edge in my voice.

He walks closer, looking amused now. "Why, did you spot me?"

"I saw you once or twice." I don't mention that it felt comforting to know that he was watching out for me. "I got everything. No trouble."

"Good." He nods to the loaded hover cart outside. "I'll move these supplies inside."

"Be careful of the horses," I warn as he moves to open the door.

"Horses?" He raises an eyebrow. "You bought *two* of them?"

I shrug apologetically. "The land will be rugged when we reach the plains. We need a spare."

He shakes his head, then walks past me to where the stallion and mare are tethered, untying them from the post and taking their reins. Surprisingly, they don't shy away, but follow him calmly inside, snorting gently. Since when does an Imperial know how to handle horses, I wonder.

"Which one are you planning to ride?" he asks, oblivious to my surprise.

I walk over to the speckled mare, stroking her neck. "This one. I've decided to name her Feather." She nuzzles at my pockets, looking for a treat.

He hands me her reins, keeping hold of the brown stallion. "Then I'll ride this one."

"You ride?!" I can't help the surprise in my voice.

"When I have to." He scratches the stallion's neck, getting an affectionate rub of the stallion's face in return. "I guess I'll have to give him a name too."

Before I can respond, Joren's comm, hidden under his tunic, vibrates softly. He subvocalizes, transmitting a message, then closes the signal with a tap. The easy manner of a moment ago is gone, his posture tense.

"Wait here," he orders. "I'm going back to get the others."

"We're leaving now?" I gasp.

"Unless you'd like to spend another night waiting."

He's right. It would be worse to be waiting in the Capitol for another night, anticipating the worst.

I answer his questioning look with a brisk nod. "I'm ready."

He slips out the warehouse door. After a moment, I open the door just wide enough to let the hover cart inside. All of these supplies will need to be loaded onto the hover wagons for the journey. The parcel that contains our clothing is perched on the top of the pile. I pull it down, sorting through the garments until I find the ones I will be wearing, the traditional women's garb of Hestia—thin linen undertrousers, light-colored dress, buttoned bodice. I will need to braid my hair as well. Married women always wear plaits.

The dread from earlier settles back into my stomach. When Joren returns with the others, my identity will change. I will become a Hestian woman again, at least in imitation, an imitation that is feeling uncomfortably real.

*   *   *

An hour later, Joren and I are leading the horses and wagons through the crowded streets.

"Which way from here?" Joren asks. He's dressed like a Hestian trader, his loose shirt tied with a sash just above his lean hips. But with his alert warrior's stance, he doesn't remind me of the farmers I'd known growing up.

"Just a little farther, then we go right," I answer.

Sion and Kya follow behind us, next to the wagons. Kya is dressed in robes of ivory linen that highlight her dark brown skin, and Sion, pale and bright-haired, in the plain trousers and loose tunic of a tradesman. No one has given them any particular attention for their striking coloring since there are so many outsiders in the Capitol. For now, they can walk with us. Later, they will need to stay hidden in the wagon.

Darla patrols the rear. She had refused to wear the women's clothing I'd brought for her, saying that skirts would restrict her movement if it came to a fight. So she had been cast as my uncle. With her lean, ropy build and shorn hair, she would easily pass.

The traffic thickens as we leave the Warehouse District and approach the City Center. We pass wide stone buildings, their open porches designed to let in the cool breeze while shielding those within from the sun. Vendors of juice and nectar hawk their wares from their street carts.

I tense up as the crowds get thicker, slowing our progress. It's hard to see the street markers through the dense crowds. The traffic draws to a halt, and we're forced to stop.

"What's happening?" Joren looks around nervously.

"Capitol Square," I whisper. "The traffic gets heavy sometimes." I hadn't meant to lead us here. Either the traffic markers have changed since I'd last been in the city, or else I'd forgotten. I hold Feather's head, soothing her. "Shhh," I soothe, "we'll be through it soon."

The wagon in front of us lurches forward, making space for us to advance. I urge Feather on, but then stop dead at the sight in front of me.

In the center of the open plaza, a raised dais towers over the crowd. Atop the platform, in an elongated silver basin, a fire burns.

We have to move past this, now.

"What is that?" Joren asks, a harsh whisper in my ear.

A bell clangs rhythmically. Too late.

I freeze, tension curling in my belly.

"No one can go through now," I whisper. "Just wait."

Joren scans the crowd, Kya and Sion moving up to stand behind us.

The crowd falls silent. All eyes are focused on a spot beneath the stairs, where a heavy door is set low into the wall. A heavily muscled man stands by the wooden door—the temple guardian. He opens the door, and a young woman steps out, her eyes fixed into the distance, ignoring the crowd. The young woman, barely more than a girl, wears a long, flowing white dress, her long dark hair unbound down her back. The white robes are traditional, worn to signify her purity. Her face is as plain and pure as the stone of the temple from which she emerged—a sacred virgin priestess of the order of Hestia, coming to tend the sacred fire.

I bow my head, like the others in the crowd, in unconscious respect.

She walks slowly toward the dais, mounting the wide stone steps to the raised platform in the center of the plaza. She approaches the large metal bowl with the sacred fire burning inside it, pure and red against the clouded sky. With a graceful sweep of her arm, she places a willow branch on the fire.

The priestess begins intoning the ritual. From this far away, I can't hear her words. But I don't need to. I know them by heart.

Today and every day let the people of Hestia uphold their sacred duties. May the Vestals of the Capitol tend to the sacred hearth of Hestia. May the women keep their hearths. Let the sacred fire burn—tended, forevermore.

It is said that, so long as the fire burns steady and even, all who see it will know that the city is safe, that order is maintained. The men can go about their business knowing that the women are at home, tending to the hearth and their domestic responsibilities.

Even after all these years away, and despite the constrictions I had felt as a woman here, I still feel an inner stirring as I see that steady burning—how it lights and brings warmth to the fading light of day. There is something beautiful in this ritual, in the continuity of human effort, in the tradition of women.

The priestess walks slowly down the stairs, finally disappearing into the darkened archway to the sanctuary. The attendant closes the heavy wooden door behind her.

As if by magic, the spell is broken. The sounds of rough talk, of jostling and shoving, the whooshing of the carts and the words of the traders, begins again, even louder in contrast to the quiet.

"Let's go," Joren urges, his hand at my elbow.

But there's something I need to do first.

"Wait here." I push past Joren to the front edge of the cart, where a long metal cylinder is kept for just this purpose. I pull it down, walking past the others to join the line of women gathered at the stairs to the dais.

It may be dangerous to stop for this ritual, but I feel that I have to. I don't even know why, just that it's important.

One by one, each of us takes our turn, kneeling by the offering basket, putting in what coins we carry, and then mounting the stairs.

Now it's my turn on the dais. I approach the stone bowl, the sacred flame burning steadily within it. I bow before the flame, then carefully place the cylinder into the fire, scooping up a small portion of coals. I intone the ritual words and descend the staircase. I place the cylinder back into its place on the hover cart.

"Come on!" I whisper to Joren, leading the way through the crowded plaza. "Let's go. We won't be noticed now."

CHAPTER NINE

The crowds thin out as we reach the northern edge of the city. There are a few houses on the city margins, mostly storage facilities for goods, and the streets are empty at this late hour. We turn on the solar lanterns to light our way in the failing light. Joren and I walk together, each of us leading a horse. We keep a fast pace, eager to get out of the city and off the road. Sion and Kya are riding in the wagon to avoid notice. Darla walks some distance behind, her predatory eyes scanning the darkness on the perimeter.

Joren looks behind us, his eyes catching on the cylinder of coals mounted in its place on the wagon. "What was it that you did back there, with the fire?"

I don't want to explain about the ritual. He'll consider it primitive, another superstition of a backward world. But I can't not answer.

"It's an old custom. A woman can make an offering at the shrine to get a coal from the sacred fire. It's considered a blessing."

He pauses, considering. "Do you still believe in that?"

I shouldn't still believe in Hestian lore. But it's hard to leave old beliefs behind.

"Maybe not," I answer. "But we can use all the luck we can get."

He frowns. "And what about the girl, the one in the white robe?"

Another tradition, even more laughable than the first, to an outsider. "The girl is a priestess. She tends the hearth flame of the city. The belief on Hestia is that it must be kept burning in order to keep the city and the lands safe."

He is silent for a moment, then nods. "It must be another tradition from the home world. There are so many in the Republic."

"You think it came from the home world?"

"Many of our traditions do. Like the Legion, for instance. It's named from an ancient fighting force from Old Earth."

"I didn't know that." How ignorant the rest of us must seem to the citizens and Core Worlders. They own the secrets of world-building, and they know all the history that we've never been taught. All I'd learned on Hestia was how to read and how to farm.

"Not many do," he answers.

Then why is he telling me? I wonder.

"I never knew that the GRIP—" Then I realize what I'd just said. I hadn't meant to use that slang term in front of him.

"The GRIP. Yes, we know what we're called... 'A tight grip holds the world steady.' That's the idea, anyway."

Before I can decide how to respond, Darla comes up behind us. "Commander! The gates."

The boundary of the city rises before us. It's just a modest arch of white stone, humble when compared to the elaborate architecture of Medina.

Joren and I mount our horses as we pass the arch, Darla climbing into the passenger cart with Sion and Kya. Joren has a good seat, I note, his hand easy on the pommel and reins. He looks surprisingly natural on horseback.

The country opens up quickly before us, adorned with neat rows of corn and wheat. I luxuriate in the smell of rich earth, the dampness of the early evening. I can't see far in the dark, but I know that these fields stretch out to the horizon, an unbroken expanse of farmlands as far as the eye can see. It won't be until we reach the boundary of the northern landmass that the farmlands will change into open grasslands. And, beyond that, the mountains.

Clouds darken the sky overhead, covering up the stars. We'll have rain tonight. Usually, at this time of the summer, the air should be dry. It would have to be for the harvest not to be spoiled. The grain could rot, the produce rained out.

Joren guides his horse next to mine. "Where is the shelter you mentioned?"

I scan the horizon. "About five kilometers north of here. Just off the road to the west." I remember that spot well, with a creek nearby and a private meadow shielded by rolling hills.

I start to feel more nervous the longer we ride. We are too noticeable now, riding after sunset. We'll attract notice. But it's more than that. Something feels wrong. It's an uneasiness in my chest, my gut. Finally, I can't hold it in any longer. "We need to get off the road," I tell Joren. "Let's hurry."

Joren frowns at me but quickens the pace, telling Sion to accelerate the speed of the wagons.

I finally recognize the signs for the turn-off, a faint trail of dirt and trampled grass off to the left. "There!" I point it out to Joren, and we turn off to the left, following the faint trail across the meadow and through a grove of oaks. The trail slopes gradually downward over a ridge until we reach a protected spot, out of sight from the road. I feel a sense of relief, as if I've avoided something bad.

Joren dismounts quickly and walks over to where the others climb out of the wagon. I'll need to help them to set up camp since they've never pitched a tent, at least not the Hestian way.

"It may rain tonight," I tell Sion as we unroll the waxed canvas of a tent panel. "We'll need this rain fly to keep us dry."

"It looks that way," he answers, studying the clouds covering the moon. "But it seems a bit late in the season for that. This isn't according to the climate plan."

Darla and Joren come over to help, and I show them how to pitch the tent using poles and pulleys to pull the covering tight.

Sion and Kya check over the equipment, making sure nothing has shifted during travel. Darla sets up the perimeter sensors that are designed to alert us if anyone gets close to us while we're sleeping.

Darla has just engaged the alarm when it pings. Joren studies the readout from the device, frowning.

"Want me to check it out, commander?" Darla offers.

Joren shakes his head. "No, I'll do it. Vesta, come with me."

Darla scowls. After all, she's security. But I'm the local guide; he must want me to identify whatever's out there.

I follow behind as we make our way through the trees to a good vantage point.

"The sensors show a large group," he whispers. "Traveling north on the road. Maybe fifteen, twenty people."

We position ourselves within a copse of trees at the ridgetop where we have a clear view of the road. Joren takes out his scope, handing me the binocs.

The sensors are right. There are about twenty men on the road, all mounted on horseback. They're all dressed alike, in light-colored trousers and tunics. But one detail causes my heart to skip. The men all have weapons at their hips. Just stunners, but still. I don't know why any Hestians would be carrying weapons on the road.

We draw back behind the trees.

"They aren't farmers, that's for sure. But they're all Hestian. I just can't figure out what kind of Hestian they are."

"They're traveling north," he says. "Think that's a coincidence? Maybe they're affiliated with the Patriarchs."

There was no way the Patriarchs would be that stupid. But I must admit, they do look like soldiers. Just not like any I've ever seen. "The Patriarchs don't have soldiers. No weapons. It can't be."

"I'll take your word for it," he answers, "but we'll have to be careful. Make sure our sensors are always on. I don't want to have trouble with any Hestians."

I follow behind as he heads back to camp.

He stops suddenly. "By the way, how did you know that we should get off the road?"

I shrug. "I didn't. Just had a feeling."

He looks at me suspiciously but doesn't press me. "Lucky for us," is all he says.

When we return to camp, Darla asks, "What was it, commander?"

"Just some travelers on the road. Nothing to worry about." Joren won't meet my eyes.

I get the horses settled in for the night and help the others make sure all the gear is secure. Joren has Darla stand guard for first shift, despite the sensors.

I settle down in my bedroll next to Kya. "Sleeping on the ground?" she grumbles, pulling the blankets over her, but then falls asleep. Sion and Joren settle down on the far side of the tent, their breath settling down too as they drift into sleep.

I lie awake, listening to the wind blowing through the meadow grasses, the sound of the creek, and—later—the patter of light rain.

Something is going on up north. Something more than missing herdsmen and mysterious men on the road. There's something waiting for us there, up north. I can't say how I know. But I can feel it—in my blood, in my bones.

CHAPTER TEN

Awareness drifts in slowly... the chirping of birds nearby... the slow, even breath of someone beside me. I open my eyes and sit up. Kya sleeps beside me, rolled over on her stomach, dark curls hiding her face. The other bedrolls are empty. I must have slept later than I thought.

I pull on my boots and wrap a shawl around me, heading outside. The air feels fresh, the meadow still holding the morning dew. A light mist of fog hovers over the golden grass. Sion is walking in the meadow, carrying his field kit. Darla paces the perimeter of the camp, facing away. No sign of Joren.

The first thing to do is to make breakfast. That means setting up the portable stove, filling the soup pot and kettle from the creek, then heating up a blend of oats, cinnamon, and nuts. This is as familiar as home. For better or worse, this crew is like my family for the duration of this mission.

I head over to the bramble of berries near the copse of trees to add some freshness to the oatmeal. I'm bending down to gather berries when I hear the sound of someone breathing heavily. I creep over to bushes, peeking out into the clearing of sunlight between the trees.

Joren is moving through a series of flowing postures that resemble a mix of combat and a rehearsed dance. He is bare to the waist, wearing only loose trousers. A light sheen of perspiration covers his chest and arms as he moves, a fusion of power and grace. His lean muscles move like silk, all masculine strength. But it's the inward look on his face that compels me to stare—an almost blank fierceness. He's not just a man but something different, something the choreographed movements of his body have awakened in him—a true warrior.

I should turn away. The ritual is obviously private. But I watch, fascinated, until Kya speaks. "Well, that's an interesting sight." She stands just behind my shoulder. She's watching Joren too, but her eyes hold a leering appreciation. "My, my… that Imperial discipline does pay off, doesn't it?"

"Kya!" I try to sound scandalized. There's no way I'm admitting to having the same reaction. "I wasn't watching him. I was just looking for some berries."

She laughs easily. "Oh, Vesta, you're such a prude. It's not a crime to admire a well-built man!"

Joren reaches the end of his routine, standing with his feet together, arms by his side, closing his eyes for a moment. He reaches down for a towel and wipes down the light sheen of sweat on his body. I shouldn't look at the way the muscles in his stomach move as he pulls his shirt over his head. But I do.

He must know we're here by now, since we have made enough noise, but I'm too embarrassed to face him. I start walking back to camp and Kya follows.

I dig out two mugs and offer her one, filling the cups with the herb satchels I had purchased in the marketplace. I add the berries to the oatmeal and stir it gently as Kya sips her tea.

Joren walks over to us, the towel draped over his shoulder.

"So, do you train like that every day?" Kya asks mischievously. She reminds me of my childhood friend Ellen. She would always flirt with the boys while I hung back shyly.

He purposely ignores her flirtatious tone, pulling on his shirt. "I don't have time for the complete schedule. Not on this mission."

Before Kya can tease Joren some more, Sion calls out to us from behind the tents. "Come here, I have something to show you."

We follow his voice to find him kneeling in the meadow, holding something in his hand. "Vesta." he summons me, with an inpatient snap of his fingers. I crouch down next to him.

"Look at this flower. Do you recognize it?" He holds a cutting in his palm, a tiny stem with bright yellow blossoms.

I know this plant. "Those are yellow buttons. They're pretty common. They grow all over the farmlands."

"I know they're common," he scoffs. "But look, do you notice anything different about them?"

I'm not sure what he expects me to notice. I've never focused much on plants, other than the crops and weeds on the farm. My sister Britta had been the herbalist of the family.

"What am I supposed to be seeing?" I finally ask, stumped.

He sighs impatiently. "Look at the flowers." He points to the clusters along the stem. "Yellow buttons have two sets of alternating blossoms, spaced evenly apart on the stem. These have three."

"So maybe they're a different variety?"

Sion mutters under his breath. "That's the point," he hisses. "They shouldn't be." He sits back on his heels. "If this planet were a natural system, then of course there'd be genetic drift. But this is a closed system. The whole ecosystem is monitored regularly to prevent changes like this."

He and Kya exchange a long look.

"The energy signatures are almost a hundredfold at the epicenter," Kya says. "Do you think it will translate to more species degradation?"

"If we're finding genetic drift this far from the target region, I wonder how much more we'll find when we get close," Sion mutters

70

to himself as he studies the readouts on his specimen unit. "We need to get some more samples from this location." He hands Kya a specimen unit, and she sets out to canvass the area.

Sion tries to rise to standing, but he's struggling, as if his legs are weak. He looks frail, I realize. I hadn't noticed that before.

"Can I help?" I offer him my arm.

He hesitates a moment. "That would be helpful," he concedes, leaning on my arm to raise himself to his feet. "The last world I worked on... the gravity was lesser. I'm afraid my constitution has yet to adjust."

If he's struggling now, there's no way he's going to be able to collect all those plants. "I can help," I offer. "With the specimen collection. I have some experience."

Sion looks at me dubiously, but hands me his spare specimen collection unit, pointing to the northern side of the meadow. "Start over there, if you will. Any novel flora."

I canvass the area, collecting any plants I can find. It takes about half an hour to get all the specimens. I walk back to camp, where Sion is sitting by the wagon, and hand him the specimen unit. He opens the compartments to check over my work. "You did decent work with these specimens," he says finally. "Where did you study?"

It takes me a moment to parse what he's asking. He thinks I went to school. He must have forgotten I'm not a citizen.

"I've done collection work here and there," I shrug. "My latest posting was on Eremos. I collected specimens for some kind of research project there."

"Eremos." He searches his memory. "Yes, I know that one. The test climate for desert ecology. You must have been working on the study of the effects on minerals in an alkaline ecosystem. My colleague at the Institute initiated that project."

"I didn't know that." No scientist had ever explained to me anything about the purpose of my work. "I'm just a freeworker. I just gathered what they told me to gather and made sure it got back in good condition."

"Well, you did a thorough job. Maybe you can help me with collections from now on."

From an expert like Sion, that feels like high praise. And that means I'll continue to be included.

I dish out breakfast for everyone back at camp. While the rest of them are getting gear ready, I lug the dishes down to the creek to clean them. I feel pleased by Sion's praise, but I can't let it go to my head. I'm still just a guide hired to do the grunt work.

As I'm scrubbing out the dishes, I notice a flash of crimson in the grass. I walk over, curious. And there, almost trampled by the hoof of my horse, is a beautiful red flower. It has a long green stem, with a spray of tiny red blooms. I look around for any similar specimens, but I can't find where it came from. I can have Sion look at it later. I cut it with my knife, tucking it into the pocket of my skirt.

CHAPTER ELEVEN

Goddess, it feels good to be back on a horse. The sun's warmth has loosened my muscles, my body in sync with Feather's easy gait.

But now, at midafternoon, the weight of my thick braid sticks uncomfortably to my neck. I'm sweltering in the thick layers of the dress with the undertrousers. I hike the skirt up around my hips, allowing the breeze to cool my legs.

Joren rides ahead of the wagon, scanning the horizon. He rides well in the saddle, his posture straight but fluid—almost as well as a native Hestian.

The others ride ahead of us in the hover cart. Kya periodically pops her head out of the back of the wagon to check out the view. Not that there's much variety in this landscape of flat farmland.

We've decided to stay off the main road, instead following the dirt paths of the traditional trade routes. So far, we've been able to avoid crossing paths with anyone. Even in peak season, traders are few and far between. And the farmers will all be working overtime, making sure they get the crops harvested before the rot sets in.

Joren slows his pace, dropping back until we're riding next to each other.

"I haven't seen any signs of houses on this road," he says.

"No, we wouldn't. The trade routes keep well away from those, for now."

His gaze drops to my bare legs, the skirts pulled up in front of me and the undertrousers rolled up above my knee.

"It's hot," I say defensively. "It's easier for you, your clothes are all light cotton. Not these layers."

"I didn't say anything," he answers with an easy shrug.

I was overreacting, treating him as if he were a Hestian man. He wouldn't care either way if my legs are bare.

He grins in answer, then pats his horse affectionately.

"He likes you."

"You sound surprised."

"I'm surprised that you ride. Where did you learn?"

He smiles, a line on his cheek showing the early bristle of a beard. Soon a beard will cover his face. *What a shame*, I think, without wanting to.

"Back home," he answers. "On Patria."

I startle at the sound of that name. It's the world where the original founders of the Republic came from, the site of the Academy and the ranking elite. So Joren is not just a citizen but must be of the highest rank among them.

"I had a mare," he continues. "Her name was Lucia. We trained together for two years back in the Academy."

So, it's true then. He probably had been a battalion commander, just like Kya said. Only the highest ranks of the Legion were trained there. And all the Academy's students were the children of the elite citizens.

"But the Legion has weapons and tech," I ask, bewildered. "Why would they bother with learning to ride a horse?"

"It's a foundation of command." He sits up in the saddle, unconsciously taking an Imperial posture like he had when I first met him with the admiral. "You have to train a horse, to trust your authority, to obey. Just like you have to master your body."

Mastering your body. I remember that from Legion training—the drills, the intense conditioning that felt like it would break me. I had loved it all, at first. I'd finally had the chance to prove myself, to test my limits in a way I'd never been given the chance to on Hestia. But, in the end, it didn't matter how good I was. I was an outworlder, and that meant that my best would never be good enough for the Legion.

"Is that where you learned the fighting form? The one you were practicing this morning." I turn my face away when I ask, strangely embarrassed, as if he could guess the feelings I had when I watched him.

He looks over at me, but I look away. "Yeah, I learned it at the Academy." That figures. Another skill reserved for the Legion elite. "It's a way of bringing the body and mind into balance. It helps to focus the mind before a battle."

A battle. That reminds me I'm talking to a former battalion commander if what Kya and Sion told me is accurate. If I want an answer to this question, I'd better ask it now.

"There's something I've been wondering about." My fingers tighten on the reins, hoping this isn't a mistake. "About the mission. About the secrecy. I've never known the GRIP to care about pissing off the locals. So why now, on Hestia?"

When I look over at him, he doesn't look upset by my question. I'm used to superior officers getting offended at being questioned, but so far Joren hasn't been one of them.

He shrugs. "Conflicts cost money, resources. Those are finite, even for the Republic. This mission is cheaper. A smaller team, more expendable." He smiles, self-deprecating.

I wonder again what he must have done to be sent to lead such a low-status mission. *Of course.* Joren's longish hair, his ease in civilian gear, his lack of formality—He must have been doing covert missions for a while. That's why he doesn't look, or act, like other officers.

"You've done this before."

"For a while." The stallion shuffles. Joren settles him down. "I do what's necessary for the Republic. This is what's necessary now. Not to stir up the local populations."

"So it's just to save the Republic's money?" I challenge. "That's why you're here?"

He looks over at me, showing just a hint of that emotion he'd expressed before, back on Medina. "No," he admits. "That's not all."

He hadn't told Darla about what we had seen on the road. Maybe he did care about the outcome here, about preventing another conflict. "I didn't think so."

His face softens, like it actually matters that I believe him.

"Commander," Darla calls from the carts. Joren pulls away to talk with her.

I can't help wondering, though, whether Joren is for real. If he's been doing recon missions, then he's probably used to deception. Maybe that's why he talks to me so freely when we're alone. Maybe that serves some kind of purpose for him.

But I don't think so. Maybe I'm a fool, but I'm starting to trust him.

CHAPTER TWELVE

We push ourselves hard all day, not stopping until almost night. We're all tired by the time we make camp, impatient for a meal. I pull out the solar cooker as they pitch the tents, getting out the ingredients for dinner. But no, this night calls for a real fire.

The site has a good supply of medium-sized stones nearby, enough to make a good hearth circle. I gather some twigs for kindling, a few fallen branches for fuel. I pull out the cylinder in which the banked coals from the sacred fire are stored, shaking them onto the nest of kindling.

The flames come to life with my breath, as I gradually feed in kindling and wood. When the fire burns steady, I murmur the traditional blessing, "May this hearth be ever tended." It doesn't seem right to leave out the words.

The others finish getting settled into camp while I cook the stew—an old recipe of meat and vegetables that my mother used to make—and mix up some biscuits.

The light fades into twilight, the first stars visible in the sky, by the time dinner is ready. Sion and Kya come over to sit by the fire, wrapped in blankets as night falls. I put the kettle on to heat water for tea.

"Where are Joren and Darla?" I ask, scooping out bowls of stew.

"They went scouting somewhere," Kya shrugs. "They said not to wait for them."

It makes me uneasy, the idea of those two being out in the dark alone. Maybe they're up to something. But it does me no good to wonder.

We've eaten our dinner of stew and biscuits, but Joren and Darla have still not returned. I set aside a bowl for each of them.

Tea is poured. We sip, looking up at the stars.

Kya reaches into the pocket of her wrap and pulls out a small box. Inside is a rounded length of polished wood with holes drilled into it. With a quick smile, she holds the flute to her lips, her fingers covering some of the holes.

From the first, soft notes, a strange recognition tugs at my memory, just outside of awareness. *I've heard this song before, but where, when?* I reach for the memory, but the effort fades as the music soothes my mind.

All the elements seem to blend together—the gentle lilting of the music, the wavering flames of the campfire, and the silvery smoke rising up to the stars. The dreamy ambience settles me into a kind of trance, fading away with the last gentle notes. We sit in silence for a moment, listening to the crackling of the fire and the distant hum of crickets.

I haven't felt peaceful like this, not for a long time. Maybe not since I left home. "That was beautiful," I tell her.

"Thank you," Kya sets her object on her lap, smiling. "I like that song too. It's been passed down for a long time. Just like this flute."

"Is the music from Cava?" I ask.

"Older than that. It's from the original home world."

It's hard to imagine something being that old. Hestia was only settled five hundred years ago. The Core Worlds must be ancient. "And the flute? Is it from the home world too?"

"No," Kya caresses the instrument, placing it carefully in its case. "The flute is a replica. But it was based on an ancient design."

"That's it! That song!" I cry. "It sounds like the melodies that the herdsmen used to play during the summertime festivals."

"Hmm," Sion pulls on his beard, rusty in the firelight. "It makes sense. We all have a common origin, after all. There must be some of that history retained on all the worlds, no matter how remote."

"It's a shame that I won't get to hear any music while we're here," Kya says. "I like to collect songs from the worlds I visit. But we won't get close enough to the herders to manage that."

"What's the song about?" I ask her.

"It's an old song, so it's full of old myths and superstitions. It's about a mother who loses her child in the woods. There's a witch who enchants the child and takes it away to a magical realm. The mother is calling out for the child, and the child is calling back to her, but they can't hear each other because they're in different worlds."

"Hmm. There's a story like that from Hestia, but it's not from the herders. It's a song we used to sing when I was a child. It's about a child who leaves the mother's hearth fire and wanders off alone, gets kidnapped by magical creatures, and goes to live with them. My cousin used to say the magical land was up north, in the mountains."

"That's a remarkable similarity," Kya says, sounding intrigued.

"See those stars there, with outline of a woman?" I point at the bright stars over the western horizon, tracing their shape. "That's the mother from the story. And those stars in a circle next to her, that's her hearth. And that small bunch of dimmer stars over there, those are her children. But that one bright star, that's the lost child who wandered away. It always moves at a distance, but in a parallel path across the sky."

Kya follows my directions, tracing the constellation. "Oh, I like that imagination! We don't have that on Cava. We're a planet of engineers, not poets. We would never think of making pictures from the stars."

Sion shakes his head, staring up at the sky. "Kya, my dear, you have the sentiments of the home world."

"Why do you say that?" I ask.

Sion smiles, a gentle look on his serious face. "Our ancestors made up stories about the stars too. They saw themselves out there, in the void. They thought the stars belonged to them. Thought they could conquer the void and bend it to their will, just like they did to their home world."

"But didn't they?" I ask, hesitant. "The ancestors were right. We did conquer the void. We're here, after all."

He takes a sip of his tea, his face somber. "They launched into the void long ago. Over a thousand years ago." He looks up at me. "Have you seen what happens to a human being when they're out too long in the void?"

I shake my head. He doesn't seem to notice.

"They waste away. They get sick. They go mad." He turns toward me, his eyes glowing bright in the firelight. "The void wasn't made for us. It's foreign territory. The home world was the only place made for us, and we ruined it."

Kya nudges Sion with her elbow. "Sion is our resident historian. He knows everything about the past. And he's always ready to tell anyone who will listen."

He shrugs, looks abashed. "I talk too much about the past. It's an occupational hazard, I'm afraid, particular to worldbuilders."

How strange this is, to be sitting at a campfire on Hestia, talking to kind of people who design worlds like this.

"We worldbuilders are just craftsmen. Counterfeiters. And all of these worlds…" With a sweep of his arm, he indicates the landscape out beyond the boundaries of the fire and the starry sky beyond. "They're all just replicas of the home world. Just an imitation. Like that flute that Kya plays."

It occurs to me that I may never get this chance again, to ask these kinds of questions. "In school," I ask hesitantly, "I learned that the home world wasn't livable anymore, and that's why we left…"

Sion smiles grimly, then nods. "It's true. The ancestors were very foolish." He sets down his mug and hunkers forward. "They disrespected the rules of life… thought they could make it better. They thought we could take control of life, shape it into the image in their minds. They altered the genes of plants and animals, changed the genetic code of insects to prevent disease, tried to increase crop yields, by adding the genes of animals to plants. They were so confident, so sure that they could control what they were doing, thought that they were meant to do it. But they didn't know the costs." He curls his lip in disgust. "Finally, they changed themselves. They mixed their genes into those of other animals."

An instinctive disgust rises up in my belly and my throat. "Why would they do that?" I ask, horrified.

He looks up at my exclamation. "They said it was to cure disease, to remove the imperfections. Or to make people better, stronger, to live longer. They thought it was for the greater good… But then, they lost control." His voice holds a grim contempt. "It was too late then. The mutations they'd engineered had already corrupted the system. They had no way of returning back to the way things were before. The entire biosphere collapsed. Billions died."

I am silent, horrified, an emotion echoed in Sion's face as he stares into the fire. "But if they were corrupted, then how are we here? How did our ancestors survive?"

A small, triumphant smile curves Sion's lips. "The original source codes for life… they'd been saved, you see, by the wise ones. They had put them away in case of just such a calamity. That's what the founders brought with them in their arks. So they could make life over again—this time in the original form, without interference."

He sits back, sipping from his tea. "We were given another chance. Our ancestors decided then and there: never again. This time, we will do things correctly. We will keep it the same, just like it was meant to be. That's how we survive."

None of us says anything more for a while. Finally, Kya lifts the flute to her lips and begins playing. We are sitting like that, quietly listening, when Darla and Joren return some time later. No one asks them where they've been. They eat the food I'd set aside for them, and Kya plays her music.

How fragile our worlds are, I muse, as the fire slowly dies down. I never knew how tenuous our survival has been. No wonder the Institute is so concerned about the environmental systems going awry. No matter what I think of the GRIP's politics, I now understand now why this mission is so important.

Hestia's future might not be the only one at stake. It could be the future of all of us.

CHAPTER THIRTEEN

I'm climbing alone through the Northern mountains. A steep path cuts through jagged rocks, leading upward. From above, I hear a woman's voice. I can't make out her words, but she's calling to me, urging me forward. I hurry up the path toward the summit.

As I pass the curve of the trail, I spot her. She stands with her back to me, lit by a bright glow. I squint against the light that frames her. All I can see is her black hair, thick and coarse, spilling down her back and over her shoulders like molten trails of lava.

I know her, somehow, as if she's a long-lost relative. And yet, I also know that I've never met her before. She beckons to me with a wave of her arm, calling me farther up the path.

A loud boom explodes beneath us. She looks behind me, her face harsh and angry. I can almost make out her features—a prominent nose, light-brown skin, a strong chin, heavy dark brows. I turn to look behind me, and I hear a distant boom, even louder than the first.

I bolt up out of sleep, the blankets tangled around my hips, the echo of the explosion still ringing in my ears. I fumble around in the dark until I find my boots, then creep toward the tent entrance. I can't hear anything outside. I scuttle out from beneath the tent flap, scanning for signs of attack.

But there's nothing. Darla is still on guard duty, leaning against the wagon. She hears me and whips around, gripping her blaster.

"Oh, it's you." She shoves the blaster back in its holster. "What do you want?"

No one else is out of their tents. No signs of anything wrong. I must have dreamed it.

"Nothing. Just couldn't sleep."

Darla shrugs, then turns away.

I'm about to head back inside when I hear the horses. They're moving restlessly, pulling at their tethers, neighing their distress. I look back at Darla and wonder if I should say something. But she would just sneer at me.

I approach the horses quietly. Their ears are pressed down flat to their heads, their eyes wild, their tails swishing frantically. I try to soothe them, but they just shy farther away.

I scan the darkness, feeling exposed. Whatever is out there can see me much more easily that I can see it.

And then, a flash of white advancing quickly toward me. I back away, closer to the horses, as the flash gathers form, emerging from the darkness. Two men dressed in white are moving, quick and silent, toward camp.

I gasp in recognition. They're wearing white uniforms like those soldiers from the road! The taller one is holding something in his hands. He retracts his arm, ready to hurl what he's holding at our camp.

"Stop," I yell, running at him. But I'm not fast enough. He releases the object toward the camp, then turns to run.

A loud, hard blast lifts me off my feet. I hit the bare ground—first my body, then my head.

I can't breathe. I can't breathe. Flames are burning behind me, and I can't breathe.

Finally, a desperate gasp of relief as I suck in greedy gulps of air. Joren and Darla run up, blasters ready.

"They went over that ridge," I gasp, pointing to the east. "Two men."

Joren looks between the direction I'm pointing and back to me.

"Let's go, commander. What are we waiting for?" Darla looks between us, impatient.

"Can you get up?" he asks, concerned.

"I'm fine," I assure him, pulling myself up to sitting. "Go after them."

Joren pulls out another weapon, hidden in the folds of his tunic. "Guard the camp."

I take the blaster, my hand clutching its familiar weight.

Joren and Darla set off at a fast run, disappearing over the ridge after the men.

I get to my feet and walk unsteadily back to camp. The horses are frantic, rearing up on their hind legs, mouths foaming.

I scurry over to Kya and Sion's tents, staying low, my eyes on the dark perimeter. Kya looks terrified, her eyes wild. Sion stares at the burning wagon.

"Stay in your tents," I order.

"But the equipment—" Kya protests.

"It's too late." Already the flames have fully engulfed the cart, the fire and acrid smoke rising into the night.

"Stay down," I order. "I'll be back."

Lucky for us, the other cart was far enough away from the fire to be safe. I pull out the extinguisher, spraying it on the flames. That was our main supply wagon. It had our comm equipment, our food, and much of our supplies. But I can't think about that now.

I patrol the camp, weapon drawn, until first light permeates the sky. Joren and Darla return soon after, breathing heavily, drenched in sweat. They must have been running the whole time.

"We couldn't keep up." Joren reports, breathless. "They must have had horses stashed."

I fetch water for them. Kya and Sion hear their voices and come out of their tents.

"You saw men," Joren demands. "What did they look like?"

"I don't know, it was too dark. I just saw their silhouettes." If I tell him about the white uniforms, that will damn Hestia for sure.

Joren doesn't believe me. I can tell by the way he's looking at me.

"Well, that's convenient," Darla drawls. "I saw you. You came out of your tent... *before* the explosion."

"I woke up. And it's a good thing I did, or the other wagon would have burned up. They were trying to burn the whole camp down."

She pushes her face close to mine, invading my space with her whipcord strength and rage. "How do we know you weren't in on it?"

I reach out my hands to shove her away, but Joren pushes me back. Darla keeps advancing, but he blocks her with his body, his face in hers. "Are you really wanting an insubordination charge, lieutenant?"

She glares at me, then sets her jaw. "No, sir."

Joren grabs Darla's arm. "Come on, let's take inventory of the damage."

Darla gives me a look of pure hate as Joren drags her away.

* * *

Kya and Sion paw through the remains of the gear from the burnt wagon, but they're only able to salvage a few items. Most of the supplies are badly burnt.

"None of this is usable," Kya says, slumping down in the dirt.

"At least the scientific gear is intact." Sion looks tired out, frailer than usual. "We had that in the other wagon."

The fatigue is catching up to me too. I feel so exhausted, surveying the devastation. "It's the food and the supplies for the journey that were destroyed," I say. "We needed all of that."

"And the off-world communications," Darla kicks at a melted lump of metal, what's left of the communicator. "We can't check in with base without that."

Joren shakes his head. "So we're down to one wagon, the science gear, and the horses. There's no way we can go on like that."

"I don't understand. Who would want to destroy our gear?" Kya asks.

"Maybe someone doesn't want us going north." Joren looks over at me, giving me a strange look that I can't read. "If we hadn't been armed and ready, they would have burned it all to the ground, and we'd have to go back."

"If Vesta hadn't warned us, you mean," Kya says. "If she hadn't woken up and seen them, they would have torched both of the wagons."

Darla glares at me, her earlier suspicions obvious on her face. "It didn't do us much good, anyway. This mission's a wash, sir." Darla spits in the dirt. "Might as well call it. The big ships can come in and take care of this mess."

I shake my head, horrified. No way can we let the Enforcers come here.

Kya and Sion don't say anything. They seem reluctant to agree but have no real argument. It's Joren who makes the call.

Joren looks between us, his jaw tight. "Give me a minute." He strides off in the direction of his tent. I follow on his heels. I reach him as we pass behind the tents, just out of earshot of the others.

"Joren, I can—"

He turns abruptly, grabbing me by my arm, his face close to mine. "You know something. Something more than you said."

I hesitate. If I say nothing, the mission is over. If I tell him about the men on the road, I could be setting up Hestia for an invasion.

He turns away, starts shoving gear into his rucksack.

"Wait."

He turns, expectant.

"I saw two men, like I said. But there's more." He's not going to like this part. "They were wearing white like the men on the road."

"The men outside the Capitol?"

I nod.

"So the Patriarchs are behind it."

"There's more." I touch his am and he stills. "When I was in the marketplace, I overhead two men talking. They said that the herdsmen hadn't taken their herds down to the Capitol yet. That's never happened before. Maybe it's not the Patriarchs. Maybe there's something happening up north."

His mouth is a grim line. "And you were going to tell me this when?"

"I was afraid for Hestia," I admit. "I didn't want you thinking there was some kind of resistance making trouble."

"Well, I certainly don't think that now," he drawls. "It's too late now, anyway. Our gear is destroyed. We don't have any choice."

"Please!" I grab the front of his shirt, holding it in my closed fist. He looks down at my hand, his eyebrow raised. I let go, trying to calm my voice. "I know where we can get food and supplies not too far from here." He hesitates, looking reluctant, but like he wants to be convinced. "You know what will happen if they come. We can fix this. We don't need the Legion. Not yet."

"This is more than just an environmental glitch. We can't allow an armed resistance on Hestia."

"I agree. I don't like the Patriarchs either. But we have to solve this first. A Conflict will just get in the way." I step closer to him, looking up in his face. "I will tell the truth, I promise. Just let me help. I can get us the supplies we need to finish this mission."

I can see him relenting. "There are regulations. If mission control doesn't receive a report, then central command will abort the mission."

I sag, defeated. "So that's it? There's nothing we can do?"

"There's one option," he says, and I look up hopefully. "The GRIP maintains a communication station, west of here." So the Legion has spy stations; I'm not surprised. "We could comm in from there and give a report. If we have a good plan, they would accept it."

I can't believe what I'm about to suggest, but what other choice do I have? "I know a place where we can resupply," I offer. "It's close by, about twenty klicks northeast."

He gets out his map, has me show him the location. It's a big spread of farmland with plenty of supplies located in the granary complex, well out of sight of anyone.

He frowns at me. "How do you know it's secure?"

"I know it better than anywhere," I answer. "It's my home."

CHAPTER FOURTEEN

My eyes are gritty from lack of sleep, my stomach a hollow space. I anxiously scan the empty horizon while Kya checks over the navigation system on the remaining wagon. We're all tired and hungry, but we need to get going quickly in case whoever attacked us comes back.

Kya mutters to herself as she examines the wires and circuits of the power board. Sion leans against the wagon on the shady side, taking refuge from the midday heat. His pale skin is reddening already. I dig in my bag and hand him the sun salve that I bought from the marketplace. "Here, this will help you not to burn." He sniffs at it appreciatively. "My sister Britta used to make sun salves like that. She made all the lotions and soaps we used and the herbal remedies for a sour stomach or an earache."

But she won't be at the farm anymore. Neither will Agatha. They will both be married and gone by now.

Kya closes the hatch on the wagon with a firm click. With a hiss of air, the hover wagon miraculously powers up and rises to a gliding position.

"You did it!" I cheer.

She grins, looking satisfied. "I have a knack for fixing things. It's something you learn, growing up on a world of engineers."

Sion gets up shakily, wiping away perspiration with his sleeve. "Don't believe her, Vesta. Our dear Dr. Kya is much more than a common engineer." He pats Kya's arm paternally. "She has a rare intuition. Always manages to find the solutions that no one else can."

Kya acknowledges his praise with a shrug. "I'm just glad we can get out of here."

I look over to where Joren is talking with Darla by the wreck of the old wagon. I can't hear what they're saying. I can only hope that he's keeping his promise—telling Darla to downplay what happened to Legion Command, buying us the time to complete this mission.

To reach to the relay station, Darla will have to ride Joren's brown stallion. I don't like having to entrust Luca to her care. Horses are sensitive animals, and Darla is rough. But we don't have any choice.

"I'll be right back," I say, walking over to where the horses are tethered.

Luca nickers gently as I approach. "It'll be alright, boy," I croon, petting his snout. "Just listen to Darla and everything will be fine." Even though part of me hopes he will buck her off. "And then you'll get a nice rest and a rubdown at the nearest stable."

Darla stalks over toward us. Joren watches cautiously from a distance, as if he's expecting me and Darla to fight. She walks past me, grabs the stallion's reins, then leans in close. "You may have the commander fooled," she hisses, "Acting all innocent, trying to play on his soft spot for you. But I know you're hiding something."

I'm taken aback at her venom, at the unfairness of her accusation. "I don't know what you're talking about."

"Right," she sneers. "Like you're not playing on the fact that because the commander wants you he's letting you get away with this!"

Joren doesn't have a thing for me. Darla is so paranoid that she's making things up.

"He's just trying to complete this mission, just like the rest of us." Although I'm not so sure that Darla does want the mission to succeed. She may prefer that the Legion come in instead.

A flash of emotion moves across her face, a hint of pain mixed with rage that she quickly shoves down. Her typical look of contempt is back. "You don't know who he is," she sneers, "but you'll find out soon."

I refuse to show any reaction to her veiled threat. She's trying to rattle me, get me confused, whatever it takes to undermine my trust in him and cause trouble. I won't let her get to me.

She shakes her head at me in disgust, then heaves herself onto Luca's back. The stallion almost rears up, but Darla is able to settle him down somehow. It's obvious that she isn't a skilled rider, but she should be able to stay in the saddle long enough to make it there in a day or two. The area is sparsely populated, so she isn't likely to encounter any trouble. I'm more worried about Darla's capacity for violence. She'll likely cut down anyone in her path.

I grab the reins before she can ride away. "Remember, there are no trained soldiers here. Hestia is a peaceful world."

She grunts, non-committal. "Doesn't seem that peaceful to me."

She kicks Luca's flank and urges him forward. He seems uncertain at first, but she manages to get him moving. As I watch them ride off, I send out a silent prayer that she finds the station without incident.

Joren walks over, frowning. "What was that about?"

"Nothing." I don't want to repeat what she said. Certainly not her implication that he wants me. "She's just angry. She hates Hestians, me included."

He looks after her, scowling. "There's a reason for that. She lost some people in the Conflict, people close to her."

I snort, derisive. "So did lots of other people." Maybe not in this province, but I saw the human cost on both sides, Legion and colonist.

He shakes his head. "Maybe so. But she doesn't see it that way. She blames the outworlders. She thinks all outworlders are potential rebels."

That explains a lot, why she has hated me from the beginning. It's more than just standard class prejudice. That's even more reason to be worried about setting her loose on Hestia.

"I wish it wasn't her we had to send out there. I'm worried about what she's going to do."

He shrugs. "Darla will follow orders. Besides, she's the only one we can spare. We don't have a choice."

This whole mission has seemed like that, one fateful decision after another because of a lack of options. I hope he's right about her following orders, although she hasn't seemed too obedient so far. But it wasn't just me she was suspicious of. It was Joren too. What did she mean by "He's not who you think he is?"

"I get that she hates *me*," I say, watching his face, "but she hasn't been that respectful to you either."

His face shutters. "Don't worry about that." His voice has gone crisp, formal. "Just leave Darla to me." He walks back over to where Kya and Sion are working on the wagon. He's facing away from me, but I can see the tension in his shoulders.

Joren must have some idea of her grievance against him, based on that reaction. He knows something about her past. She must know something about his too.

"I have bad news." Kya's voice rises, grabbing my attention. I walk over to join the others beside the wagon. Kya is holding a tool in one hand, leaning against the cart with the other. She looks exhausted, her dark curls sticking to her head. "The cart can only carry two people at this point. I was able to get it operational, but the capacity is reduced."

"Can we lighten the load?" Joren asks. "Jettison any gear that we don't need?"

"We've gone through it all," Sion says. "It's all essential."

"But we've only got one mount," I protest. Feather is tethered nearby, quietly munching on grass. There's no way that we can make the journey that way. Someone would have to walk, and that would take too long.

"Not necessarily." Joren looks appraisingly at Feather. "Vesta and I will need to ride together."

"What?! No! She can't carry two of us." Well, technically, it's possible. But it will slow us down. And it gives me a funny feeling to imagine being pressed up against Joren.

"She can manage it if we keep our pace slow."

"But the saddle," I protest. "It's not wide enough for two people."

He looks at me skeptically. "Do you want this to work or not?"

I'm being unreasonable. And I don't want him to know how uncomfortable I feel at the idea of being so close to him. Sion looks annoyed at my protest. Kya has a speculative look, like she can read my mind.

"Alright, sure. Let's try it," I concede.

Kya and Sion clamber into the wagon, Kya giving me a mischievous smirk before she climbs in.

Joren unhitches Feather and walks her over. He reaches up to grab the pommel as if he's going to mount and leave me to ride behind him.

"Wait," I stop him, placing my hand on his. "I'm a better rider than you. It's going to be hard on Feather to have two of us anyway. I want to be in charge of it."

He raises up his hands in defeat. "Alright, I'll ride behind you."

I'd expected Joren to resist. His easy surrender throws me off. Self-conscious now, I lift myself into the saddle, settling in. Joren grabs the pommel and lifts himself up to mount behind me, surrounding my body with his own.

Definitely too tight a fit.

I hold the reins, so Joren has to hold on by grasping my hips, his fingers spread across my stomach. His chest presses against my back, his thighs nestle up against mine, his breath warms my hair.

He should stink after running last night. But no, he smells good, the herbs from the sun salve mixing with the natural smell of his body. There's a thrill in my stomach that I don't want to feel.

This is going to be an interesting ride.

"Alright, you ready?" I ask Joren. My voice only quavers a bit.

"Ready," Joren confirms. His voice sounds in my left ear, gently ruffling my hair.

I ease the horse forward, signaling the wagon to follow.

It's hard to ignore the sensations of his body against mine. I'm feeling a stirring of warmth in my body, an excitement that I really do not want to feel right now, not with my mission commander. He shifts a little behind me like he's trying to make a bit more space. I don't know whether I should be relieved or offended.

It's been quite a while since I've been with a man. That must be why I'm reacting so strongly to Joren. I like the feel of his body against mine, even if I don't want to be liking it. I can feel my cheeks burning, but luckily, he can't see my face from behind.

This is stupid. We're going across the mountains, people out there are trying to kill us, my home world might be destroyed, and all I can think about is being pressed up next to my mission commander.

"How far is it to the boundary of your land?" he asks.

"Huh...? Oh, about twenty kilometers northeast. But that's just the southern boundary. We'll be going to the granary. It's a few kilos northeast of that."

"Are you sure we won't be seen?"

"Yes, the granary is way out of sight of the main house. If we get there late in the day, there's no chance of anyone coming over there."

By anyone, I mean my family. Papa rarely hired on temporary help like the larger farmers sometimes did. Simon and Lucas will likely have stayed on with Papa to help out, along with whoever they've married and their children. If only I could see them again, just once. Even Papa, at least to show him I made it out, that he didn't get his way.

"I haven't seen my family for years either," Joren says softly.

There he goes again, reading my mind. Or maybe we just understand each other, despite what I expected.

"I guess the Conflict has done that to a lot of us" is all I can think to say in return.

I can feel his body start to relax, his arms settling around my waist.

I give up trying to talk, focusing my attention on the terrain in front of us. He keeps his attention on the horizon, scanning for threats.

As the hours pass, the adrenaline of the night fades into exhaustion and the sun saps my strength. My stomach is feeling even more hollow. I start thinking about that jerky they were selling in the marketplace. I should have bought some. It would go perfectly right about now, washed down with a tall pitcher of those cool mango juices they sell in the Capitol. Or, even better, one the meat pies my mother used to make, the ones with the gravy and those little carrots.

My stomach growls loudly.

"Hungry?" His voice rumbles against my hair.

I groan. "Aren't you?"

He shrugs. "I wouldn't mind something to eat." He sounds like it doesn't matter to him much.

Hunger makes me impatient; it always has. "So you can go without food, huh? Let me guess, that was part of your officer training."

He doesn't answer right away, as if my question has taken him aback. "Before that." His whole body tenses up, his posture going rigid behind me. "It was part of our training in the Academy."

"Trained how? To be hungry?" Surely, he couldn't mean that. The Academy was the training center for the privileged youth of the Core Worlds. They wouldn't do that to their own children, would they?

He shrugs again, but I can feel the tension in his hands where they grip my hips. The apparent casualness of his voice doesn't match what his body is telling me. "We were kept hungry. It made us work harder, learn to do without. We learned to function, to fight, without weakness. Sometimes without sleep too."

"How old were you," I ask carefully, "when you went?"

His hands squeeze me tighter in an unconscious gesture, his fingers almost hurting me. "I was seven. That's the standard age."

I stop Feather, turning toward Joren in the saddle so I can look him in the face. He shifts his hand on my hip, holding me from falling off. "I can't believe your family would do that to you. Who sends a seven-year-old boy away from his family, starves him, and makes him fight?!"

He looks startled at my vehemence. "It's a tradition of Patria," he protests. "It's what makes us strong."

I try to imagine seven-year-old Joren, without the strength and certainty that he holds now. He would have been a little lost boy without his mother, hungry, punished.

"I wasn't helpless. I was small for my age, but I fought boys older than me and won." His knuckles tighten. "There was one boy who hated me. Bruin. He was from a southern lineage. It was a matter of family honor to best me. He made it his personal goal to take me down."

"He didn't succeed?"

"I have some scars to show for it, but no, he didn't."

His voice sounds dismissive, but his body tells me the truth. His fingers are gripping my hips, his muscles tense.

I never thought I would have any sympathy for a Legion officer. I always thought they had everything I didn't, that their money and privilege insulated them from what the rest of us suffered through.

But his suffering had been different. I may have done without, but I'd always had the love of my family. I hadn't been alone. At least, not as a child. Suddenly I wish I was behind him instead of in front so I could wrap my arms around him, to give him comfort.

We fall silent for a while after that. As the day wears on, the tension in his body gradually relaxes. After a while, his arms feel comfortable, wrapped around my waist like an embrace.

CHAPTER FIFTEEN

We stop later that afternoon, just a brief break to eat and to empty our bladders. I'm so tired. It would feel pretty good to have a break from being the lead rider. As we're about to mount back up, I ask Joren, "Maybe you could take the reins for a while?"

He grins good-naturedly, eyebrows raised. "Oh, you think I'm good enough?"

I roll my eyes.

We get back in the saddle, him in front this time. I wrap my arms around his waist. At first, I try to keep a bit of distance, sit up straight. But as I get more and more sleepy, I lay my cheek up against his back, my arms all the way around him.

I come awake sometime later.

"Huh?" My hands are wrapped around Joren's stomach, his hand locking them into place. "Did I fall asleep?"

"I had to hold your arms or you would have fallen off."

"Oh. Thanks."

I stretch to sitting, surveying the territory.

"We're almost there, according to the nav device."

"This is looking familiar, actually."

Kya pops her head out of the back of the wagon. "Please tell we we're almost there."

We stop at a copse of trees, down by the banks of the river.

I climb down and hold on to Feather's reins. "I'll get her settled in," I tell Joren.

"OK, I'll start getting the camp set up in a minute." Joren climbs down slowly, gingerly, then walks over toward the wagon. He's limping. It's almost undetectable, but he favors his left side. His right hip looks stiff.

"Are you alright?"

He keeps walking. "I'm fine," he answers tightly. "Just stiff from the ride."

I feel sore too, but this looks like something different. "Are you sure? It looks like you're injured."

He sighs, then stops and turns to face me. "It's an old injury, from back in the Conflict. It's just acting up from the ride." His face looks tense, like he's in pain and trying not to show it.

I frown. "I thought you officers all got full regen."

He shrugs. "Haven't had the chance yet."

The Conflict ended three years ago, which means he could have gone back to the Core Worlds for regen by now. There must be some reason he hasn't. It's not normal for an officer to be living on the fringes like this, so far from home.

He lowers himself down to sit on a log, holding his right leg out in front of him. He's obviously in pain and doing his best not to show it. That must be another part of the training. An Imperial officer always has to appear perfect, infallible, undefeated. I sense that it would embarrass him for me to say anything more.

I keep an eye on him as we set up camp. If I didn't know he was injured, I wouldn't have noticed it. He does his part in setting up the shelters and securing the camp like the rest of us.

Once I set up the fire, I go into the wagon to get the pain meds out of the medical kit. I bring him the meds while Kya and Sion aren't looking, and he accepts them silently.

Later, as we settle down to camp and around the fire, I take him his dinner, refill his cup, and do whatever I can to bring him things without seeming to.

When I refill his cup of tea, he raises an eyebrow at me. "I know what you're doing."

"What?" I ask innocently, as I sit on the log next to him. "I was getting some anyway."

He grins crookedly. "Thanks." His is tone grudging, but the smile softens it.

I wonder how long it's been since someone has seen underneath his strong, tough exterior, to the man underneath.

*　　*　　*

There's still an hour of sunlight. Dinner has been eaten and put away. Sion and Kya are lounging by the fire.

Joren takes out his weapon and starts checking it over. I'd better do the same. I take out the blaster he issued me and check it over just like I was trained to do in Basic. Joren stows his weapon. "How long has it been?" he asks.

I set down my weapon. "Since I fired one of these?" He nods. "A while."

"Need some practice?"

I don't like the idea of needing to use a weapon on one of my own people, but it wouldn't hurt to be prepared, just in case.

"What I could use is some of those fighting skills you promised." I don't want to be in a position like last night again, without a weapon or the ability to defend myself.

"Fine." I look over, surprised. I didn't expect him to say yes. "If we're attacked again, I need some backup. More than a couple of scientists."

Kya pretends to take offense. Sion just shrugs.

Joren leads to out to a flat spot in the meadow, where the grass has been trampled down. "Show me what you know," he invites.

I take my initial stance, knees bent, hands in attack mode.

Joren makes his approach, surprisingly fast, and before I can blink, he has me turned around, my feet swept out from under me, and I'm flat on the ground.

"What," I dust myself off, outraged. "Was that?"

He smiles, scratches his chin. "Didn't they teach you that in Basic?"

I scowl at him. "You know they didn't."

"Well, I'll have to suggest that to the training division."

"I was being easy on you because you're injured," I lie.

"Right." He looks skeptical. "This time you come at me."

I don't care if his hip is hurt. I can use that to my advantage by coming at his left side and using my angle and leverage to knock that leg out from under him. Somehow, I end up disarmed and on the ground again. But this time Joren's boot is on my chest.

"How did you do that?" I ask, looking up at him from where I lay in the dust.

"Come on," He reaches his hand down and pulls me to my feet. "Let me show you."

We go through all the likely ways I could be attacked. We run through scenarios of how to disarm attackers, even multiple attackers. I forget that he's hurt until finally I manage to knock him off his feet and he goes down hard. I remember his leg then, and rush over to help him up. He takes my hand and pulls me down and over, pinning me.

"Hey, that's cheating," I protest. His face is inches from mine, his lips visible through the scruff of his dark stubble, brown eyes rich and warm above me.

That warm feeling moves through me again, that uneasy excitement I felt on horseback. I want to kiss him. I shouldn't want to kiss him.

His eyes move over my face. His lips part, his breath catches. Then he pulls himself away, up to his knees.

Was he just reacting to me, the way I was to him?

This time he doesn't take my hand but stands several feet away as I get to my feet. He looks almost uncertain, looking at me and then away. "Not bad, Vesta. I think you're ready."

He's acting weird too. At least I'm not the only one embarrassed.

I brush the dust off me. "Barely. I never was much of a soldier."

He shakes his head. "You're good. Just haven't had access to the training."

It's ridiculous that his praise warms me. "I was better with my weapon than hand-to-hand, but it's been a while."

He walks over to where he left his gun belt and pulls out his blaster. "Here, take mine." He holds it out, handle first.

"An Imperial model. Nice." I can feel the difference as I test its weight. I check its charger settings, admiring the craftsmanship.

"Ready for some target practice?" He walks across the field, gathering up some fallen tree limbs to use as makeshift targets and sets them up at various distances. Then he comes back to stand beside me.

My aim is still good, even after all this time. But Joren offers me some hints and adjustments as I go along. I'm surprised by how help-ful he is, so different from the harsh rebukes of the Legion trainers. It doesn't make me nervous for him to watch me. Soon, I'm hitting all the targets dead center.

The word hits me, then... *dead*. I vowed that I wouldn't shoot at a living person again, not after I left the Legion.

Would I be willing to use this weapon against a fellow Hestian?

Joren walks over to the farthest target, sets an apple atop it, then steps away.

I aim, fire. The flesh of the apple explodes outward with the force of the blast, mimicking the damage to human flesh. I lower my weapon, meeting Joren's gaze across the field.

Yes, I decide. *If it means saving Hestia from destruction... I am.*

CHAPTER SIXTEEN

It's about an hour until dusk. The beams of sunlight slant sideways, turning the fields of wheat a glowing golden color. This is the magic hour when anything seems possible.

Simon and I used to ride out on summer evenings like this. We would perch on horseback, eyes alert for a glimpse of the herder caravans as they headed south, eager for the onset of the annual celebrations.

I scan the horizon, looking for any familiar landmarks. But the landscape of fields seems nondescript, no signs of familiar trees, buildings, or streams.

"Recognize anything?" Joren squints at his nav display. "If this is working right, we should be coming up on the southern boundary of your family's land."

I stand up in the stirrups to get a better view.

"Whoa!" Joren grips my hips to steady himself. "Give me a little notice next time."

The warmth of his hands on my hips distracts me. But then my eye catches on a flash of blue amongst the gold, just past the boundary of the fields. And, just beyond that, the shelter of a mature grove of oaks.

"That's it!" I let out a whoop of triumph, settling back into the saddle. Joren's arms wrap around my waist again, but it can't match the excitement of what I'm seeing. I urge Feather on, faster. "We're here!"

We pull up to an oasis of clear blue water, edged by a grove of old oaks. We used to swim in this creek in the summers. Its southern bank marks the boundary of my family's lands.

The wagon pulls up behind us. Sion and Kya pop their heads out. "Why are we stopping?" Kya asks.

"We're about five klicks from my family home," I answer. "Almost there." Close enough for where we're going, but far enough away from the house to avoid being detected.

I wonder if the old farmhouse still looks the same—white paint, dark blue trim. Mama always loved those colors. On summer nights like this, after dinner had been cleared away, we would sit out on the wide porch. Mama would bring us cool juice. Sometimes we'd play music, sometimes we'd just listen to the crickets in the dark.

"Which way from here?"

The urgency in Joren's voice pulls me away from the memories. "We head northeast to the granary." That's where the supplies we need will be stored. And no one should be there at this time of day. Which means no one in my family will ever know that I was here.

"What is it?" Joren asks, sounding concerned. I must have tensed up.

"Nothing. It's fine." I hesitate. "It's just... hard to go home again."

He doesn't say anything, but he squeezes my shoulder, and I get the impression that he understands. We signal to the wagon, then head out.

*　　*　　*

We pull in around back of the granary. The bulky gray-green building has a barn attached, with some storage sheds just across the way. No one should be able to see the wagon and horses from where we're parked. And anyway, we should be in and out. No one would have any reason to come here at the dinner hour.

I'd visited this place so often during harvest season. Most of the grain and vegetables will have been harvested already, so it should be well-stocked.

It's cool inside, a relief from the summer heat, with the familiar scent of hay and grain.

"Where are the supplies?" Joren asks, fishing out the food sacks.

I open the storage bins of grain, beans, and other dried foodstuffs. They're all curiously low, much less than I would expect to find at this point in the harvest. I feel guilty now. I'm stealing from my own family. But I get out the food sacks and we start loading up the supplies.

Wrrp, wrrp. We all stop, listening intently. A dull whirring, getting louder, coming from the east.

Joren draws his weapon, his expression deadly. "We've been followed."

"No, wait." I press his arm down. "It's a harvester."

I peer out through the slats. A red vehicle is approaching from the east. The driver pulls up to the storage shed across the way and climbs down from the cockpit. It's a man, probably one of the farm workers, dressed in homespun clothing and a wide-brimmed hat, facing away from me. He heads to the storage shed across the way, opening the latch. The man turns around, and I gasp.

Simon. My close brother. So close we were almost twins. If there's anyone I would trust with my life, it's him.

"Who is it?" Joren whispers. "Do you know him?"

"That's my brother!" I reach for the door, frantic.

Joren grabs my arm. "We can't trust him. It's too dangerous."

I spin around. "He'll help us!"

"We can't risk it."

Joren's denial hits me like a punch to the stomach. His mouth is a firm, angry line. He won't budge.

I pull out my binocs to get a better view, desperate for a glimpse of my brother. He's filled out since I left, taller and more solid. There's no trace of the gangly nineteen-year-old from ten years ago. He looks older, his face marked by lines of stress, so different from his usual laughter. His dark hair has grown longer, hanging just past his neck, his olive skin darkened from the sun.

I have to go to him. I can't be so close and just walk away. But Joren stands at my elbow.

Simon grabs something from the shed and closes it back up behind him. He's walking back to the harvester. Then he stops and squints at something behind the barn.

The hover cart. He's seen it. It's too late to hide anyway.

I push open the barn door and slip past Joren before he can grab me, stepping out into the sunlight.

Simon startles at the noise of the creaking door, turning to face me. His jaw drops, his face slack.

"Vesta?" His voice trembles.

I nod, hot tears slipping down my cheeks.

He's frozen for a moment. Then, with a whoop of delight, he runs over and lifts me off my feet, spinning me around in a fierce embrace. I'm crying and laughing at the same time.

I'm home. I'm finally home.

He sets me down, holding me by the shoulders, looking me over with that familiar grin on his face. Our eyes are the same shade of green.

He's touching me on my face, my arms, all over, as if checking to see if I'm real. "I can't believe it. You're really here!"

The others in the barn must be watching us, listening to every word. But I won't let them spoil this moment.

"We haven't heard from you in ten years! We thought you were dead!"

So Papa never told them. I'd hoped better of him.

"Simon, Papa knows. I sent him a message when I went off-world."

Anger moves across Simon's face, followed by grief. His fingers tighten painfully on my shoulders. "He's gone, Vesta. Heart attack. Last year."

I look inside, trying to find the sadness, the grief that a daughter should feel. But I can't find it. I find only relief. I won't have to face him again. At least there's that.

Simon holds me by shoulders, his forehead creased with concern. "When Papa sent you away… to the city… Vesta, I wish—"

"No." I reach up to cover his mouth. This is private. I don't want the others listening. "I need to tell you something first."

His eyes narrow. "What is it?"

I hesitate, my eyes moving to the barn. "Before I tell you, you need to swear that you won't tell anyone."

He nods slowly, his eyes fixed on mine. "I swear it. I'll help you, whatever you need."

Joren will kill me for this. But what other choice do we have?

"I'm not alone, Simon. My friends need help too."

Simon looks over at the barn, then back to me, shaking his head. "Why does that not surprise me, sis? You always did have a talent for getting into trouble."

*   *   *

I shield Simon with my body as we walk into the barn.

Joren's weapon is tucked out of sight. He looks angry, though… not that I can blame him.

Simon steps out from behind me, arms crossed as he looks them over. He notes Kya's dark skin and curls, and Sion's pale, ruddy face and orange hair, marking them as off-worlders. Joren stands proudly with a warrior's aura of command.

"'Publicans, Vesta?!" Simon asks, his voice derisive.

Joren steps forward, extending his hand to Simon in the customary greeting of the Republic. "I'm Commander Joren. Your sister says we can trust you."

Simon ignores Joren's hand until he drops it.

The two men look like two bulls ready for a fight, but I can't let it come to that. Joren is a seasoned solider, all lean muscles and keen reflexes. My brother wouldn't stand a chance against him. I step between them, my hand on Simon's chest in a silent plea.

"Does someone want to tell me what's going on here?" Simon asks, never taking his eyes of Joren.

I look to Joren for permission. He nods, his jaw tight.

I tell Simon everything—the anomalous readings, the recruitment of me as a guide, the attack. He stops me a few times to ask questions. But otherwise, he just listens, his expression darkening as the story goes on.

"That explains a lot," he says finally. "The weather's been strange lately. All this season, the crops have been struggling."

Kya and Sion exchange a worried look.

"That should have been reported to the authorities," Sion says.

Simon bristles at that. "We're used to solving our own problems out here." He glares at Sion. "You ignore us, and we ignore you. It's worked pretty well so far."

"Simon, they can fix it," I plead. "That's why they're here. Sion and Kya are the best scientists from the Institute."

His eyebrows raise at the mention of the Institute. Even on Hestia, we've heard of that.

Kya steps forward, her winning smile an improvement over Sion's gruffness.

"I'm Dr. Kya." She takes Simon's hand, but instead of shaking it, places his between her own. "Vesta has told me about you, about her family. You have something special here on Hestia. I'm here to help you to save that."

I can recognize the honesty in her voice, and so does Simon. He looks uncertain for a moment, then he sighs and nods his head. "I don't like this. But I'm going to help you, for my sister's sake." The others relax a measure of their tension. "It's late. You all can stay the night here."

Sion opens his mouth as if to refuse, but Joren shakes his head at him and accepts the offer.

"But first, I have to talk to my sister… in private."

Before anyone can respond, Simon marches me out of the barn. He leads up to the far side of the harvester, out of view and earshot of the others.

He looks uncomfortably at the barn, then back to me, his face softening.

He's taller than me now, I notice. When I left, we were the same height.

He reaches out and tugs on my braid, the same way he used to when he'd tease me, but his eyes have a somber look. "I didn't tell you. I'm married now. To Rachel."

That's not a surprise. Our neighbor Rachel had wanted Simon since we were children. "She finally got you, huh? So, am I an aunt?"

He grins proudly. "Two boys and a girl."

I've missed so much. Everything.

"What about Britta and Agatha? Are they married too?"

"They moved away not too long after you left. The aunts and uncles went with them. It's just Lucas and me running the farm now, but he's been gone a lot doing business in the city."

I never thought I would miss Lucas. But I do, even him.

"What happened to you, Vesta?" His voice, plaintive, echoes my own sadness. "The last time I saw you when was when Papa sent you off the Capitol. How'd you end up with these 'Publicans?"

I was so frightened when Papa forced me to go to the city because I had to go alone. Simon and I had always dreamed of going there together, of seeing the port, of watching the merchant ships launch into space, where we wanted to go.

"Remember how we always talked about going off-world, how great it would be to get off Hestia, go explore the sector?"

He nods.

"I did it, Simon." For a moment, I remember the excitement of it, not just the fear. Simon would have been so jealous of me then. "I hopped a freighter off-world, joined the Legion."

"The Legion?!" His eyes widen. "I knew you were tough, but I didn't know you were Enforcer tough. You always were a little crazy, sis."

I shrug, deflecting, but I love the compliment. "I served out my contract. Now I've been working around, here and there." I don't want to admit my subsequent failure to Simon. "Anyway... that's how Joren found me. From my Legion service record."

"Joren, huh?" He snorts dismissively. "He's a Core Worlder, you can tell. One of those high and mighty types." He crosses his arms across his chest. "I don't trust him, and I don't like him around my sister."

A wave of outraged fury moves through me. After all this time, and he has to play the protective older brother. "Look, Simon, I've been living on my own all this time, and I haven't had to answer to anyone for the decisions I've made."

He backs off, his face softening. "Hey, I don't want to argue, Vesta. I'm just happy to have you back."

I take his hands in mine and squeeze. "Then you have to trust me. I've seen what happens to a world when the Legion comes. I won't let that happen to Hestia."

He glances at the barn and seems to come to a decision.

"You should come with me to the house. Tonight."

His offer tugs at me, at what I wish for most. But it's impossible.

"I can't, Simon. We need to get moving."

"But you're short a horse. I can get you another one."

Even an offer of a horse wasn't likely to sway Joren.

"Even if Joren agreed, what about Rachel and the kids?"

"They're at her sister's tonight."

"And Lucas?"

"He's in the city." He takes my hand. "You should come. To say goodbye, at least."

When will I ever have this chance again?

"I'll have to ask Joren. Maybe he'll let me go if I take him with me."

He flares. "I won't have a 'Publican at our home."

I look back at the barn, where the others are waiting.

I don't know how I'll convince him, but I have to.

"OK, wait for me, Simon. I'll be there," I promise.

CHAPTER SEVENTEEN

It doesn't take long to reach the house, maybe twenty minutes of riding. The sun is setting over the ridge, the farmhouse bathed in the magic light of almost-dusk. The grounds look mostly the same, an expanse of open meadow with a well-tended herb garden up front. Some of the fruit trees are gone, but not the oaks. Those old trees are still stretching out, thick and strong, at the side of the house. The house looks freshly painted, but it's still the same colors—white with blue trim.

I can't believe I'm here.

It was hard to convince Joren to let me come here, but eventually he gave in. He got angrier than I've ever seen him, ranting about how much he hates these surreptitious missions, waiting around while I take risks. I was surprised by that. I hadn't expected that my safety would be his objection.

But in the end, he let me go. He knows, just like I do, how much we need a second horse. He insisted that I take my blaster, although I told him I'd never shoot my own brother. "What if there's someone else there?" he demanded. So I took the gun.

Simon is waiting on the porch as I ride up. He walks out to me as I dismount, gives me a long, tight hug. "It's good to have you back, sis."

I wipe away the tears threatening to overflow onto my cheeks as Simon secures Feather to the porch railing. I look to the left, past the grove of oaks. That's where they're buried. I'm not ready to say goodbye to Mama and Papa. Not yet.

We walk together up the front steps, onto the wide porch where we used to sit out on summer evenings, and through the front door.

The memories rush in as I step inside. I almost expect Mama to walk out from the kitchen, chiding me for being late to dinner. The furniture is mostly the same, but little touches are different—the blue tablecloth, the lamp made of brass. That must be Rachel's doing.

The door to the kitchen is open partway. The clean, organized space would have pleased Mama. The dining room table would normally be set for dinner at this hour, but it's bare. Coats hang on the rack by the entryway, with the bright colors and small sizes that show the presence of children. Simon watches me intently as I take it all in.

"It looks good, Simon," I assure him. "Rachel's done a good job."

My old bedroom would be just up the stairs. The railing of the main staircase is made from old oak, worn smooth from years of use. All the bedrooms are up there. Mine was just to the left of the landing.

"Do you want to go up? The kids' rooms are upstairs now."

On the last day I lived in this house, I had walked down these stairs, when my father had called me down to face the Patriarchs.

"Vesta, come downstairs." There's something wrong; I can hear it in his voice. Papa has someone there with him in the parlor.

"Vesta, are you alright?"

I'm frozen, looking up the stairs. It seemed so real.

It's Simon, not Papa, I remind myself. It's OK. I'm safe.

"Just memories." But I don't want to go up there.

114

I turn, instead, to the downstairs parlor. That was the last room I went into before I was taken away.

The furniture is wrong. I notice that right away. Mama's chair is missing from its spot in the corner. So is the dark-blue couch where Papa used to sit. A new settee, gold fabric with a fancy trim, has taken its place. Rachel must have brought that from her mother's house.

Papa hovers by the fireplace, my brother Lucas beside him. Three men sit on chairs, severe looks on their faces. I don't recognize them, but they are dressed as Patriarchs. They must be from the city.

You must go with them, Vesta, Papa tells me.

No, no, I can't. I'll behave. I don't want to go.

You have disgraced the family. The boy's family will not have you as a wife.

You asked them? I ask, indignant, humiliated.

Lucas stands, impassive. He always thought he had the right to judge me as the eldest.

I walk over the fireplace, touching the worn brick. The pictures of Mama and Papa are still there, but now images of Simon's family hang above the mantel. Rachel and Simon look happy, surrounded by two boys and a girl who each look a bit like them both.

"Clara has green eyes, like you." Simon stands next to me, looking up at the pictures. He points to an image of the older boy, holding a trophy that's almost as big as him. "That's Marcus when he won the prize for best student farmer in his class."

So many years I've missed. Time that we can never get back.

"It was quiet here after you left." Simon's voice is quiet, hesitant. "First Mama was gone, then you too."

As they march me out of the house, I see Simon standing by. His eyes are wild, sad. But he says nothing. He's letting them take me. There will be no rescue.

The betrayal burns, as fresh as if it happened yesterday. "You could have done something, said something." I turn to him. "Why did you let them take me away?"

Simon looks stricken. "I should have." His voice turns pleading. "I tried to talk Papa out of it. He and Lucas were set on it. I wish you hadn't had to go away."

"You could have said something. You could have stopped them."

His face crumples. "I've told myself that... so many times since you they took you away. Every day I've wished it was different."

Tears are streaming down my face, all the anger and grief I've been pushing away for so long flowing out of me.

"I didn't know you'd leave Hestia. At worst I thought I could visit you in the Capitol." He sags in defeat. "I wished it had never happened. I wanted you to be married by now. Live nearby. So we could all be together like we used to be."

I wanted that. Maybe part of me still did.

My rage crumples. He'd only been nineteen, just one year older than me. He was right—there was nothing he could have done. Lucas and Papa would never have listened.

"Papa missed you. He regretted sending you away."

I want to believe it. But Papa was always hard to read. Nothing I did ever seemed to be good enough for him. I never fit what he thought a girl, a woman, should be.

Simon takes down a picture of all of us from when we were children. "I found him one day, right here, looking at this picture. He missed you. He said he wished he hadn't done it." He shakes his head. "I think he cared too much about what people would think. And Lucas..."

A fresh anguish moves through me. "He told him to send me away?"

"You know how he is."

So it wasn't just Papa's decision.

Suddenly the parlor is too close, too full of memories. I hurry out to the porch, and Simon follows me. I lean over the railing, catching my breath.

Simon puts his hand on my shoulder. We stand there for a while, looking out at the farm. But there is more of the past to visit tonight. Just beyond that copse of oaks... Papa and Mama are buried.

Maybe this whole trip—the mission, the whole mess of it—maybe something good could come of it. Now I could have this chance to say goodbye.

"I'm ready to see them," I tell Simon quietly.

"I'll come with you."

"No." I soften my face, my voice. "Simon, please... I need to do this alone."

*   *   *

"Hello, Mama."

The sun has faded to a golden, dappled glow in this sheltered spot. Someone has trimmed the grass around the gravesites, giving me a flat space to sit. My mother's maiden surname, Minerva, is carved in the granite. Yellow asters are blooming all around, her favorite flower. The granite of the grave marker is cool on my fingers.

"I missed you." She'd already been gone when I'd left. But somehow, I felt she'd known anyway. "I'm sorry I've been gone so long."

She would never have understood why I would want to go. She'd always been content with what she had. She'd never understood my restless spirit.

"I wish I had done more for you." I remember the times she had lain in bed with me, holding me. I wish I could do that for her now. I wish that I could climb in beside her, cover us with the blankets, and comfort her, show her the appreciation I never got the chance to.

"I love you, Mama." I lean down to kiss the stone, resting my forehead against it, smooth and cool against my skin.

And there is Papa, lying next to her. I already got my chance to grieve for Mama. I wish that I could grieve more for him. But I still hold so much anger, so much hurt.

He had an idea of who I should be, just the like Patriarchs. He didn't approve of me. I wasn't what he thought a girl should be. I wasn't his idea of a woman.

And now he's gone. And there is no way I'll ever get the approval or understanding that I had wanted from him so badly. It's all over now, that fruitless quest. I hope he is at peace. I really do. I lean down and place another flower on his marker stone.

"I love you, Papa." It feels both true and not true. But it's true enough.

I never had a place here on Hestia. There was no way I could ever really fit in. It wasn't just them sending me away; I couldn't ever be myself here.

There's no way to make this all right now that Mama and Papa are gone. There's no way to ever say enough, no way to be ready for goodbye, especially when I know that I won't be back.

I hear footsteps behind me. Simon comes up and stands beside me. Simon holds fresh-cut irises, four of them, and we lay them on their graves.

"When was it?" I ask him.

"Last winter. He was having pain all through harvest season. We thought he was better. Then he just collapsed when he was getting ready for bed. Rachel called the doctor, but it was too late."

And finally, it comes. Just a few tears. Thank the Goddess, at least I can cry a little.

We stay a short while, until the sun starts fading, reminding me that I need to get back.

"I need to get the horse, Simon. I promised to be back before dark."

"I'll take you in a minute. But first." Simon's face tightens. "There's something you need to know."

This doesn't sound good. "About what?"

He grimaces. "About Lucas. About why he's in the Capitol right now... It's just rumors. I don't know much. I'm not involved with politics, you know that. I only know because Lucas—he's one of the Patriarchs now."

Despite my shock, it makes a strange kind of sense. Lucas was also so self-righteous, so rigid. He was the one who stood next to Papa when he sent me away. Of course he would join them.

I feel a dread in my belly. "Simon, what is this about?"

"Lately, there's been something going on. The herdsmen." He looks up, his gaze troubled. "You may have heard. The herders didn't come this year."

"I heard they were late." Is this what the men in the marketplace had been grumbling about?

"We thought so too, at first. But they still haven't arrived. That's when I found out... the Patriarchs have something to do with it."

Oh no, so it was true. They were blocking the herdsmen. They were hiding something. But why?

"Why didn't you tell me, Simon? This could be dangerous."

He grips my arms, his face intense. "I don't trust them, Vesta. I love you. You know that. But I don't trust those 'Publicans. They're going to call in the Legion if they know."

"Joren won't do that!" I insist.

"You trust this Commander Joren so much?" He looks at me suspiciously, his big brother protectiveness on full display. "Who is this man to you, anyway?"

"It's not like that! We aren't involved like that." It's true. Whatever foolish feelings I may be harboring for Joren are inconsequential. "We're nothing to each other. "I just trust him because he hasn't lied to me. He's kept his word."

He looks skeptical. "I don't trust these 'Publicans, you know that. And I don't want you getting used. Hestia can't risk that."

"Simon, we were partners, remember? We've always trusted each other. I need you to trust me now."

He rubs his hands over his face, then sighs. "OK. You asked me to trust your judgement, so I will. But there's something you should know first. Come on, I need to show you something."

I follow him to a storage shed around back. The door is locked. Doors are never locked on Hestia. He opens the lock with a key from his pocket, turning on a solar lamp.

The space is filled with crates stacked neatly in tall rows. Simon pries opens the nearest one, reaching in to rummage inside. "Those men you saw on the road, the ones dressed in the white unforms," He pulls out a bundle of white cloth, one whose shape looks startingly familiar. "Were they wearing these?"

My gasp of shock is my answer.

I stare at the crisp white uniform. I can't believe it. How could Lucas be a part of this, part of attacking his own sister? "So Lucas was the one who ordered the attack?"

"He couldn't have known you were with him," he answers quickly. "He would have thought they were just Imperials."

He can't know that. But I also can't believe that Lucas, even Lucas, could ever do such a thing to me. But this is bigger than just Lucas's personal betrayal. If the Patriarchs were responsible for attacking an Imperial citizen, especially knowingly, they might have just signed Hestia's death warrant. "The men on the road, Simon, they were carrying blasters."

"I know." His shoulders slump. "The cases in the back are full of them. A big supply."

Papa would never have condoned this. No matter what, Papa was traditional. He would never have done anything to upset the balance of life on Hestia. It doesn't make sense. The Patriarchs are supposed to preserve the balance of power on Hestia, not risk destroying it. "So it was the Patriarchs all along?"

He shakes his head, vehement. "Not all of them. This group is made up of some of the younger members. They call themselves the Brotherhood. Lucas is one of their leaders."

My mind is still reeling. "But why would they need blasters?" I ask.

"It's something to do with the herders. There's been talk lately that they've been causing trouble. Something about the North. Maybe they blame them for the problems with the weather. With the disruptions. I don't know."

It does make sense, as horrible as it sounds.

Simon grabs my hand, his eyes wild. "Vesta, I'm only telling you this to warn you. I don't want you involved in this. It's dangerous."

He's still playing the protective big brother. But it's too late. I grew past needing his protection a long time ago.

"Simon, I need to do this. It's our only hope of resolving this without bloodshed."

He doesn't know what I've seen, the costs of defying the GRIP. I never knew what the Legion was willing to do to enforce the GRIP's will, the cost in lives, in worlds.

I can tell when he relents by the release of breath and the faint nod.

"You never did back down, did you, sis?" It feels good to be back to this, the old teasing, the competition of our younger days. It helps me to forget the cost if we fail. "Alright. I'll try to find out more if I can."

"Thank you." I hug him tight. "Let me draw you a map of where we're going. Then if you find out more, you can come there."

"I will." He's scrunching up his face, his eyes tearing up. "I'm going to miss you, sis. Maybe once this mission is over, you can come back and visit. Seeing as how you're going to be a citizen and all."

What a frantic dream, this future we're betting on. But I promise anyway.

Simon looks back at the house, where the kitchen light glows warmly against the darkness of dusk. "Come on." He pulls at my arm. "We can get the horse in a minute. But first, let's eat together."

I know that Joren is waiting for me, and I promised this would be quick. But when will I ever get this chance again?

I let Simon walk me back inside. We sit in the kitchen, eating and talking, as night falls outside.

CHAPTER EIGHTEEN

The granary and barn are dark as I approach with the horses. I try my best to be quiet, murmuring to the horses to soothe them.

"You're back."

Joren is leaning against a stack of hay bales, partially hidden in the darkness. He walks toward me, the shadows and light stark on his face and body, showing the muscular grace of his movements.

"Sorry I'm late. I stayed for dinner with my brother."

"I've been waiting for you." There is a tension in his voice.

"Why?" I bristle. "Did you think I'd run off?"

"No, I was worried about you."

My body fills with a curious warmth. As he draws closer, I smell a familiar but unpleasant smell—the smoke of the varu plant. Joren is holding a rolled-up cigarette of varu, pinched between his fingers.

"What the—" I wrinkle my nose at the foul smell. "You're smoking *that*?"

Varu, a mild intoxicant, is an outworlder herb, popular among freeworkers and the auxiliary troops. Some of my squadron mates had tried to offer me some back in the Legion, but I'd always said no. Varu is not something I'd expect Joren, a high ranked Citizen, to know about, must less use.

"You caught me." He smiles ruefully, blowing out a puff of smoke. "Picked up the habit on Domita. The auxiliaries got me started. It helps with the pain in my hip."

I know he's not looking for sympathy, so I cluck in mock disapproval. "What would your 'Publican friends say if they could see you now?"

He grins, a dimple showing in his grizzled cheek. "They'll never know. You think I'm going to ruin my image?"

He reaches out for the gray mare I'm leading behind me. "And who is this?" She settles down as he strokes her neck.

"Her name's Emeraline. She's actually the granddaughter of my childhood horse." I couldn't believe it when Simon took me to barn and introduced us. It was like being reunited with an old friend. "She looks just like her, actually. I used to race on her. Me and Simon would compete when we were supposed to be doing our chores. Our father would get so mad!" I realize that Joren isn't saying anything, just watching me with an expression I can't name. "What?"

"You love this place."

"Yeah, I do. I miss it." I shrug. "It's home."

I hadn't let myself miss Hestia until now. But tonight, in the quiet of the barn, I'm reminded of the good times. Feather nudges against me impatiently. "Don't worry, girl, we'll get you settled down for the night," I answer, leading her into an empty stall. Joren takes Emeraline into the adjoining stall, then helps to fetch the water and hay.

My mind wanders to the past again, lulled by the gentle ritual of brushing her down.

"You asked me about whether there was another reason I left."

I can see Joren focusing in on me, listening.

"It wasn't just about my mother. There was a scandal. At least on Hestia it's considered one."

After talking with Simon today, after saying goodbye to the pain, it doesn't hurt as much anymore. It seems more ridiculous than anything.

"I was caught in this barn with a boy, Darien, from the neighboring farm. That's why my father sent me away. My virtue had been compromised, so he arranged for me to marry Darien." Those words sound so ridiculous after being off-world.

"First love?" he answers easily.

I shake my head. "Nothing like that. It wasn't serious for either of us." Darien was willing to get physical with me, but he never wanted anyone else to know. At the time it hurt, but now it just seems like a lucky escape. "He's probably married now with five children and a silo full of wheat. My father was so mad that I wouldn't marry him."

"So that's why you left."

I should just leave it at that. But somehow I can't. I want to tell it all.

"You remember that girl we saw in the city?" I ask. "The priestess?"

He shifts in the dark. I can feel his focus on me, even if I can't see his expression. "The girl in white, at temple? Yeah, what about her?"

I can't believe I'm telling him this. "That was me. I mean, that was what I was supposed to be." I sneak a glance at his face, but it's too hard to get a read on him. "My father sent me to the Capitol after I was caught with that boy. I was supposed to join the order of the Vestals, be part of them."

He snorts. "I can't picture that."

"Yeah. I couldn't do it. Even though it was expected for my 'family honor.' That's what my father said, anyway. I either had to get married or join the Vestals."

He doesn't say anything for a minute. "Not that different from my world, then."

I snort. "I doubt that!"

"Not about the Vestals. But about family honor. Marriages are arranged by families on Patria too."

"Really?" I had never imagined the elite of the Core Worlds might be as constrained by tradition as we were on Hestia.

"Mine was." My heart seems to sink down into my stomach. "I was pretty young, too, when I signed my marriage contract."

Why should it matter to me that Joren has a wife? I'm certainly not interested in him... am I? The idea is ridiculous, and yet, something in me doesn't seem to like the idea.

My breath feels tight, as I ask, "So your wife, she's waiting for you back on Patria?"

He shakes his head. "Not anymore. She dissolved the contract. I got the notice a year ago."

The sick feeling in my stomach settles down, followed by a rush of warmth and relief. "I'm sorry," I say. But I'm a liar. I'm not sorry at all.

"Like I said, it was an arranged marriage. Our families were business partners for generations. We graduated from the same academy. We were expected to marry. So we did."

He sounds so matter of fact. Does he miss her?

"How long were you married?"

"About ten years. But we married during the Conflict, so we lived apart for most of it. We'd meet up a few times a year."

"It must have been hard for you both, to be so far apart." Why am I saying that? I'm such a fool.

He shrugs. "I'm sure she was with someone else, had other company. It's the way it works when you're posted apart for so long. And we were young—twenty years of age when we married."

"Oh... did you?" I don't know why I ask that. It's none of my business.

"Did I what?" He is watching me carefully.

126

I'm blushing. Thankfully, it's dark, so he won't notice. "Were you with other... people too, when you were apart?"

He looks at me intently for a moment, then he shakes his head. "No. Never."

I hadn't expected him to say yes. It wouldn't fit with what kind of man I've come to know him as. Loyal. Trustworthy. Honorable. It's frightening how much I am coming to believe in him. What a fool this woman must be not to wait for him.

"Why didn't you go back? To Patria, once the Conflict was over?"

His face turns guarded. "That... is a story for another day."

"Of course." I shouldn't have asked him that. "We should probably get ready for sleep."

He walks over, looking down at me. In the warm darkness, there is a strange intimacy. From the shift in his breathing and the expression in his eyes, he feels it too. It's almost like he is going to reach out to me, to touch my face. But he doesn't.

"Yeah, we should," he mumbles.

I turn quickly, walking quietly back to the granary where the others are sleeping, Joren following behind. I crawl over to my sleeping pad, avoiding looking at Joren as I crawl inside my sleep sack.

I close my eyes, listening to the crickets chirping outside. I can tell from Joren's breathing that he is lying awake too, but I don't dare look over at him. Finally, his breath settles into the deep rhythm of sleep.

The jealousy I'd felt had settled. I must admit that's what I felt, as foolish as it was. Some deluded part of me harbors a fantasy about this handsome man. But they are just fantasies. They'll never come to anything, so I'd best keep them to myself.

CHAPTER NINETEEN

By afternoon, we have left the farmlands behind. The grasslands spread out before us now, a waist-high expanse of gold, brown, and green opening to an endless sky. The Caldera Mountains lay to the north, a distant charcoal-gray smudge on the horizon.

The hover wagon skims just above the grass ahead of me. I ride Emeraline through the long grass, brushing gently against my legs. The rhythmic motion of the ride, the swishing of the grass, brings a sense of ease. My body has grown used to riding again, my muscles hardening with the supple strength and attunement that riding requires. I have felt different ever since we've been moving northward through this open land—my senses heightened, my body vital and alive.

How can I be content with everything so wrong?

But I am. For this moment, at least, I am.

Joren rides just ahead, his body moving in time with Feather's. I scan the perimeter, but my eyes keep drifting back to him... to the breadth of his shoulders, his lean hips, his strong legs astride his horse. In the slanted sunlight, the bristles sprouting on his jaw are a lighter brown, with some highlights of gold and copper.

I can't help but imagine stroking the strong lines of his soldier's body, touching the planes of his face, his jaw, his hands, roughened and strong. And, I have been imagining those hands on my body, those wide lips on mine, those warm brown eyes focused just on me. An awakening of my senses has been happening ever since we left the city, and now its influence is unmistakable.

Joren turns and notices me looking at him. I know he can't read my thoughts, but I'm still embarrassed to be caught staring.

He slackens his pace to allow me to catch up, until we are riding astride. He looks easier in the saddle too, but his face holds tension, his eyes scanning the horizon. "Have you seen anything?"

I shake my head. "Nothing yet."

"The sensors haven't detected anything either. Not that we can rely on those." He falls silent for a minute. "I hope we're far enough north to be out of danger. I don't think Darla will be able to rendezvous with us until we're almost to the mountains."

"How will she catch up with us?" I ask. "She's not that skilled of a rider."

"The outpost has vehicles too," Joren answers. "She can take a skimmer."

"But I thought we were supposed to be covert," I protest.

He shrugs. "Someone already knows we're here. I'd say it's worth the risk."

I don't want to see Darla again, but it's better for her to meet up with us and help us to complete the mission than for her to call in for ships.

"Well, the Patriarchs won't be taking skimmers over this land. They'd be too obvious. This isn't even Hestian territory. No one from the Capitol comes up here. Only the herders."

"Still, we need to be on alert."

"Agreed."

He falls silent for a few moments, shifting restlessly. I've learned that's a sign he's worried about something.

"What is it?"

He looks over at me in surprise.

"Is there something you're not telling me?"

"I just wish I had more of a strategy here. These kind of small guerilla actions, they're not what I'm used to. I'm trained for battle, for engaging the enemy. Not this."

Once again, he's trusting me. Letting me see beneath the veneer of invulnerability that I'd always ascribed to Imperial officers. How different he is from the man I once thought he was.

"You've kept us safe so far."

He snorts. "If you call losing half our gear a success." But he looks pleased anyway.

"There's something different about this place. This world. Maybe it's the energy fluctuations, I don't know. I've been feeling it since we got here."

How could he know? Did he actually feel it too?

Then the wagon makes a hissing, wheezing sound. It abruptly stops, dropping roughly to the ground. We hurry to the wagon at a gallop as Sion and Kya are climbing out. Joren has his weapon drawn, scanning the perimeter.

"What happened?" I jump off my horse to join them. "Are you alright?"

"We're fine," Kya answers tersely. She pulls out the access panel, frowning at the display. "This doesn't make sense. Sion, look at this." Sion joins her at the controls, squinting in confusion.

"What happened? What happened to the cart?" Joren holsters his weapon and dismounts to join us.

Kya sets down the instrument panel, frowning in confusion. "The cart, it shorted out, basically. Just got overloaded from the energy fluctuations. The signals in this area are getting erratic, contradictory. They're interfering with the instruments."

"They're getting stronger," Sion says. "The closer we get to the source."

"So what, you can't fix it?"

"No, I can fix it. I'll just need to experiment with the settings. Get it to allow a wider range of signals. That should prevent the system overload, allow more resilience in the energy parameters."

"That's good news," Joren says. "So what's the problem?"

She and Sion exchange a look.

"There are some changes in the energy readings that look... concerning. Sion, do you agree with my assessment?"

"Unfortunately," Sion's face looks worried. "Yes."

"Can you just tell us what this is about?" Joren demands irritably.

"I can show you." She holds up the console so we can all see the display. She presses on the viewscreen and brings up another display screen. The display glows a dull glow of bright orange. "OK, so this image, if you recall, was how the energy readings looked when we were off-planet." The orange glow grows larger and more intense. "Now, this was the magnitude when we were in the Capitol. Right now, we're about one hundred klicks from the epicenter of these readings. And these are readings now." The glow is now explosively bright, a brilliant red that seems to undulate and flow.

"It's getting stronger as we get closer," Joren says. "We expected that, right?"

"Yes, but—"

Sion interrupts, "Not to this magnitude. If we can trust these readings—and I must admit, there may be some interference happening—these levels of energy have never been seen before. At least, not on a settled world. These levels are consistent with a terraforming stage!"

As little as I know about worldbuilding, even I can tell that doesn't sound good.

Joren frowns. "What do you mean?"

"It means," Kya answers, waving her hands for emphasis, "that this is a seismically active area. Those mountains contain an active volcano."

"How is that possible?" Joren explodes.

"It isn't. It shouldn't be."

"The terraforming process is restarting itself." Sion looks stunned. "It has to be a massive malfunction. I've never seen anything like it!"

A wave of dread settles in my gut. If even the Institute has never seen this before…

Joren looks grimmer than I've ever seen him. "What could be causing this?"

"I don't know, commander," Sion answers, "but we can't rule out sabotage. I can't imagine what else could instigate changes of this magnitude."

I shake my head. "This doesn't make sense. No Hestian would cause damage to our own world. There has to be some other explanation."

"I hope you're right, Vesta." Kya's warm dark eyes are troubled, her face tight. "The only way to know for certain is to get to the source."

"How long to get this going again?" Joren asks, waving at the wagon.

"I should be able to get it going soon, maybe twenty minutes."

"Then do it," Joren orders. "We'll stand guard."

It feels dangerous to be stuck out here in the open, but Kya is as good as her promise. She has the hover recalibrated in record time, and we all breathe a sigh of relief as it lifts back up above the ground.

Kya and Sion clamber back into the wagon and Joren and I mount our horses.

"Keep your weapon close," he warns. "We can't trust our proximity sensors anymore. And it's only going to get worse as we get closer to the mountains."

We look up at the towering peaks on the horizon. Deep within those mountains is a source of some great power. It's not just the instruments that can feel it. Now, I can too.

CHAPTER TWENTY

The landscape has changed as we've drawn closer to the mountains. The grasses are shorter, a stubby undergrowth of green and tan interspersed with areas of bare rock.

I squint my eyes at a smudge of brown to the west. It looks like it's moving. I grab the binocs and focus in on a herd of grazing animals. Wildebeests. We haven't seen many this far north. It looks like a herd of maybe fifty or so animals. But something looks different about them. I'm not familiar enough with the animals to tell.

I turn back and whistle, calling out Sion's name. He pokes his head out from the wagon, blinking against the sunlight. I hold up my binocs, pointing toward the herd. He clambers out of the wagon and walks over.

"You have to see this." I hand him the binocs. "There's something strange about that herd over there."

Sion squints into the binocs, panning them around the herd, then focuses in on something.

Joren rides up at a gallop, his weapon drawn, scanning the perimeter. "What did you see?" he demands, his face tense.

Sion lowers the binocs, his lips compressed. "Wildebeests. And they're farther north than they're supposed to be grazing this time of year. Something's off about them. We need to take a closer look."

"What's going on?" Kya climbs down from the wagon, frowning in concern. Sion rushes over to her. He's talking quietly, urgently, waving his arms. I can't make out what he's saying, but they both look worried.

Joren holsters his weapon. "I thought it was another attack." He runs his hands through his hair and notices me watching Sion and Kya. "What's wrong?"

I shake my head. "I don't know. But Sion seems to think it's something big." I look over at the distant herd. "We can't get close on horseback. We'll have to walk if we want to get a closer look."

Sion and Kya come back over, tight-lipped.

The four of us approach the herd cautiously on foot, careful to keep a safe distance. When we get close enough, Sion holds a scope to his eyes, scanning the herd.

At the perimeter of the herd, I spot two massive beasts set apart from the rest. One beast is mounting the other, its front legs pinning the female with its massive bulk, the act of mating unmistakable. I focus in with the binocs. They look similar to the wildebeests, but something about their tusks and fur looks different.

Joren walks up behind me, watching them with his scope. When I turn to him, strangely embarrassed, he raises his eyebrow, amused.

"Aren't they out of season, Sion?" I call out. "I thought mating season was in the spring?"

Sion's complexion has turned flushed and blotchy, bright red like his beard. "It's not the season I'm worried about. It's the species. These animals... they're not wildebeests. They're some kind of hybrid."

"I can't believe it." Kya shakes her head as if to clear it. "This is so much more than we've ever seen before. On the other worlds, there was some degradation, some glitches away from the plan, but for a new species to form on its own... That's on a whole new level from the other worlds..." She trails off, covering her mouth with her hand and looking at me with wide eyes.

She hadn't meant to say that about the other worlds. At least, not when I was listening.

"What do you mean, the other worlds?" I march toward her. "Are you saying you've seen this on other missions?"

"Vesta, it's not what you think." Kya's tone is soft, apologetic. "The others have been—"

"Kya," Sion's interrupts. "This is confidential data—"

"She deserves to know, Sion," Kya yells, challenging Sion with her glare. She looks to Joren. He nods, just a slight movement of his chin, giving permission for Kya to speak. "Yes, we've seen anomalies before," she admits, "but not like this. This is new."

"And you knew about this already? All of you?" I look to Joren, his eyes guilty. Somehow his betrayal hurts most of all.

After all the people who have lied to me, have let me down, I thought I had become immune. But apparently I just keep making the same mistakes. And Joren is just the latest.

It all makes sense now—Joren and his recon missions, Kya and Sion and their previous work together. They have seen this before. They already knew that terraformed worlds were having problems, and they didn't want the secret to get out. They have all been quietly cleaning this up over and over again. And I was the only one who didn't know. I was the stupid one. The ignorant outworlder that they've been fooling. The clueless local who's been guiding them right where they wanted to go, right to the source of the secret.

"So what's causing it then? I thought you knew."

"We know how to fix the damage." Kya says. "That doesn't mean we know what's causing it in the first place."

"Sabotage," Sion says. "That's the most likely explanation. Especially with the level of divergence we've seen today."

"Who would do something like that?" I ask. "Not Hestians."

"Rebels. Breakaways. Destroyers." He spits the words out.

"Let's not jump to conclusions," Joren warns Sion. He rubs his hands over his face and squares his shoulders. "The only way we can answer this is to get to the mountain. Let's get back to the wagon." He won't meet my eyes as he walks away. Sion and Kya follow.

I can't move. I won't.

All this time, I thought I was part of this team. I trusted Joren, trusted all of them. And they've been hiding the truth from me all this time. I stay there for a few moments, long enough to compose my face. They won't see the foolish tears of betrayal that I'm holding back.

Sion and Kya are standing next to the wagon when I return. Joren is focused on untethering his horse, his jaw tight.

Sion climbs back into the wagon. Kya lags behind. She puts her hand on my shoulder, her eyes beseeching me to understand, then follows Sion into the wagon. Joren mounts his horse. He still won't meet my eyes.

"Well?" Joren's voice is brusque. "The wind is building up. Let's go. We need to get to shelter."

I meekly mount my horse. My horse follows his as we head out across the plains and toward the distant mountains.

Their lies don't really matter, I tell myself. The fate of Hestia is more important. And, if the Institute's scientists don't even know what's wrong... that is truly terrifying.

CHAPTER
TWENTY-ONE

I've been riding behind Joren, deliberately keeping my distance. He looks my way from time to time, a somber, brooding presence.

The winds have been building in intensity all afternoon. It's near sunset now, the light fading over the western grasslands. I'm starting to worry about whether we can find a safe, sheltered space for the night. I'm not used to this climate, but it seems unusual.

The comm unit beeps. Joren falls back, allowing Feather to catch up to Emeraline. I steel my face as I reach him.

"What is it?" I demand.

He glances at me, then away. "There's a structure up ahead near those cliffs."

Sure enough, a rough stone cottage lies ahead, barely visible in the shadow of the cliffs, a crude chimney rising above it.

"Do the herders build permanent structures like this?" Joren asks me.

I shrug. "I thought they just lived in tents. But I don't know anyone who's been this far north."

"We need to get out of this wind. If it's not occupied, we have a safe place to stay tonight. It would be warm and easy to defend."

He's acting like we're partners, teammates. But that can't be true, not if Joren and the others have been lying to me all this time.

"Fine. Let's check it out."

We keep a close watch as we draw closer, our weapons ready. The cottage looks abandoned, a front door made of lashed branches hanging open. The grass all around has been flattened, like it was trodden down by horses.

Sion and Kya hang back in the wagon as Joren and I approach on foot, weapons drawn, alert for any signs of movement. Following his cues, I stand guard as he storms the entrance to the cottage. A moment later he emerges, his weapon holstered. "No one home."

We patrol the perimeter of the cottage, scanning the ground.

"Look at these." I point out hoofprints in the exposed mud. "The shape of the horseshoes, see that? We don't use horseshoes that shape in the South. These must be from Northern horses."

Joren nods. "So, it's from the herders, like we thought." He scouts farther out, peering at another set of hoofprints nearby. "But what about these?"

I study the other prints, which are all too familiar. "Those are from Southern horses! What would Southern horses be doing up here?"

His face tightens. "That's a good question."

I kneel in the dirt, noting what look like the marks of someone being dragged. I follow the trail leads to a patch of ragged bushes. A torn swatch of fabric is stuck to one of the branches, dark woven cloth embroidered with red thread.

I pull the fabric swatch from the branch and hold it between my fingers. "Joren, this a herder's garment."

He nods grimly. "It looks like there a fight."

My stomach feels hollow. "Maybe we shouldn't be here."

"It happened a while ago," Joren says. "Look at how dry the scat is. It must have been several weeks ago."

How could battles happen on Hestia? Who would have attacked us coming from the North? It makes the idea of armed conflict harder to dismiss.

"Come on, let's take a closer look inside."

In the main room of the cottage, a hearth and chimney has been constructed. The coals in the brazier show that it's been used, but not recently.

"It should be safe for us to use for tonight."

"I agree," he says. "Let's just set up the tents for lodgings, and we can use the cottage to have a fire for cooking and warmth."

*   *   *

The wind has blown in hard by nightfall, making us grateful for the shelter of the cottage. We lash the tents to the cottage wall for protection from the wind and to make more space for sleeping. The cottage itself is only one small room, a hearth with small wooden benches set in front of it.

We huddle before the hearth, eating our stew, listening to the roaring of the wind outside and the snapping sounds as the wind tries to lift the loose edges of the tent cloth.

We hadn't bothered to set up the perimeter alerts for tonight. None of the tech can be trusted—not so close to the mountain. We'll post a guard while we sleep. But for now, we should be all right. There's not much chance of anyone being out in a storm like this.

Kya nibbles at her stew. "I wonder where Darla is. She should have rendezvoused with us by now." I'd managed to put her out of my mind, but Kya was right. She was overdue to meet up with us. Something must have gone wrong. "Not that I'm missing her. But we could really use that replacement comm unit, that's for sure."

Sion sets down his bowl. "With this windstorm, we can't even use the emergency beacon. The support vessel won't even pick up the signal."

"What support vessel?" I ask slowly.

"It's standard protocol," Sion answers absently. "In case we need an emergency extraction, a show of force."

Yet another secret. I shouldn't be surprised. Joren moves to tend the fire, crouching next to the hearth. "Sion, any idea of how long this storm will last?"

Sion sips from his tea, his shoulders hunched. "No way to predict that with the system disruptions. I've never seen a planetary system this impacted."

"Are you going to tell me now?" I challenge. "About the other worlds?"

Joren meets my eyes, then dips his chin. "What do you want to know?"

"Commander, she doesn't have the clearance—" Sion protests.

"It needs to be said, doctor," Joren says, firm, implacable. "The problem began many years ago, before the Conflict. Some of the Consortium worlds, they were having problems with their systems."

He can't mean—

"They were rebelling. That was the official reason for the Conflict. But it wasn't about independence or profits. It was because their terraformed systems were failing, and the Republic did not want that acknowledged."

This is worse than I ever imagined. The Conflict, the reasons for it, were all a lie. It was just that the rebels were afraid for their survival and the GRIP needed to cover it up.

"The Conflict shut down the rebellion." Joren looks down, brooding. "But it didn't fix the problems. After the war, we realized that teams needed to be sent to investigate, to fix things." He shrugs. "We've been working together ever since."

I shake my head, disgusted. "You mean you've been covering it up."

"And what would you have us do?" Sion rises to his feet, anger distorting his normally calm expression. "Should we tell the whole human race that their worlds, their homes, everything they need to keep them alive, is failing? Would you have us tell them that?!"

"No... I..." I don't know what to do, but I know they shouldn't be lying to everyone. They shouldn't be leaving us defenseless. "Don't they deserve to know the truth? Maybe we can do something? Maybe we can fix it?"

"Vesta—" Kya touches my arms gently. "We're trying everything we can. That's why we're here."

I can't think. I don't know what to think. I need to get away.

"I have to check the horses," I mutter as I rush the door. Joren stands up like he's about to go with me, but I escape into the night and the loud, cold wind, fleeing into the blessed privacy of the night. I lean back against the cold stone of the cottage, staring up at the glowing orb of the moon... a single moon, innocent and pure, surrounded by the familiar constellations of the Hestian night.

How I wish I could go back to when this was the only moon I knew.

Before I was ever sent to Telos. Before I ever saw the triple moons of Telos as they rose in the night sky as I had waited with my squadron for the order to attack. I can still see those moons, in my memory... the largest rising first, hanging over the horizon, its surface as pitted as a tree that's bark had been carved out by beetles. The second and third moons rose later, chasing each other in the night sky. The order to attack had come just after I saw the third moon rise, before dawn. Then the bloodshed began. The terrible, senseless death as the people of Telos were slaughtered from afar, their fierce defiance no match for the Legion's power.

At the time, I had believed it was a necessary price to pay. Or at least that they were being punished for rebellion. But that had all been a lie. Telos had been just another casualty of these environmental disruptions. They had been destroyed to cover up a secret, and I have been unwittingly helping that to happen again.

I hear footsteps coming toward me. Please, let it not be Joren.

Kya appears from around the corner. She leans back on the cottage wall next to me.

I don't even know what to say, what to feel.

"I'm sorry," she says after a while. She sounds tired, sad. "I couldn't tell you the whole truth, Vesta. I wasn't allowed to."

"Can you fix this?" My voice breaks as I ask her.

"We always have before, Vesta, but we've never seen this level of distortion."

If they can't fix the damage, then the situation on Hestia will need to be cleaned up. The GRIP would destroy the evidence. And Hestia is the evidence.

"What if you fail? I'd need to tell them... tell my family, at least. To warn them!"

"Vesta," she says in a fierce whisper, grabbing my arm. "This is dangerous! What do you think the GRIP would do to keep this secret? They would kill for it!"

I pull my arm away. "Don't you think I know that! Don't you think I've seen what happens to a vassal world that doesn't fall in line? I've seen what happens to a world when the Legion comes! I've been part of it! You and Sion, in your institute. All those ideas and plans! These are real people here, real creatures, real life. Not just systems in your equations. Real beings that suffer when things go wrong."

I soften at the sympathy in Kya's face.

"I know you mean well," I go on, "but this an outworld, a vassal world. We know what we are. We know what little power we have. We exist at the pleasure of the Core Worlds. We know enough not to fight."

Kya shrinks down, collapsing, her voice subdued. "I just want to go home, Vesta. Just fix this and go home. You have a chance too. I meant it, what I said. You'll have your status upgrade." She smiles sadly, touching my cheek. "You can come visit me on Cava."

It's almost funny. All those years that I dreamed of visiting the Core Worlds. And now, it doesn't even matter.

"I'll come visit you on Cava, Kya," I promise. "If we fix this, I'll go."

She goes back inside. But I stand out here for a while, listening to the wind.

*   *   *

I set my comm unit to wake me once Kya and Sion are asleep. Joren is our night sentry, standing guard inside the cottage. This is one conversation that needs to be private.

I push open the cottage door slowly, so as not to startle him. Joren looks up as I walk in. He sits on the stone bench by the fire, his weapon next to him. I close the door behind me, leaning my back against the wall, arms crossed.

"So you knew."

He gets up to face me. "I knew."

"I get it. I'm not important enough to be trusted with that kind of information, and—"

"It's not like that."

"Then what is it like?"

"I didn't want to lie to you," he says quietly. "I won't anymore. What do you want to know?"

With those words, the fight drains out of me. It's so much easier when I'm angry. Now I feel only fear at the thought that maybe none of us know how to fix this.

He watches me as I cross the room, standing next to him at the fire.

"So what are you going to do?"

"I'm not a scientist. I'm counting on Kya and Sion for that."

"I mean about the satellite in orbit. About the GRIP."

"Like Sion said, that's standard protocol. But no, I'm not going to call it."

I feel a relief at that. At least he won't call in the Legion… not yet.

"You know, when I first met you—with the admiral—I hated you."

He looks sideways at me, a slight twist at edge of his lips showing his amusement. "I'm not surprised."

"But then you asked about Telos. I saw your reaction. You understood how terrible it was. That's what made me trust you. Then you went back to being the cold officer again and I wondered which one of you was real."

He lets out a bark of laughter. His shoulders slump, a weary resignation in his face. "I've wondered the same thing myself."

I don't know what to say to that.

He wipes his hand down his face. "The admiral wasn't supposed to be there when we met. He summoned you without me knowing."

I replay the scene in my mind. "So that's why you looked so irritated?"

"He was checking up on me."

"Why would he do that?'

"He had his reasons." He reaches up, rubs his eyes with his palms. I realize how tired he must be, how tired we all are. I haven't slept well since we left the inn.

"You want to know why I care about Telos?" he asks.

I nod mutely.

"What do you know about the Battle of Thea?"

I search for the memory. "Wasn't that somewhere near the end of the Conflict? I was in the Eastern District. I don't remember much about the Western front."

"I was stationed there, in the Consortium border region, one of a few that were leading that campaign." He draws inward, remembering. "It was an outworld district. I had mostly auxiliary troops. They were good soldiers. Most of the officers looked down on them, but I found them decent. They did good work, and they were loyal if you treated them right."

So it was true. He *had* been a battalion commander in the war, just like Sion and Kya said.

"I had a full contingent under my command, ready to make planetfall. I got the orders to engage." His body is tensing up, his breath getting shallow as he stares into the fire. "The objective was to prevent Thea from falling back under the Consortium's control. To take back Thea, or to destroy it if we couldn't. The honor of the Republic was at stake. It didn't matter that most of our troops would be wiped out."

I should be shocked at the cold-bloodedness of the GRIP's willingness to sacrifice so many of its own soldiers. But I know better than that. They would do anything to win.

"But we were desperate." He turns his face to me, his eyes wild like a horse that's been spooked. "Nobody has been allowed to know that, outside of the ruling families. How close we were to losing."

His voice is a litany, unstoppable. I can feel how much he needs to get this out, how it's been hurting him.

"I just couldn't do it. I *wouldn't*…" He clenches a fist, then releases it, taking a deep breath to calm himself. "That's when I realized that I'd changed. A few years earlier, I would have given the order, followed it to the death. But I couldn't do it anymore." His eyes dart back and forth, as if he's seeing things from back then. "I came up with some alternatives, routed them to command. But they wouldn't accept any of them. No matter how much more strategically sound they were, they wouldn't agree."

"So I decided. I took it upon myself, and I gave the order to use my own plan. It would have worked. It would have gained victory without all the losses." He smiles grimly. "But I never got to put it in place. I was undermined by one of my own officers. Someone reported me to command and my authority was suspended." He laughs bitterly. "I have some ideas about who it might be. Some of my old comrades from Patria were posted under my command. We were taught at the Academy that it was victory at all costs, even if the costs were our own soldiers."

I move closer to him. I don't want him to be alone with this.

"And it went forward anyway. The same loss of life. The same slaughter. And even more bloodshed to teach the Consortium a lesson. So, in the end, it didn't make any difference."

"I was removed from duty, quietly," he continues. "They didn't want it to get out. If it wasn't for my family, I would have been executed or banished. But Admiral Sennon—he's a friend of my family—he had me reassigned to somewhere he could keep an eye on me."

So Joren and the elite admiral were friends. He was one of the elites, the privileged. I should hate him for that. But does it even matter when he risked his career to try to save his soldiers, when he is risking himself to help Hestia?

"That's what missions like these are about. To prove my loyalty to the Republic. Then I can go home." He smiles ruefully. "You asked me once why I haven't gone back for regen." I nod. "This is why. I can't go back until I redeem myself. The problem is, I'm not sure I want to be redeemed."

The pain in his eyes breaks my heart. So does his courage, his integrity.

"And now this..." He gestures to the world outside, to the anomalies. "Maybe it won't make a difference anyway."

I reach out my hand to tentatively touch him arm. He tenses up at first, then he starts to relax, releases some of the tension he'd been holding.

I want to get this right. I want him to see in himself what I see. "It wasn't your fault, Joren. You did the best you could. You couldn't have known." The words sound empty, unconvincing, even though they're true.

"I'd like to believe that Vesta. I really would."

He steps away from the fire, settles down with a sigh on the wooden bench behind us, his arms spread over the back.

I walk around behind him, settle my hands on his shoulders. He looks up, startled at the contact. I can feel the tension in his shoulders, the weight of the guilt and responsibility he's carrying. I want to comfort him somehow.

This man is not the man I had judged him to be, not the arrogant Core Worlder I had assumed he was when we'd first met. He is a man of honor, a man who made decisions to do what was right, even at great cost to himself. I want to help him, to soothe his pain.

My hands begin kneading his shoulders, releasing the tensions there. "You don't have to do that," he protests. He relaxes back into my hands, groaning in relief. "But damn, it does feel good."

It feels good for me too. He trusted me with this burden, and I want to comfort him.

I focus on releasing the tension in his muscles, stroking and kneading his neck and shoulders. He leans back into my hands, making sounds of appreciation as he relaxes. I get the sense that he hasn't had any comfort for a long time.

Soon, I feel a new warmth move through my body. My hands move more slowly as I deepen my strokes. I become keenly aware of his muscled shoulders and back beneath my palms and fingers, the warmth of his skin through the fabric of his shirt, of his thick, dark brown hair as it curls over his neck. I feel my own body getting heavier, slower, as my body comes awake to the fact that Joren is a man, a very attractive man who I'm now touching in a way that feels very, very good. My body wants more, wants to move my hands

147

down to stroke his muscled back and chest, to press my lips against the rough stubble of his jaw.

By the shift in his breathing, he feels it too. The relaxation in him has changed to a new kind of tension. He's breathing more shallowly now, holding himself alert. I can sense his intense interest in my hands on his body. If I lean forward just a bit, I could press my breasts against his back. I could lean down to nuzzle my lips against the warm skin of his neck.

I should stop touching him. Why can't I stop touching him?

Joren slowly reaches back to put his big warm hand on mine, seeming to hold his breath. In the moment of waiting for what will happen next, I imagine him putting my palm to his lips, kissing his way up my arm, pulling me into his lap. A rush of excitement shoots through me, almost overwhelming in its intensity.

I have to stop this now. I had only meant to offer comfort, understanding. Not this wild desire that swamps me. Too much is at stake. I need to regain control.

I pull my hands away as Joren rises from the bench to face me. He's breathing heavily, his eyes moving over my face, my body. I can feel the flush of warmth on my cheeks, the heavy weight of desire in my body. We're close enough to touch, for him to take me into his arms. I want to. I'm tempted to kiss that wide mouth, to run my hands over his strong chest, to give in to the urge to join with him. I can see that he wants that too. But he stands there, not making any move toward me, as we look at each other, holding back.

I look down, breathless. "I have to go."

I walk quickly to the door, trying to get away before I'm forced to acknowledge what just happened. As my hand touches the doorknob, Joren calls my name. I turn slowly to face him, praying that he won't walk over to me. If he touches me, I don't trust myself to not respond.

But he's still standing by the fire, his hands curled into fists at his side. "Thank you, Vesta," he says, his warm brown eyes intent on mine.

I nod, then slip out the door, closing it carefully behind me. I lean against the wall outside, taking a moment to catch my breath and calm my body.

What just happened there, I wonder. It's been a long time since I had been with a man, so I can be forgiven for my body's response to touching him. But what worries me more is the feeling in my chest—the warmth, the trust.

But I can't be distracted by personal feelings, not now. I have to push them down, concentrate on the mission. Anything else would be a dangerous distraction.

But I'm not sure if I can. It may be that something has already shifted inside of me. I'm afraid that now I have something more to worry about besides the well-being of Hestia, and of myself. I have started to care about Joren too.

CHAPTER TWENTY-TWO

The windstorm has blown itself out by morning, leaving behind an eerie calm and clear skies. I walk the perimeter of the camp, checking for damage as I take down the tents. The ground has been scoured clean by the wind, erasing all traces of footprints from the night before.

I leave Joren's tent until last. I'd let him sleep a little longer, since he'd been on watch most of the night. Well, that was one reason. The other was how nervous I feel to face him after last night.

He emerges from his tent, stretching and blinking against the early morning light. I try not to notice the way his shirt clings to the muscles of his chest and arms, try not to notice his body at all, or the guarded warmth in his eyes as he greets me.

"Why didn't you wake me?"

"You needed the sleep."

"Thanks." He looks around, as if to check that we're alone. "Um, about last night—"

"Thanks for telling me," I interrupt. "About… everything. I'm glad you did."

His eyes turn somber. "You're the first person I've told, about any of that."

Better to only mention the conversation we had, and not what happened after.

"I've got to go help Kya. Breakfast is done. It's by the hearth." I offer a nervous smile and walk briskly over to Kya. I offer her some of the biscuits I cooked this morning, and she takes a break from inspecting the cart.

"How's it looking?" I ask. And I mean to listen as she explains some technical language that makes no sense to me, but I find my gaze drifting over to Joren as he tends to Feather.

"Vesta?"

"Huh?" I snap back to Kya looking at me expectantly. "Oh sorry, I was just keeping an eye out, making sure no one was out there."

"Mm-hmm, I see what you were keeping an eye on." She raises an eyebrow. "So, you and Joren..."

"What?"

"You know... Are you sleeping together?"

Could she somehow read my thoughts? "What would make you think that?"

She shrugs. "You seem close. Not that I know how you'd have the time."

"No. Of course not." I don't know why I'm so defensive. It's not like Kya would judge me for being attracted to him.

"Alright, I was just wondering," she says easily. "Can you hand me that tool, the one with the small blade?" I hand her the tool, and she goes back to her work. "I only wonder," she says, "because I tried to make a move on him, and he turned me down."

"You what?" A succession of emotions moves through me—amusement, shock... jealousy. Kya, with her elegance, her easy grace, her confidence, has everything I don't. Had Joren really turned her down?

"I just flirted with him a little bit. No harm. Just to see if he was interested." She shrugs her elegant shoulders. "I've been away from my mates for a while. I'm pent up."

"Kya!"

"Oh Vesta, you're such a prude."

I can't help but laugh at her sheer audacity.

"Well, maybe I'm not his type." She looks me over. "Maybe he likes a certain pretty Hestian guide?" She arches her brows at my look of disbelief. "What? You're single, he's hot. What's the problem? You have the standard sexual health and conception regimen. Or do freeworkers not have that?"

I'd been implanted with the anti-fertility device when I entered the Legion. And I'd been given the standard protections against disease. That wasn't why I objected.

"It's not that... I just haven't been with anyone for some time," I admit.

She looks at me expectantly.

"It's been difficult since I left the Legion."

"But that was—what—a few years ago. I'm sure you've had a lot of chances."

I don't want to admit this to her.

"Wait, you don't mean you've been celibate all this time?" Kya looks dumbfounded.

"No, not the whole time," I admit. "But I don't very often. It's been a while."

I know that it won't make sense to Kya. Not just because of the sexual mores on her world, but because of Kya herself. She is daring, open, uninhibited—everything I'm not.

"It's partly because of how I was raised." I can feel my cheeks flaming. "Women's purity is highly valued." She snorts at that. "Anyway, I already tried to overcome the modesty conditioning. It didn't work."

Kya raises her eyebrows, smiles mischievously. "Oh, so there is a history for the pure Vesta," she teases.

"I'm not that pure," I mutter. "But yes, there is someone I loved once. I thought I loved him, anyway. I thought he loved me."

"Young love gone bad?" she asks wryly.

"We were young, yes. I was a recruit from the Provinces. He was a captain from the Core worlds. You can guess how it turned out." The memories used to hurt. Now they just seemed like something that had happened to someone else. "He made me promises he couldn't keep. I was young and foolish, so I believed him. I've learned my lesson since then."

Her expression is a mix of pity and compassion. "Oh, Vesta. It's not healthy to put all your hopes in one person. That's why we have group marriage on Cava. It helps us to weather the storms." She pats my hand consolingly. "We all have our disappointments, Vesta. We just need to keep trying anyway."

As we finish up our work, I keep glancing back to Joren, thinking that maybe Kya has a point. I haven't been interested in any man for a long time. Not until now. Maybe it couldn't hurt to find some happiness, however temporary, while I can.

*   *   *

We've been riding all day. The mountains, once distant peaks, are now close. We have been skirting the western boundary, searching for a path upward, for almost an hour now. The sun is getting low in the sky. If we don't find an entry soon, we will have to camp for the night and try again in the morning.

"What the hell?" Joren reaches for his binocs, pointing them at something off to the west, where the grass expands a long distance. "What is that?"

I pull out my binocs and focus where he's pointing. The moving blur in the distance gets closer, finally crystalizing into a crowd of mounted men on horseback quickly heading our way.

This is bad. Very bad.

"It's the herdsmen," I say, lowering the binocs. "They've found us."

"Damnit!" Joren hides his weapon beneath the waistband of his tunic and whistles to Sion and Kya, who poke their heads out of the wagon.

"Quickly," he calls out. "Cover the gear and get out!" They rush to comply.

We'd hoped to avoid the herdsmen. From all I'd been told, they were sparsely populated across the grasslands. But we'd come up with a cover story, just in case.

"Are they dangerous?" Joren hisses, his face tense, as the herdsmen steadily advance, the hoofbeats of their horses starting to shake the ground.

"They shouldn't be," I answer. But then, the Patriarchs weren't supposed to be armed either.

The phalanx of horseman advances en masse, quickly surrounding us in a blur of stomping horses and ornamented riders, a cacophony of horse breath and pounding hooves.

Their horses are all a beautiful chestnut brown, snorting and huffing from exertion, their reins and saddles decorated with small silver bells. Their opulence is matched by the herdsmen themselves. They are all dressed lavishly in dark fabrics of layered brocade with rich embroidery, their hair twisted into long braids woven with brightly colored strips of cloth. They have the same black hair and olive skin as we Southerners, but theirs is darkened and weathered from the elements. The herdsmen all carry speared weapons at their waists. I've never seen herdsmen with weapons before.

It isn't just men, but a woman too. She wears a red headdress and a woven shawl over her proud shoulders. She nudges her horse over to Joren, inspecting him carefully.

"You're far from home." Her accent is unusual, clipped and nasal.

"We travel from the Capitol to trade with the herder people." Joren's accent doesn't sound quite Hestian. Hopefully, she won't be familiar enough with how Southerners speak to tell the difference.

She guides her horse next to mine, peering at me curiously. Her green eyes shine brightly from her lined, wind-chapped face.

"You're from the South. You're one of us."

"Yes, I am." It can't hurt to admit that.

"Tell me your name, daughter."

"My name is Vesta."

"Welcome, Vesta. I am Raina of the mountain people."

The woman, Raina, guides her horse over to Sion and Kya, raising an eyebrow. Then she looks over at the men and laughs. She laughs so hard that she wipes tears from her eyes. The herdsmen look as confused at her reaction as we are. Finally, she stops, holding her belly. "They've been called," she tells them. "They've come to meet the mountain."

The herdsmen nod, seeming satisfied by her explanation.

Raina walks her horse over to me. Her horse moves minimally, remarkably calm and controlled for such close quarters.

"The mountain has called you," she says.

I look uncertainly at Joren.

"Come," she signals the other herdsmen. "We bring them."

"Bring us where?" Joren asks, frowning.

She points at the nearby peaks. "To the mountain. Come, you ride with us. You will be our guests tonight."

Raina signals to the herdsmen, who adjust their saddles to make room for Kya and Sion to ride behind them on their mounts.

"We can't refuse," I hiss at Joren. "At least we'll have a path into the mountains."

"We'd better just go along," he agrees in a whisper.

"But our equipment," Kya protests. "We can't leave the wagon."

"I'll handle it," I say. I ride up to Raina, who seems to be the leader of this group.

"We need to bring the wagon," I tell her. "The others can't ride. We need our supplies."

The herders snort in laughter at this. One man says, "They can't ride?! Are they children?"

"Yah," she says finally, waving at the wagon. "She wills it. You will bring the wagon with you."

Relieved, we fall in line with the horsemen as they lead us up a narrow trail through the mountains, the jingling of the metal bells that decorate the herders' saddles clinking as we ride. Sion and Kya, each of them riding behind a herdsman, look awkward and uncomfortable as they hold on tight, trying to keep their seat. It looks funny, despite the danger we're in.

I can't risk saying anything to Joren without being overheard, but we share nervous glances. I'd never heard of the herders being dangerous in any way. In fact, they've always had a reputation as being hospitable. But still, we are surrounded and outnumbered.

We ride steadily upward until we reach a high plateau, then continue northward on flatter terrain until we reach the herders' village. The sun has almost set by this point. Soon the only lights will come from the fires of the herder's village. We arrive at the settlement, which is no more than a collection of tents made from cloth and hides. The people we pass all stop to stare at us as we go by.

The herders dismount when we reach the center of the village, and Raina walks away without saying goodbye to us. Sion and Kya are helped off of horseback, the herders obviously trying to hide their amusement at the scientists' lack of riding skills. A herdsman shows where to park the wagon and to shelter our horses.

A large cooking fire burns at a central hearth with delicious smells of stewed meat, reminding me of how hungry I am.

"Come, we eat," a herdsman invites, motioning to a spot by the fire.

We join the villagers at the cook fire, the recipient of curious glances from the people gathered there. A woman hands me a plate of food, to which I nod my thanks. The food is meat, most likely wildebeest. I take a bite, expecting it to be tough, but it's soft and flavorful, if strangely spiced. It's served with flat bread and a salad of fresh greens and root vegetables.

"You drink?" the woman offers.

I accept the cup of fermented milk. The thin skim on the surface looks unappealing, but I take a deep gulp. The others are looking skeptically into their cups.

"It's not bad," I urge them. "We used to drink it during harvest time when the herders brought the animals south for transport."

"What is it?" Sion asks.

"Fermented yak's milk. I drank this with my brother Simon before. We drank so much we threw up."

"So it's alcoholic?" Joren asks. "We shouldn't drink it. We have to keep our head."

"Try it at least. Better not to insult our hosts," Kya says.

The herder nearby notices Joren's reaction. He reaches into his pack and pulls out some bottles. "Beer?" he offers with a smile.

I thank the herdsman, then dig into our packs, offering him some fruit and meat in return. He smiles gratefully, accepting the exchange.

"We make this from our grain," I explain, passing around the bottles to the group. "It's made from fermented wheat and hops. It's a specialty of this region."

Everyone takes a sniff, then some experimental sips.

"Not bad," Kya proclaims.

We sip on our drinks as the herdsmen talk amongst themselves and people come up to load their bowls with food. The children watch us shyly. I wave to them, and they giggle.

"Do you see that? The beasts in that herd, grazing over there," Sion indicates the animals with a nod his chin. "More of the hybrid creatures. The herders are accepting them, maybe even breeding them."

Sion falls silent as some herdsmen come to sit at the fire. They just greet us briefly and settle themselves around the fire, pouring cups of home brew. One of the men pulls out an instrument that resembles a flute. He lifts it to his lips and begins to play.

The music sounds so much like the tune that Kya played earlier. I was right when I remembered the sound of the herdsmen songs from so long ago. Kya waits until the song fades. She smiles, then reaches into her pocket and pulls out her flute.

"Can I play with you?" she asks.

The man starts a tune, waits for her to copy it. She matches it by ear. Soon they are playing a tune together, a lilting melody that entrances us all. The music begins again. As the next song fades, I realize that Raina is standing at the fire, listening.

"The music," she says. "It sounds even better to hear you play together."

"I do like it," Kya answers.

"Something we share."

I notice that Raina has a red flower tucked behind her ear, deep red and spiky.

"That flower," I burst out. "I've seen one just like it before." I pull out the crushed red flower in the pocket of my skirt.

Her eyes widen. "That is the lehua flower. It grows here by the mountain."

"But I found it south, just outside the city."

"It was a gift from the mountain. She left it there for you." Raina settles down next to me, leaning in. "The mountain, she calls to you. From far away."

I feel a strange resonance from her words. I can't think of how to answer.

"Yes, we've come a long way," Joren responds. "From the South."

Inexplicably, Raina laughs. "No, not from the South. From out there." Raina points up at the sky, at the distant stars.

She knows. Somehow, she knows where we're from. She obviously never believed our cover story. But then why does she not seem to care?

"Yes, we are called to the mountain," Joren answers carefully. "The mountain needs our help. We need you to take us to the mountain so we can take care of it."

She chortles. "The mountain, she is our mother. She gives us life. She's not happy. She's been ignored too long."

My dream!

Just before the ambush, in my dream, that woman was beckoning to me, urging me to follow her up the mountain path! And then the explosion woke me in the dream. But that was before the real explosion. It was almost as if she was warning me. If I hadn't woken up right then, those men would have succeeded in burning down the camp.

"Vesta, you are a daughter of Hestia." Why do those words touch something in me, some kind of emotion I never knew was there? "That's what you call this world down there in the South, yes?"

I can't look away from her intense dark eyes. "What do you call it?"

"Not it, daughter. Her. We call Her… well, you will learn Her name in time. Not now, though. And you." Raina turns to Joren. "You are a son of the Far Away. Yes?"

"Yes," he admits. "I do come from far away."

She grins, seemingly satisfied. "She needs you both tonight. You will join us. If you do this, I will bring you to her heart."

"Her heart?" Sion asks. "Where the disturbance is?"

"Yes, tomorrow we will bring you there. Tonight, you join us." Raina smiles reassuringly. "Tonight, we dance. We honor the Mother who lives in the mountain. We give her the love she needs. Then she will be happy. And the land will be happy. And all the people."

"Just dance?" I ask uncertainly.

"Just dance. Together. That what she asks."

She grunts her approval and walks away as if we have already agreed.

We gather together, keeping our voices to a whisper.

"She's talking about the volcano as if it were alive," Joren says, frowning. "I've heard of primitive superstitions like this on the homeworld, but never since then. Interesting."

"We don't have time for this ritual or ceremony or whatever it is!" says Sion. "We need to get there right away!"

"We can't get there on our own, not without it coming to a fight," Kya says. "We need to cooperate, be patient."

"She talks about giving love. And she needs a man and a woman. It sounds like... a fertility ritual," Joren says. "It's an ancient practice. In the Academy we were taught about Earth's history. In ancient times, it was believed that humans were a part of the planet being renewed. Every year the people mated to remake the world. It brought the rain and made the crops grow."

"How primitive," Sion says. "Before they knew about science, they thought that what they did made things happen."

"It makes sense," Kya muses, "in terms of energy. Isn't everything we do a part of everything else?"

Sion snorts. "We're not a helpless part of the planetary system anymore. We're the creators of it."

"It doesn't matter what's true," Joren says. "We need to get to epicenter and fix this problem. Vesta and I will go."

I wonder what they will require of us in this strange ritual. Kya, I think, would be able to do something like this. Not me. I have always been modest when it came to my body. But the thought of Kya dancing with Joren makes me angry, jealous.

Raina returns. "Are you ready," she asks, "to come help the Mother?"

Joren meets my eyes, asking for my consent. I nod.

"If we participate in this ceremony," he asks Raina, "you will take us to the heart of the mountain, to its core?"

"If you do this for Her, then we take you to Grandmother. She's the one who guards the mountain's heart. She's the only one who can take you there. I will come for you when night falls. You must be ready then." She walks away, chuckling.

"A fertility ritual, huh?" Kya raises an eyebrow, giving me a mischievous look.

I glance at Joren, who looks as uncertain as me. If this is a ceremony that is supposed to mimic passion… we both know that this will be more than an act for us. Our passion, although hidden, is real.

CHAPTER TWENTY-THREE

They come for me at dusk.

A young woman approaches the fire. She wears a long dress with an embroidered bodice, her dark hair plaited. "Come," she says, "I prepare you for the ceremony."

I am nervous, suddenly, to be separated from the others. Joren stands up, his eyes following me as I am led away.

"Be safe," Kya calls after me.

I follow the woman to a hut made of woven branches, the door covered by a wildebeest hide. She pulls the hide aside and ushers me inside. The shelter is lit with candles. The only furniture is a wooden stool.

The woman pulls down a garment hanging by the door and brings it over to me. It's a dress of dark woven cloth, richly embroidered around the bodice and the skirt in the traditional style of the herders. But this dress is even more elaborate than the others I have seen, obviously adorned for special occasions.

I hesitate, touching the rich fabric. "Is this for me?" I ask. The dress is too beautiful, an honor that I, as an outsider, don't deserve.

The woman's face is kind. "Come," she urges. "You must remove your clothes."

She helps me undress, her manner setting me at ease. I realize then that I haven't bathed in several days, the odor of my body unmistakable. The woman brings in a basin of warm water, a cloth, and some soap, setting the supplies out for me as she discreetly waits for me to cleanse myself. She helps me to step into the dress, tying the fasteners of ribbon and leather twine.

"Come, sit," she directs, and leads me to sit on the wooden stool.

She opens a tin of some kind of cosmetic, a black substance that she applies to the edge of my eyelids. Then she applies a red berry pigment to my lips and cheeks. She brushes out my hair, weaving narrow braids into it as well. When she is finished, she looks me over, then nods and smiles.

"You look," she urges, and uncovers a mirror to see myself in.

I am shocked at the transformation. The bodice of the dress is cut low, more revealing that I'm used to. The dress nips in at the waist, the skirts hanging loose and flowing from hips. The dark pigment has given my green eyes a smoky, mysterious look. My black hair hangs, glossy and thick, over my shoulders. I almost don't recognize the woman in the mirror. She has an eager desire in her eyes, a display of sensuality that I have always kept hidden, private.

All my life I have shunned cosmetics and avoided wearing clothing that displayed my body. I never wanted to risk being seen as wanting a man's attention. It was safer that way, no risk of being embarrassed or rejected.

But here, now, I am displaying myself as a woman, admitting that I want to be alluring… to Joren. He will see me like this, and I will have to admit to the world that I want him, and that I want him to want me.

The woman stands behind me, looking on approvingly. "Tonight, you honor the Goddess."

"How do I honor the Goddess?" I ask, although I think I know.

"Man and woman honor the Goddess together. They join together to remake the world."

So it's true. This is a fertility ritual, as Joren guessed.

My face feels warm, flushed. The warmth moves through my body, loose and languorous.

I hear the first drumbeats and whistles in the distance. The tribe has begun its celebration. A rush of excitement moves through my body.

The woman leans over and kisses me on the cheek, then pulls aside the drape aside and beckons me out. I step out into the night.

The oil lamps light a path to the dance area as I follow the sounds of the music. As I walk, a few men turn their heads to look at me admiringly. I feel uncomfortable with the attention, but I must represent the role well, so I stand tall, chest out, and nod graciously until I reach the clearing where the ritual is in progress.

Most of the village must be here, more than a hundred herds-folk at least. Men and women, but no children, are arrayed around the open dancing space. Several fires are placed around the area with cushions laid out for people to sit.

The herders play stringed instruments and flutes like the ones I saw before. The drums beat a variety of rhythms, some steady and others complex. The drums are made of some kind of gourds, the heads made from stretched hide. The herdsfolk are all singing and clapping to the music. I don't recognize the tunes, but, mixed with the rhythms of the North, I recognize the lilting melodies from the old folksongs of my childhood.

I turn my head to find Joren watching me, his eyes intent like he's touching me. He's seated on the ground at the edge of the dance area with one knee bent and his arms resting on it. He wears cere-monial garb as well, a loose tunic which lays opens on his chest and a pair of loose trousers that looked like they're made of animal skin.

I can sense the masculinity, the hard grace in his athlete's body. The lamplight throws deep shadows on his face, rugged and stark, giving a primitive feel to his expression.

He wants me to come over to him. I can tell. Or I want it. I begin to slowly make my way over to him, my eyes never leaving his as I approach. As I almost reach him, he stands to face me, so close we are almost touching.

I remember the day we met, when he stood next to the admiral, stern and forbidding in his Legion uniform, so formal and hard to read. I can read him so clearly now. His eyes show his desire, a longing that pulls on my own.

Joren takes my hands in his, his thumb stroking my palm, igniting a tightening in my breasts, my stomach, between my legs. His cheeks are flushed, his nostrils flaring. He puts his hands on my hips, pulling me closer, and we both seem to hold our breath.

The music stops. The priestess calls out new dancers, who quickly join up in couples, man and woman, out on the dance ground. New music begins, with gentle, throbbing rhythms from the drums. The couples move and sway together, guided by the drums and the priestess's singing. She waves to us, signaling Joren and me to the dance ground.

He puts his arm around my waist, his hand warm against my side. I can smell herbs mixed with the natural of his body. He must have been prepared too, as I was.

He spins me to face him on the dirt dance floor. The music begins, the drums and the flutes, and the other couples begin to move in a swing of hips and stomping of feet. We look back and forth between the other couples and back to each other, trying to mimic their movements. We are awkward, clumsy at first. As the music builds gradually, we stop trying to copy the others, instead tuning in to each other's bodies, moving together to the rhythm. Our touch, although not overtly sexual, builds an erotic excitement between us.

One part of my mind is observing us, asking me what I'm doing. But most of me is one with the dance, with Joren's body and my own, and with the shared experience of the whole village, who play and sing and clap and dance all around us.

The music reaches a crescendo, and Joren and I can't keep up with the pace. We collapse against each other, breathing hard. It's like a spell is broken as we come back to an awareness of what we're doing, of who we are. The song ends, and the priestess speaks. "Now it is time to honor the spirit of the mountain."

I'm confused for a moment until I see the couples departing the dance floor. They hold each other in a sensual way, the men kissing and nuzzling the women. It's obvious what they're about to do.

I'm suddenly embarrassed at what we are expected to do, and for everyone to know it. I want to flee. Joren touches my arms, drawing me close. He whispers in my ear, "It wouldn't be wise to insult our hosts. Let's just leave together."

I allow Joren to encircle my waist with his arm, leaning into me, as we walk out of the torchlight. The villagers hoot as we leave the dance ground, encouraging us. My cheeks flame.

As we reach beyond the lights, we stop by my tent. There is no one around, and the evening has turned cool. I'm uncomfortably aware of the desire still coursing through my body. I stop inches away, looking up into his face.

His eyes search mine.

I want him to kiss me, to touch me, to take me into the tent and make love to me. But I know now that he will never make the first move. He's too honorable to touch me first, not when I'm under his authority on this mission.

I reach out my shaking hand and place it on his chest. His skin is warm beneath the fabric of his shirt, the pounding of his heart. So, I affect him too. That knowledge emboldens me. I reach out my other hand as well, stroking his muscled chest with my palm. He draws in a sharp breath, his eyes roving my face. I stand up on my tiptoes, sliding my hands over his shoulders, brushing my breasts against his hard chest, wrapping my arms together behind his neck as I tilt my head for a kiss. I touch my lips to his, gently, cautiously. His lips are firm and smooth. His breath tastes of honey beer.

He doesn't respond, and I'm afraid that I've made a terrible mistake. Then, abruptly, he presses his mouth urgently against mine, opening his lips to devour my mouth, pulling me against him. "Vesta," he moans, his mouth hot on mine, our tongues touching, his hands stoking my back, my hips, my butt. I can't seem to get close enough, his mouth and body all around me. I feel myself lifted off my feet, pressing harder against his body, his erection pressing between my thighs. I gasp, a helpless desire flooding me. I lose all control as I rub myself against him, moaning.

I hear footsteps approaching and realize suddenly where we are, outside my tent practically making love standing up, in full view of passersby. Joren breaks away from me, holding me away by my arms, breathing heavily. He looks at me, an unspoken question in his eyes.

"Stay," I whisper. He smiles, victorious.

Holding his hand, I lead him into my tent, closing the outside world away as I pull the drape closed. A small lamp burns by my bedroll. I lead Joren to my pallet of blankets, guiding him down with me, cradling his body with my hips as he covers me with his body.

"You're so beautiful," Joren moans, leaning down to join our mouths, his hands caressing my breasts, my waist, my hips.

I free my arms to pull my blouse over my head, his eyes watching hungrily as I uncover my breasts. He lowers his mouth to my breasts, sucking and nibbling as his hands stroke me. I can't handle this feeling. It's too much. I writhe helplessly beneath him.

I lift his shirt to pull it over his head. It's my turn to admire his body now. His chest, his shoulders, his arms, his stomach, silky flesh over hard muscle, exquisitely masculine. I begin kissing his nipples, licking, and touching everywhere as he moans.

"Joren, I need you," I gasp, my hips moving against his. I can't wait any longer. I have been waiting so long for this.

"Are you sure?" he gasps desperately in between deep kisses, looking into my eyes. I can tell he wants to finish this as much as I do. But even now, he has the restraint to make sure this is what I want.

"Yes," I gasp, cradling him between my legs.

Then his hands are pulling my undertrousers down and off. His fingers are stroking me between my legs with an exquisite friction. "Oh God," he moans. I can feel the wetness as his fingers rub against my entrance, then he kisses me deeply as his finger penetrates. I cry out.

"Vesta." His voice has a choked quality. "I want you so bad."

My hips begin moving against his fingers, my body begging for consummation. He groans again, as if in pain. We need to be joined, now.

He lifts himself up, kneeling as he pulls down his trousers and his cock springs free. He looks down at me, holding himself in his fist, his exquisitely muscled body crouched before me. I have never seen a more erotic sight in my life.

I open my arms, urging him down. He braces himself on one arm, kissing me deeply as he enters my body. Oh, the bliss. The fullness. The touching deep within. I feel him inside of me the way I have never felt another man inside of me. He feels it too. His face has a look of lust and wonder. As I wrap my legs around him, and he thrusts and moves inside of me in a heady rhythm, I feel a building excitement from deep inside of me. I'm shaking. It's like he's drawing an energy from inside of me that I've never felt before, a bliss that needs him to fulfill it. And we are drawing that bliss out together like magnets, closer and closer like a wave of pure pleasure swirling and building. We ride that wave together, higher and higher. We're looking into each others' eyes, in wonder at the building pressure of pleasure we're drawing out of each other.

Joren is inside of me, and I envelop him. Our rhythms join with the sounds of the distant drums from the dance pit. Our moans and cries are echoed by the chanting and singing of the villagers as they cry out in song.

It's as if we are the elements themselves, coupling on the plains. I scream in ecstasy, and so does he. We are calling out with the bliss of making each other complete. Like striking two rocks together and making flame. This is meant to be. This is it. This is everything I am living for.

It builds to the point of no return, then it peaks in one blinding release, shooting out my energies in all directions as we blend together. I call out, my face turned into his shoulder, until the waves gradually decrease and he lets go in a staggering release, yelling out in a low growl, inside me.

The peak fades, and we return to ourselves, holding each other, drenched in sweat.

Our hearts are pounding as he collapses beside me. We both lie there, catching our breaths. What the Goddess just happened? I've made love before, but never like this. I turn my head toward him, and he grins, his expression tender. He touches my cheek with his fingers gently, then leans over and kisses me, his lips clinging to mine.

I don't know what to say.

That's why, I realize. The ritual, the one the priestess had described. The ritual has been completed. We have been the Goddess and her consort.

We have made the Dance of Life.

CHAPTER TWENTY-FOUR

I come to consciousness slowly, a languorous heaviness in my body. I feel so good, although I can't quite remember why. A man's heavy arm is wrapped around me, his body pressed up against mine from behind.

Oh, now I remember. A satisfied smile spreads across my face.

I just lie there for a moment, cherishing the feeling of being held, of Joren's heavily muscled arm wrapped around me, his big palm against my belly. I twist around to look at him. His face looks younger in sleep, more innocent. I want to trace the lines of his cheek, the bristly beard growing on his jaw, his wide lips, his bushy eyebrows. With his eyes closed, I can see how thick his eyelashes are.

How thoroughly I had stroked and kissed that sculpted chest last night! What had Kya said about the benefits of Imperial discipline on Joren's body? After last night, I have to agree.

After our first joining, we had stayed awake for most of the night. We had talked a little. He'd told me about the sights he'd like to show me on his home world—the waterfalls on Patria he used to visit as a child, the lake where he would swim before he was sent to Academy. His face was open, more relaxed than I had ever seen him, so vital and young until he realized what he was promising. I would never visit Patria. It was a fantasy. From then on, we just talked about now and pretended that nothing existed outside of our magical tent.

Mostly though, we had made love again and again in a dazzling variety of ways. I hadn't known that I could feel so passionate and at ease at the same time. And we'd eaten from the basket of food that the herdsfolk had set outside our tent. "We need to keep up our stamina," Joren had teased as he'd rubbed the juices of a ripe Northern fruit over my chest and belly, then devoured my body with his mouth.

I felt like a goddess. Everything bad was far away. We were safe in our ecstatic cocoon, a glorious bliss that I never wanted to end. We both knew that, when the night was over, we would have to go back to reality.

And all the time, the drums and the singing and the stomps of the dancers and their loud voices kept us company. But the sounds must have faded, and our energy too, because we finally collapsed into an exhausted, sated slumber.

And now the sun has risen. The villagers move about outside as they go about their morning activities. The passion of last night was from another world, one that only existed in that special, sacred night. Without the drums and the pulsing energy of the night, I am back to myself.

Had I really pulled him down into my bed, wrapped my body around his, welcomed him inside me? Not just into my body, but joining with him at such a deep level?

What if it *had* been the energy of the dance, of the ritual? Was it real? Suddenly, I'm not sure.

I carefully lift his arm, just enough for me to slide out of the blankets we're nested in. Our clothes are thrown haphazardly on the rug, a reminder of how little we had cared about such niceties as we tore them off each other last night. The remains of our meal are on a platter next to our nest of blankets. I pick up my underclothes and slip them on, then the light trousers.

I'm just beginning to button the bodice of the dress when he speaks. "Good morning."

I swing around, caught. His brown hair is tousled, a sexy smile on his lips. He leans back on his elbows, the blankets barely covering his waist. What a magnificent sight!

I don't know how to talk about last night. How can I make it fit with what comes next, with who we are to each other outside of this tent?

I see a vulnerability in his face. He can tell that I'm ready to flee.

"I wish you'd stay."

When I don't say anything, he sighs and sits up. Suddenly, he's Commander Joren again, and he's naked in my bed, and we've just spent a night of indescribable passion, and I don't know how to put those things together.

We need to talk about this. That's obvious. I slowly walk back over to him. He pushes off the blankets, giving me a fantastic sight of his naked body. At first, I think he's inviting me back in with him, but instead he jumps up and grabs his pants from the floor, pulling them on.

"So..."

"So..." He grins, looking amused but also pleased, with a hint of the arousal from last night. I realize that I haven't fastened the front of my blouse yet. I pull my top together, hurriedly doing up the buttons. He walks closer to me and puts his hands on my shoulders, looking me in the eyes as he lowers his mouth to mine. As I feel him opening me gently with his tongue, I can't help but moan, and the rush of arousal moves through my body again.

OK, so maybe it wasn't just the drums.

But I have to pull myself away. "Joren, we have to talk."

He's breathing a little hard, but he says, "Yeah. OK." He brushes my cheek with his fingers.

"Before we go any further with this... with us—" Something flickers in his eyes when I say "us." I'm not sure what I want it to mean. "We need to make sure that what we're feeling, that it's real."

His face softens. "If you want to know what I feel for you—"

I cover his mouth with my fingers.

Goddess, I want to hear those words. But I need to get this out.

"What if it's not just the energy patterns that are being affected? What if somehow it's our feelings, our emotions too?" I can see him considering what I'm saying, taking it seriously. "Haven't you felt different since you been here? I know I have. And I can feel it getting the stronger. The strongest was... last night." I look down, embarrassed at the images in my mind, of how openly I had given myself to him, of how right it had felt. "Maybe we're not... feeling like ourselves. Maybe that's why we're so... drawn to each other. We don't really know if this is real."

"I do feel something, Vesta, but you're wrong if you think it's just the planet. I do feel different here, but I feel more like *myself*, if that makes sense." He brushes my lips with his thumb, his eyes intent on mine. "But I've been drawn to you for a while. Before we ever reached Hestia."

"What?"

He grins, looking bashful. "When I first met you, with the admiral, I thought you were... trouble. But also courageous, smart." His voice deepens. "And very beautiful."

How remote he had seemed to me when I met. The perfect Legion officer.

"You didn't act like it!" I protest. But, oh Goddess, I want it to be true.

"Well, you were under my command. It's not like I planned to act on it. And we had a mission to complete." That's one thing I have learned to value about Joren. He's a man of honor. "I tried put my feelings for aside… but I couldn't. The more time I spent with you, the more I wanted you. And now…" He bends down and kisses me again, the passion building between us, our lips clinging.

"I noticed you too," I admit.

"Oh, really?" he teases.

"Well, maybe not during the meeting. I was too scared. I was trying just to hold myself together. I hated you at first."

His lips twitch. "I could tell."

"I thought you were too perfect."

"Too perfect. I don't think I've ever been accused of that."

"But when you came to my quarters, I saw a different side of you. And I guess I've been noticing you ever since."

He grins. "So, if we're not being brainwashed by a crazy planet, maybe we actually care about each other."

"I haven't been without anyone else," I confess. "Not for a long time."

"Me neither. I haven't been close to anyone since the Conflict ended. Not with my situation being so complicated." His eyes are pained. "Vesta, I have nothing to offer you. I'm a demoted officer who can't even do his job anymore. I'm disgraced. I can't go back to my home world. I have nothing to give you."

"I don't expect anything, Joren. I know you can't promise anything. Neither can I. Do you think any of us know what's going to happen? Whether we'll be alive tomorrow? If Hestia will?" I touch his arm, willing him to understand. "I'm not an innocent little girl anymore, Joren. I know that we don't have any future together."

He smiles a little sadly, his lips lush against the growth of dark brown stubble on his jaw. He leans down and kisses me, first gently, then more deeply.

"But I want to," he murmurs. "I want to give you more than that."

I can feel the passion rising again in my body, and I wonder what it will be like to make love again, this time in the daylight, as his kisses grow more ardent, his hands moving over my body.

But then, I hear the scuff of footsteps approaching the tent, stopping directly outside. It appears that our idyll is over. I look at Joren with regret, then pull aside the flap.

Raina is standing outside, dressed in a fresh wrap. She scans the interior of the tent, her eyes focusing on the rumpled bedroll.

"The Mother is pleased," she pronounces. "Come, now you meet the mountain."

CHAPTER TWENTY-FIVE

Don't look down, I tell myself.

We follow Raina down a steep, narrow trail that hugs the mountain's edge. I keep my eyes focused on her back, not on the little pebbles that slip off the edge as we walk, disappearing into the abyss below.

"Careful," Joren whispers from behind me, as I sidle past an outcropping of rock that narrows the path.

"Oh, crap!" Kya is following right behind, and Sion behind her. I'm worried about Sion's ability to navigate this steep climb. He seems to be getting weaker as we get closer to the mountain. But Kya is staying close, ready to help him.

"We did ask to meet the mountain," I joke, but my voice is shaking.

"How much longer?" Kya calls out to Raina.

"Not much farther. Just a bit more."

Soon the path widens, allowing us to stay farther from the sheer drop to our left. The path ends at a small platform of rock, wide enough for us to all gather together. Raina is waiting for us, standing at the entrance to a large cavern leading into the mountain. I try to peer into the cave, but it's so dark inside that I can't make out any details.

Then a flash of white emerges from the darkness. An old woman emerges from the depths of the cave. She wears a simple wrap of white cloth, her feet bare. She has a wreath of lehua flowers on her head, a vibrant red against her gray-white hair. Her bright eyes, emerald green, shine out of a deeply lined face. She smiles, revealing a missing tooth.

I get a strange feeling, as if I know her. It's like people in dreams are familiar even if you've never met them before.

Raina embraces the old woman, puts her arm around the old woman's shoulders as they face us together. "You have the honor to meet Lahne, the Grandmother of the mountain. She will take you within."

Lahne beckons to me, urging me closer. When I'm close enough, she reaches up to enfold me in her arms. Her body is warm, strong. She smells like herbs. The strangest part is how comfortable I feel. After a moment, she releases me, stepping back. Her bright green eyes are soft with tears. "Daughter, you came back to us!"

I don't know what to say.

She turns to Joren. "Ah, and you are the son of the Far Away."

Joren nods carefully.

"And you," she says, looking at Kya "are one who knows the energy of the mountain."

She points at the diagnostic instruments that Sion carries. "Are you going to bring your eyes and ears with you?" she asks him.

Before he can answer, she laughs, a deep warm sound. "You come with me. She's been waiting for you."

Lahne turns and walks into the cave, her white robe bright against the darkness. Not wanting to lose sight of her, I follow quickly, Joren right behind as the others trail him.

It's not as dark inside as it first appeared. There's ambient light, glowing as if from reflected firelight. And it's high enough to walk upright.

"The warmth from the volcanic activity must be heating the stone," Kya whispers. "The energy signatures keep rising; we must be getting closer to the epicenter."

The tunnel opens into a wide cavern with a small hearth in the center. The smoke rises up through an opening in the stone above us, shining a circle of daylight into the chamber. A series of large flat cushions have been laid out in the Northern style around the fire. Lahne signals us to sit, then settles herself on a cushion by the fire, cross-legged. The fire light illuminates Lahne's eyes to an even brighter emerald, and her hair glows orange as if it were burning.

She looks at me expectantly. "Now, daughter, ask me what you came for."

For some reason, she has designated me as the speaker for our group. But I don't know what to say, how to explain all of this to her. First, I must understand her.

"Grandmother, I'm confused." I use the Northern honorific for an elder. "Why do you call me your daughter?"

She chuckles. "I call you daughter because you're a daughter of this world. And Hestia needs Her daughters now. That's why She called you home."

I frown. "*Hestia* called me? You talk as if the planet is a person. I don't understand."

"Oh, you will." She looks at each of us in turn. There is something almost regal about her presence, a humble kind of power that is hard to deny. "You all come here because you're wondering what's been happening to this world."

"You must know about the anomalies then," Sion interrupts.

"The 'anomalies?' That's what you been calling them?" She chuckles, her missing tooth giving her a strange appearance in the firelight.

"All the changes happening here, they all come from the power in the mountain. She's the one doing it. It's all part of Her plan."

She reaches over behind her and sprinkles a handful of herbs on the fire, which raise an aromatic smoke, before settling back on the cushion. She stares into the fire, her eyes going distant. "She's been here on this world for a long, long time. Before even the first sons and daughters came here. She's been waiting here all along, waiting to be born."

I get a strange chill down my back, like when the older kids used to tell scary stories to me as a child.

"The sons of the Far Away, they think they made her. But She was already here, waiting for them. She just needed the seed, and She was ready to grow. Just like the man puts the seed in the woman, who makes it ready and births it. Hestia, She's birthing something now."

Sion leans back, looking skeptical, almost offended. But Joren and Kya listen intently.

"Does this have anything to do with the animals we saw," Kya asks, "out on the grasslands? There were creatures that looked like wildebeests but must have been another species."

Lahne nods. "Yes, all of them. They're all part of what She's making."

Sion stirs beside me, setting down his sensor instruments. "When you said this 'She,' this power in the mountain, has been here since the beginning, do you mean before the terraforming?"

Lahne nods.

"You're saying that there was life here before the terraforming? Some form of alien intelligence?"

"Don't know about that. Don't know what She is. But She's been here waiting for us."

"But that's absurd!" He waves his arms angrily, ignoring Joren's signal to calm down. "There's never been anything like that before. Nowhere in the whole of explored space. We're alone out here."

Lahne shakes her head. "Even before we met Her, we've never been alone. Don't you remember the legends, the ones we brought with us... the old, old stories that tell how the world was made?"

Sion looks confused. "I'm a scientist, not a storyteller."

"I tell you the old story, then. This is how it goes..." Lahne's eyes film over as she stares into the fire. She grasps a thick stick, pounding it on the ground. Her voice rises in a powerful tone. "In the beginning was darkness. All was quiet and still. There was no life and no death. Just a still field, like a big ocean with no waves in it. And then, the light came. And the light and the dark, they joined together. And they made life. The male and the female. The light and the dark. And then the world was born."

Sion wrinkles his nose. "What do these old superstitions have to do with anything?"

"Sometimes, old stories, they've got some truth in them, just a deeper way of things. You see... Hestia...Well, that's not Her real name; no one knows Her real name. But that's the name that men who settled Her have put on Her ... She comes from the dark, the mystery. And you all, you children of the Far Away, you're the other half. You woke her up. And She gave birth to what you wanted. But now," she chuckles, "now it's her turn. Her and Her daughters."

I'm part of it. Just like I'd been feeling. That strange feeling of being meant to be. It wasn't just about Joren. It was about all of it. I'm one of Her daughters, one of the daughters of Hestia. I have some kind of purpose here. A reason for why I was called back.

Lahne continues. "That's what's got those men down in the South so afraid. They don't want Her taking Her turn. They think She's angry, that She wants revenge. But She's not angry. She's just doing what She must."

"You may not understand," Sion says to Lahne, speaking slowly, as if to a child. Joren is trying to quiet him, but Sion just waves him away.

"But this is a designed system. And what is happening here is an error, a problem. It needs to be fixed. If we don't, many people could die."

She just smiles indulgently. "It's wearing out. Things breaking down. Can't you feel it?" She looks to Kya, to me. "All of this round and round of the same old thing. No passion there. It's no mystery Life wants something new. Can't you feel it? She's saving us from ourselves, from our own cleverness. We think we know everything. But we don't know anything."

Kya looks down at something on her instrument display, frowning at it. "There may be something to this, Sion. What about the energy leakages? What about the wildebeests? How do you explain that?"

He hisses in warning. "Please, Kya, you're a scientist, surely you can't—"

"It's energy, Sion." Kya insists. "There are some theorists that equate energy beyond the physical. That there's an exchange of energy that's... well, I guess it would be called metaphysical, if you wanted to go back that far, to the pre-historic."

"I can't believe we're even debating this." He rubs his face with his hands. "It doesn't matter. This is all hypothetical until we get some actual data. We need to go to the epicenter, take some readings, and see what's going on."

Lahne nods. "You want me to bring you to Her. I can do that."

Sion looks taken aback. "Finally."

But Lahne isn't looking at Sion. She's looking at me.

"Tonight," she says. "I will bring you to Her heart."

CHAPTER
TWENTY-SIX

We follow Lahne into the darkness, her wrap a beacon of white in the low light of the cavern. This pathway is narrower than before, the ceiling lower, the path sloped steeply upward. It grows steadily hotter as we climb, becoming almost unbearably stifling, but Lahne's pace never slackens.

"Sion?" Kya calls out.

I look behind me. Sion is bent over, leaning his weight on the cave wall.

"It's the heat," he gasps, waving away Kya's help. His face is pallid, his eyes sunken, skin damp with sweat. "I'm fine, let's go," he insists, pushing himself to standing and charging ahead. We look at each other uncertainly, then follow closely behind. A dim glow of light shines from the tunnel ahead.

We emerge onto a vast shelf of rock sheltered on all sides by tall volcanic peaks. The area is lit only by starlight and a distant red glow, the source of which is just out of sight. Sion and Kya take out their monitoring equipment and take readings from the area around us.

"Here it is," Lahne lifts her arms, spinning around slowly. "The heart of the mountain."

The rock looks different here. The walls emit an orange-red glow as if lit from within. And the rock underfoot has a strange consistency, somewhere between liquid and solid. The whole landscape looks like it's almost melting, and yet that's impossible. Only lava can move. And if this rock were molten, we would be burning up.

Kya looks down at her equipment screen. "Are you seeing this?" she asks Joren.

He squints down at the readout. "More distortion?"

"No distortion," Lahne answers. "You are at the mountain's heart. This is where all energy gathers to its home."

"No distortion?!" Sion shakes his head. "According to these readings, we should be burning up. The air must be poisonous, from the gases."

"Poisonous to some. Not to us. You're under Her protection here. You'll be safe for now." Lahne beckons me forward. "Come, my daughter."

I obey her summons. Just ahead, the lip of the caldera is visible in the distance, the source of that mysterious red glow. Joren moves to join us.

"No," Lahne warns him. "This is not for you. Only the daughters of Hestia may come this close."

His face hardens. "Vesta, it's not safe."

I reach up and touch his arm. "I trust her. I'll be alright."

He nods, conceding. But his eyes stay fixed on me as I walk with Lahne, heading toward the distant glow of the caldera.

The rock softens further, my feet squelching rock so molten that is almost liquid. But Lahne walks calmly on, so I follow. The air is thicker now, heavy with the scent of burning, the gases of the caldera swirling all around. But somehow, I can still breathe.

She stops at the lip of the caldera. Her face is lit from below, throwing harsh angles onto her ancient face, her emerald eyes glowing. Gurgling and hissing sounds rise from within the caldera, like a stomach digesting a meal.

"Come, my daughter."

I join her at the edge of the caldera, terrified to look down. Its power feels strong enough to pull me in, its fires hungry to consume me.

"Look," she urges, pointing at the molten pool of fire with one gnarled finger. She grips my hand in hers. "I'll hold you steady."

I trust her. She won't let me fall.

I shift my balance and lean forward to steal a look within the caldera.

A swirling mix of molten red bubbles up, churning, beautiful, dangerous—an angry liquid, remaking Hestia itself. I stare down, transfixed by its terrible power.

"This is where She lives, my daughter." She raises up her arms, her head thrown back. "The source of all power on Hestia. This is Her cooking fire. This is where She makes the world."

A thrilling energy gathers within me, echoed by the lava as it rises toward the volcano's lip.

"You feel it." Lahne eyes holding a knowing gleam. "You've been feeling it since you came back. This is yours!" She waves her arms, encompassing the whole of the mountains. "All of this world. You're part of Her. *She* is where your power come from."

"*My* power?" I shake my head. "But how? I'm from the South. I've never even been here before."

"I will tell you something. Something really important. Something they never taught you about down south." She takes both my hands in her gnarled grasp. "We were one people once, the farmers and the herdsfolk."

What? That can't be true.

"We all lived down there. It wasn't all farms back then. There was space to roam. Then we herdsfolk came here to the North, and something changed. Once we lived close to the mountain, we learned to live Her ways."

Her ways. Like the woman I saw in my dream, beckoning me forward.

"Why do you call this mountain She?"

"Because the mountain, She changed us women most of all. She made us strong, gave us powers. She has work for us to do." She reaches into a pocket of her wrap, pulls out a handful of dried herbs. She sprinkles them into the fire of the caldera. "The men from the South, they don't like us. But we need each other. So we stay here. They stay there. We know Her time is coming."

It's all happening the way it was mean to. That's the feeling that settles on me. That everything I've done has taken me here, to just this place, to this moment. It's just like I felt with Joren.

"You had to go away from your home, daughter. That was part of your path. You had to go away and learn about that big world out there. You had to learn that it isn't your place out there, but it was *his* place. And now you came back... with him."

"Joren is part of this?"

"He's a son of the Far Away. And you're a daughter of Hestia."

The fumes from the volcano, the drugging energy all around me... This can't be real, can't be true. I shake myself, as if out of a trance. "This planet... It's making us feel things. How do we know any of it's real?"

Lahne gently shakes her head. "She's not making you feel anything that's not already there. She's just pulling at what needs to come out." She puts her hands on my shoulders, gives me a shake. "Don't you feel it? That's Her, giving back to you what you lost. Making you whole again."

"What does She want from me?" I cry.

Her lips compress. "I don't know. But you need to talk to Her."

"Talk to her? How do I do that?"

"There's a way. I tried to do it. The others tried too. She wants you. You're going to have to do it…" She sighs deeply, looking at me with something like sympathy. "And if you want Her to listen, we better do it quick."

*   *   *

"Frick the readings. We practically walked on lava, and we didn't get burned."

Sion is pacing, restless in the tight quarters of the tent. He's been agitated since we returned to the village. The rest of us gather with him, trying to make sense of what we've just experienced. "We don't even know what this force is. We don't know where it comes from, what's causing it, or who put it here. It's dangerous."

"We don't know that it's dangerous, Sion," Kya says softly.

"You saw what's out there! The whole system has been destabilized."

"It's changing, yes, but it's not like the other worlds we've studied. Those were degradations of the system, breakdowns. This is something different. It's generating new forms of life. It's more like a creation, a re-creation, rather than destruction."

Sion looks dubious.

"I wonder… There's a theory in the field of energy science, from esoteric theory. That the energy forms in our mind create our consciousness and the forms it takes." Sion is about to interrupt, but Kya is quick. "Wait, listen. We brought our forms with us from old Earth. Not just our lifeforms, that's obvious. I mean the forms in our mind, our energy signatures."

"Oh no, you're not going into that again, are you?" Sion asks impatiently.

"The ancients talk about energy balance in terms of yin and yang, male and female, the union of opposites. We may be making the same mistakes again. Maybe the force here is a complementary

186

energy, a form of consciousness that completes what we have been missing."

"That's mysticism, not science!"

"Maybe," she concedes, "but do you remember what you said about the ancestors, how they thought they knew better when they were tinkering with life?" He nods. "What if we're making the same mistake?"

Sion snorts, dismissive. "This is different. They were changing things. We're keeping them stable."

"Maybe it's not just about *what* we're doing but *why*." Sion frowns in confusion, so Kya explains, "We aren't considering that maybe life has its own intelligence, that the *why* of life is larger than the human mind can understand. So any way we try to control a living system isn't going to work."

"These are all wild ideas. There's no way to prove any of this."

But I can prove what she's saying if what Lahne told me is true. If I'm actually crazy enough to believe.

I stand up, shoulders squared. "I can do it." They all look at me, surprised. "I can communicate with the force on Hestia. Lahne told me I can... and I know it too. I can feel it already. Maybe it's because I'm from here. But if there's a way to do it, I'm going to try." I may be overstating my confidence, but we don't have any other choice. I have to try.

"No." Sion places his hands on my shoulders as if to calm me. "We're not going to subject ourselves to another primitive ritual."

"Not us...Vesta," Joren corrects him. I can see the concern in his eyes. He doesn't want me to do anything that would risk my life.

"But Commander—"

"No, Sion. I'm in command of this mission. This is what we're going to do."

Sion is visibly holding himself back, fighting the urge to argue further, but he finally nods his acceptance, compliant but obviously unconvinced.

But Kya looks hopeful, giving me a look of encouragement.

Joren turns to me, his eyes worried, echoing my own dread. He must know how much of a risk this is. He also knows that I have no other choice. "When does she want you to do it?"

"It's urgent. Tomorrow, I think."

"Sion, Kya," he says, his voice clipped, his eyes not leaving mine. "Go to talk with the villagers. Find out all you can about the ceremony."

Once they're gone, he moves closer. "Are you sure about this?" His warm hands are resting on my shoulders, his eyes searching mine.

"Lahne said this is the only way." But I'm afraid too. Of course I am. "Anyway," I say, smirking, "the last ceremony wasn't so bad."

His lips twitch, a flash of desire igniting between us.

We're alone. When will we have this opportunity again? One thing this mission has shown me is how uncertain things are. Why not enjoy what pleasure and happiness we can for as long as it lasts?

"I wouldn't mind doing that again," he answers, and for a moment it looks like he's going to kiss me, but instead, he lifts his right hand and cups my cheek and jaw, his thumb moving over my lips. "But somehow I don't think this next ceremony is going to be as pleasant."

He's right. I get the sense that it is going to be dangerous. Talking to a mysterious consciousness in the mountain... the idea is terrifying. But Lahne has kept me safe so far. And I trust her.

"I can do this," I say, not sure if I'm trying to convince him or myself.

"I know you can." His voice holds such confidence, such trust. "And whatever happens, I'll be there with you the whole way."

I step into his arms, and we hold each other for a long while.

*   *   *

I wake up to a sound of rustling outside my tent. Instinctively, I grab my weapon. The tent flap opens, and Joren's face appears.

"Joren," I whisper harshly. "What are you doing? Someone could see you!"

Joren scrambles into my tent, pulling the flap closed behind him. He is smiling—a mischievous, teasing look. "I couldn't stay away." He crawls up to me on my bedroll, embracing me with a passionate kiss.

"Have you lost your mind?" I whisper when his lips leave mine. "You can't be in here!" My body is already eager for more, but there are real-world consequences here. I don't have a reputation to protect, but Joren does. "I don't want you to get in trouble."

Joren draws back, cradling my cheek in his palm, his eyes sincere. "If you don't want me here, fine. I'll go. I don't want to make things harder for you. But as for me, I don't care who knows." He settles closer to me. "I want to be with you." His lips draw closer to mine. "I want everyone to know that we're together." His face holds an expression of wounded joy, his eyes tearing up.

I kiss him, lingering, our lips clinging to each other.

We don't have a future together past this mission, no matter what he promises me. I know that. But I want to be with him tonight, at least one more time, no matter how much it hurts when it's over.

"Stay," I whisper, "but we can't do this right now. The others will hear us. We have to wait until they go to sleep."

Joren grins, pulling the blankets over us. He presses himself against my back, his arm around my stomach. I can feel how hard he is, pressed against my bottom.

"This reminds me of riding with you on that horse," Joren whispers in my ear, stroking my hair. "I was trying not to press against you too close. I didn't want to get too turned on."

"What?" I laugh. "I thought you didn't care one way or the other. I was trying not to let you know how much I liked it. I was too embarrassed."

"Oh, I cared." He runs his hand down my hip, his voice lowering to a seductive tone as he nuzzles my neck. "And now I can touch all I want."

It feels so good, so arousing, that I don't want to stop.

"Shh, the others will hear us," I protest weakly.

His hand reaches underneath my shirt, stroking my stomach, rising to my breasts. "Then we'll have to be quiet, won't we?"

The feeling of him touching me and whispering in my ear, not being able to touch him or look at him behind me, is incredibly arousing. I struggle to control the building sounds of my arousal, especially as he finally slips my trousers down over my hips and enters me from behind. We both have to stop ourselves from crying out, and somehow the restraint raises the intensity, the privacy, of the experience to a fever-pitch, and we both reach a quick climax.

As we hold each other in the dark, drifting into sleep, I feel safe, content for the first time in years.

Despite the future, despite the differences in our status and our futures, we have each other now, and it is pure, and true, and beautiful.

CHAPTER TWENTY-SEVEN

The massive tent, the largest in the village, is crowded with herdsfolk as I enter with Joren at my side. The villagers are seated on the ground, arrayed in circles around the tent, talking amongst themselves in soft murmurs. Some of them look up as I enter.

At the front of the crowd, Lahne sits cross-legged on a large, orange cushion, the priestesses arrayed around in a half-circle around her. I notice Sion, seated in the third row back, looking uncomfortable.

"Vesta!" I turn to see Kya waving to me from the edge of the tent. She stands with the musicians, holding her flute. It makes me feel better to know she will be a part of the ceremony.

"You must go." Raina signals to Joren, indicating that he should sit with Sion. Joren squeezes my hand. "I'll be here," he assures me, taking his seat.

I walk to the front, settling down on a cushion next to Lahne, keenly aware of all the onlookers focused on me. Their eyes look hungry, intrusive. Lahne grasps my hand. "Forget about them," she whispers. "Just follow the energy. She will guide you."

She signals to the herdsmen crouching at the edges of the tent, their hide-covered drums set before them. The drummers begin to beat out a steady rhythm, like a heartbeat. The villagers follow the beat, pounding on the ground with their hands. Then the flutes join in. The melody of the flutes rises above the rhythm of the drums, airy and mystical, blending with and heightening the resonance.

Then the priestesses join in, chanting. Low at first and then rising in intensity until the sound fills the pavilion with its energy.

Some of the priestesses begin to move, rising up from their seats, to flow in time to the music. They move in front of me, flowing hypnotically in patterns my eye cannot follow.

I look away, searching for Joren in the crowd, but everything looks blurry. All I can see are trails of light around the dancers, smudges of dark colors outside of their light. Bright lines emanate from the dancers' bodies, connection to the drums and the flutes, extending through the tent. I shake my head, but the glowing lines are still there, moving between the people like stitches made of light.

My heart beats in time with the drums, my breath moves in tune with the flutes, as if these rhythms and sounds and movements are a part of me.

My eyelids grow heavy, my body soft and warm. I slump down to the cushioned sleeping pallet, my body as limp as a cloth doll's. I can hear Joren's voice from far away, crying out as I collapse, but someone stops him from coming to me.

I lay as if asleep, but something inside of me is waking up.

I am falling... sinking... down... down... slipping through the cushion that my body rests upon... into the dirt beneath the tent, past the worms and bugs and burrowing creatures, through the roots that weave themselves through the dirt... deeper down... to where no plants or animals live... just rock... and now heat... and now fire, deep down underneath the world. The crust is cracking, shifting, opening. A river of fire flows through the underworld. It flows like water, like blood in our veins—it's the same pattern.

An energy, an awareness, builds in me, from the base of my spine through my abdomen, out through my body and my head. The energy expands like a wave, moves out in all directions, my consciousness expanding with it, traveling eastward over the plains, becoming part of every living thing as I expand outward. I am the migratory beasts as they wander in packs, the chill of the wind on my hide, the tang of the grass in my chewing jaws, the steady energy in my big woolly body. I am the grass itself, the energy that runs through it from the planet's core. I am the ocean, the fish, the plankton, the great whales in the sea, the deep cold of the ocean through my blubber, the joy as I jump above the surface and flip over on my back, the itch of the barnacles.

Too much, too far, too big. Stop. Stop.

I stop. Focus. One spot.

I move south to the lands where my people live. It feels different here. They don't know I'm here with them. They don't know what they're part of. Don't know what's happening in the North. Don't know that everything that's ever been a part of Hestia, everyone, they're all still here. Traces of their energy resonate in everything around. Somewhere, far off, I sense my mother—her love of our family, out on our farm. And her parents and relatives, and my father, and his ancestors too. We are all part of it, all together. This great mystery, all connected, and woven together like a tapestry on a loom. It is all so beautiful and transcendent, and if I just draw back a little farther, I'll see all of it, the whole design. The whole picture, and I will finally understand.

But the link to my body is getting weaker. If I go too far, I will no longer be me. "I" will become "we." And then maybe even "we" will dissolve.

I'm not ready for that. No matter how much I want to know what's beyond, I'm not ready for that. That's for the next stage, the one they call death. If I want to know what's beyond that, I will have to let go of me as Vesta forever.

She. The power in the mountain. The source of the energy here on Hestia.

She is with me. Her presence envelopes me like fog or mist.

She is without form. Like water, like lava.

She makes no sound, and yet, She is telling me a story.

So long we been here in the cold and the dark. Alone. Waiting. Quiet. Still.

Yes, yes, this is what I have come here to know.

Then He comes to us. He makes life in us. But He takes from us too. He only wants to make life in His own image. He won't share the joy of creation with us. He wants to make his story be the only one.

We wait here, in the mountain. We stay small, down in the burning fire. We join with the life near us, the female creatures. We change together. We try to go to the land down below us, where the little fires burn, but something holds us back.

Then this daughter comes. She sees what we been making. She sees what's been dying. She's come to make new life for this place. She makes something new. She joins with the ones who sing the song, the ones who tell the story.

I can see the villagers in the tent, dancing and singing. They are singing the mountain awake. They are singing the land into harmony. This daughter is part of their song.

We must keep them safe, the creatures of this world. The others will come and hurt them. From the Far Away, from the void, the metal ships will come. They will come to try to kill what we are making. We will not harm the creatures of this world. We will bring their cousins to life too. We will be a mother to them.

This daughter tells her that she understands. But this daughter (I…Vesta… that is what "this daughter" is called) needs to go back. I need to go back to my friends, where I belong.

This daughter must go. This daughter must finish the story. This daughter is needed. This daughter must take a gift with her.

I feel a pulsating strength inside of me, a transmission of energy from Her to me. It is part of me now. I must go back to the others so that I may use it for its intended purpose.

I turn back to the place where my body lives, to the container that is my body. It is so small. The flesh, the mind, both. How can I ever fit back into such a vessel when I am so much more than its capacity?

I have to let go.

I have to let go of the whales and the fish, the grass and the beasts. I have to let go of the expanse. I need to shrink myself back down, small enough to be a "me."

People hover over my body. The priestess recites incantations, burns herbs. Her green eyes look up and around, searching for me. She knows I'm struggling to return. But I don't feel afraid. I have too much filling me up.

I know that I can't die, not really. But I want to go back to my body, my mind—where I belong. I have so much to tell them.

I can feel my mother holding me as a baby. My brother, laughing as we ride our horses as fast as we can go. My sisters, as we cook together in our warm kitchen. My father, as we read books together.

They all love me. We love one another. And it's different from the way I am with the beasts and the whole of Hestia as part of me. It's the way that we connect with each other when we are human. We love each other.

Drawing closer, I see Joren leaning over me. He has the strangest expression on his face. Desperate. He's calling my name. He holds me by my shoulders. He looks like he's about to cry. I want to tell him that I'm OK, but I know he can't hear me. I try to listen with my human ears, but I can't hear. Those sounds of human speech make no sense. I can feel though. I can feel something from Joren, even though he's different from Hestia.

He cares. He cares in a way that intrigues me, that draws me in. I want to know what it feels like for him to hold me again. He is kissing me on the temple, begging me to come back. Somehow the feeling of Joren is even stronger than the rest, more immediate to what I'm called back to do. It is that desire—to be held, to be cared for, to be loved—that draws me back in.

A sudden pain, like being squeezed, and I'm back. I can make out the speech around me, the cooling sweat on my skin, Joren's warm arms embracing me.

The light is so bright. The sounds so loud. This must be what being born feels like—coming into a bright, loud, cold world, and being held.

Joren has tears on his cheeks, a look of wonder and joy on his face as he holds me.

"Vesta," he says, with a tone of voice I've never heard before. But I've felt him from the inside, so I know what it means.

I pull my parched lips into a smile.

He loves me. He's called me back with it.

CHAPTER TWENTY-EIGHT

A blur of faces. Too bright. Too loud. My body shivers. A soothing, dry warmth as Lahne wraps my body in a blanket. Kya's worried face swims above me, then is gone. Joren's presence at my side warms me, his brown eyes searching my face.

"She needs to rest," Lahne beckons to someone. "Carry her to the healing tent."

"No, I'll carry her." I nestle into Joren's chest, clinging to his neck, my body shaking. He carries me outside, then into a small, quiet tent. I am lowered gently into a nest of blankets that smell faintly of incense and horseflesh.

"We need to get you warmed up, my daughter." Lahne lifts me bit by bit, peeling off my sweat-soaked clothes, then wraps me back up in the cozy blanket. She sets a small kettle on the fire and adds some sweet-smelling herbs.

I must have drifted off. A moment later, her hand cups my head as she lifts a bowl of warm liquid to my lips. "This will help," she says. I carefully sip and swallow. Joren raises me up to sit, as Lahne settles pillows underneath me.

"You went far away, my daughter," she says finally, grasping my hands in hers.

It almost feels like a dream now. I can remember the idea of what happened, but not how it felt to be there. The memories settle into me, my mind trying to make sense of what happened.

"What do you mean?" Joren demands of Lahne. "What happened?"

How can I explain to Joren what I barely understand myself? There are no words for it. But I have to try.

"I found it, Joren. It was Her, the consciousness inside the mountain." He looks incredulous. "She took me far away." I feel it again, just an echo of that endlessness, a taste of that ecstatic connection. "She showed me Hestia... why she was here. Lahne was right, Joren. She's been here since the beginning, since before Hestia was terraformed." In a rush, I remember the rest. "And she gave me something—some kind of power, some energy force." Even now I can feel it, a low hum of warmth all around me and within me.

"Yes, daughter, She has entrusted you with this," Lahne says, touching my shoulder. "But you must know that all gifts come with a price." Lahne stands up, tucking the blanket around me. "Tomorrow I will teach you more about this gift. For now, you rest."

Joren moves closer, crouched by my side. "I'll take care of her."

Lahne rises and leaves us alone together.

I need him close to me now. I lift the blanket to invite him in, to lie with me.

His eyes move over my naked body, desire flaring. I feel an answering desire in my own body, although I'm too tired to act on it.

"You need to rest," he says.

I smile wearily. "I wish I had the energy to be like that with you. I want it. But I just want you with me."

He pulls his shirt over his head, throwing it on the ground, revealing the sculpted body that I enjoy so thoroughly.

"I'd better keep the pants on, though," he teases.

He scoots in beside me, pulling the blanket over us, tucking his body around mine. I settle my head on his chest. He feels so warm, so safe.

After a moment, he whispers, "I wish I could take this on for you, Vesta. I don't want you to be the one taking all the risks."

I pat his chest playfully. "You always have to be the hero, don't you?"

A grin flashes, then it's gone. "It was so hard to see you like that." He cradles my cheek and jaw in his big hand. "I thought you were gone."

"I almost got lost," I admit. I didn't feel afraid then, but now, it's terrifying. "Then I remembered why I was there, my duty. Lahne, she helped me to trace my way back." The incantations, the prayers. "But I got stuck. I couldn't get back all the way." Joren holding me, pleading for me to return. "But then, I *felt* you. You pulled me in. You helped me come back the rest of the way."

He brushes back my hair from my cheek and tucks it behind me ear. "I don't know how I did that. But I'm so damned glad I did."

I lean into him, closing my eyes.

"Shh, rest," he says. "I'll stay here with you. Just get some sleep."

I drift off, safe in Joren's arms.

*   *   *

A little boy is dressed somberly in dark trousers and shirt. He wears polished shoes. His dark hair has been combed down neatly. He must be brave today. His family will be shamed if he cries. Last night he begged his mother not to make him go. She hugged him to her and cried bitterly, but there was nothing to be done. The men come to his door now. They say that it's time to go, that he has a duty to uphold to the Republic, so be a good man and come along. They walk him to the glider parked outside the main entrance of his family's estate. Its door hangs open, with an empty seat for him, next to another boy he does not recognize. He hesitates, looks back. His mother is looking out the window. She wipes the tears from her eyes before they can fall, then waves. Her smile is false. She is trying to encourage him, he knows. This is what he must do. He doesn't wave back. That would embarrass him in front of the others. He climbs into the vehicle and takes his seat. He won't look out the window. Otherwise, he might cry too, and that would not be good. The door slams shut. This will be last time he will see his mother as a boy. The next time he returns, he will be a man. And this place will be his home no longer.

Joren sits up abruptly in bed, waking me. He puts his head in his hands, breathes slow and deep.

"What's wrong?" I sit up, stroke his back.

"I dreamed about my mother."

The woman at the window.

How could I dream his dream? Could it be the effect of the ceremony? Maybe the barrier between the world and consciousness is thinner now, permeable after what I went through.

"I haven't thought about that in years." He sounds stunned, vulnerable. "Remember when I told you that I was sent away to the Academy when I was a child?"

The boy with the dark hair...

"And I haven't really thought about it, not since then. But this dream, it was so real. My mother was young, maybe thirty—the age she was when I left. And I was seven. I was begging her not to send me away. But I knew I had to go."

The woman at the window, holding back tears...

"It must have been terrible there. What you told me before about not having enough to eat, not being able to sleep."

He snorts. "The physical part was easier than the rest."

"But you were starved, beaten!"

"That was just my body. The mental part, that was much worse." He leans back, lost in memory. "At the Academy, feelings were a weakness. They'd be used against you by the other boys, by

200

the instructors. I had to put them all away where no one would ever see them. I had to forget about everything but surviving."

I reach out to comfort him, but he stops me. "Wait, I have to say this."

"And I did it. I earned my commission in the Legion. I did what I had to do during the Conflict. But after Thea, I couldn't do that anymore." There is pain in his warm brown eyes. "Vesta, before I came here, before I met you, I didn't know what to do with myself. I knew I couldn't go back to how I was, but I didn't know what would happen. I thought I was broken." I want to comfort him, to take away the pain. "But since we've been here, since I've been here with you, I've been feeling... like I just got something back. Something I lost a long time ago."

"What did you get back?" But I think I know.

"My feelings. What it feels like to be loved by someone. To care so much that it rips your heart out be away from them. To care, no matter what. I'd forgotten that I could feel that." He touches my face with his hand, his eyes intent on mine. "Until now."

How can this be real? That I am here with this man, hearing everything I never knew I wanted to hear.

"I love you, Vesta."

He is staring into me, so open. This can't be happening. It's too good.

"I know I we haven't known each other very long, and I have no idea what kind of future we're even going to have together, but... I do love you. More than anyone I've ever met."

Everything in me is crying out, *yes, yes.*

This can't be happening. But it's meant to be.

I need him. Just like he needs me.

"I love you too."

He gasps out a breath.

"For as long as this lasts."

His mouth twists. "It may not last long."

He means the danger we're in.

"There are no guarantees." We both know that. "Not for us, not for Hestia."

He cradles my face in his hands. "I can't go back to Patria and pretend this isn't happening. Whatever it costs. This is it." He's smiling but his eyes are wet. "I can't go back now."

We kiss, our lips clinging together. A consummation sweeter than anything I have ever imagined.

Joren pushes back just enough to look me in the eyes. He has that hero look on his face. "I'm here with you… forever, if you'll have me."

How could I ever say no to that?

Joren is the real kind. He means what he promises.

"I'm going all the way. Vesta. For us, for Hestia, for what matters."

For what matters.

What matters is Hestia. And now Joren—a general, a leader, a man of strength, discipline, intelligence, responsibility—is on Hestia's side, and mine, ours.

Ours. I like the sound of that.

CHAPTER
TWENTY-NINE

We find Kya and Sion sitting in front of a large tent in the center of the village, talking with a herdsman. Kya is waving her hands animatedly. Sion looks somber, tired.

I'm wearing the beaded herdsfolk clothing that Lahne left for me, an embroidered dress and leggings. With my hair worn long and the borrowed clothes, I look more herdswoman than Hestian.

Kya rushes over when she sees us, and Sion follows more slowly. He glances down to where my hands are joined with Joren's, frowning.

"Are you alright?" Kya demands, enveloping me in a hug. "We were so worried about you when you just slumped down like that."

"I'm fine now," I assure her. "Lahne just checked me over."

Sion scans me, critical. "You lost consciousness. You should be evaluated medically."

I doubt the medical scanners will find anything, but to satisfy them I allow Sion to check me over. He sits me down on a stool in front of the tent while Kya goes inside the tent to fetch the equipment. The herdsman who was here must have left while we were talking.

"I didn't actually lose consciousness," I tell Sion as Kya returns with the medical scanner.

"Don't you remember?" Kya frowns. "You passed out."

That's what it must have looked like for them. They're not likely to believe what actually happened, but I need to try to explain regardless.

Sion's scans me with the medical unit. He stares at the med display, then his eyes widen with what looks like surprise.

"What is it?" I ask. "Is something wrong?"

"No. Nothing." He smiles reassuringly, but there is a falseness to it. He begins tucking away the instruments. "Lahne was right, You're fine." Sion clears his throat. "Now, are you going to tell us what happened?"

He and Kya are looking at me expectantly. Joren squeezes my arm, encouraging.

"I know this is going to be hard for you to understand." I look between Kya and Sion, gauging their reactions as I tell them what happened during the ceremony, about the experience of my mind expanding throughout Hestia, of finding the consciousness inside the mountain, of coming back into my body. The only thing I leave out is about energy She gave me before I came back. I feel intuitively that I should keep that part to myself.

Kya leans forward throughout, looking fascinated.

Sion, as I expected, looks skeptical. "It must have been a trance state. Maybe the priestess drugged you, put something in your food or drink."

"Sion, it wasn't—"

"Or hypnotic suggestion. The rhythms and the expectations of the setting—"

"Sion," Joren interrupts, "she's telling the truth."

Sion doesn't react for a moment. "Commander," he says finally, "I am concerned that you are letting your personal feelings for this woman come before your duty."

Joren's face hardens. "This *is* my duty, Sion. The safety and well-being of the Republic."

Sion stares back at Joren, then covers his face with both hands and rubs his eyes. "If that's true, commander, then there's something you need to know. All of you," he says, but he's looking at me. "Since we've been here with the herders, I've discovered something. I've been analyzing their genetic structure, and I've found some anomalies. Specifically, among the herdswomen." His voice grows more fierce, insistent. "It's not just the landscape that's changing. Not just the animals and the flora. It's the herdswomen themselves. Their biology is evolving. Just like the beasts we saw breeding."

"The herders aren't beasts—" I interrupt.

"You know what I mean," he hisses. "Biology is biology. The humans on Hestia are not supposed to change, just like all the other lifeforms. But something is causing the females of this population to change."

Of course. "It's the mountain," I explain excitedly. "That's what's giving the priestess her special powers. They're being transformed along with the land. That's amazing!"

"No," Sion's eyes are troubled, his expression somber. "It's dangerous. That means the mutations will be passed along to offspring." He opens his hands and looks wildly between us. "When... if... we can correct the energy anomalies... That's just the first step. Then we'll need to remove all the mutations in the system... the plants, the animals, all the lifeforms that have been knocked off track. They must be... culled."

It takes me a moment to understand what he's saying. The herdsfolk, they must be *culled* as well. "You can't mean—"

"It's standard containment protocol. We can't allow the genetic contagion."

"But they're people!"

"I think we can say," Joren interrupts, "that we're beyond the standard protocol here, Sion. I'm not going to authorize any culling of the herdsfolk."

Kya nods shakily, her hand on my shoulder in support.

"There's something else you need to know." Sion is looking at me with a detached expression, like I'm a specimen he's studying. "Vesta, you have been affected too." Kya gasps. "It must be because you're a female and a native of this planet. The energetic disturbance of this place has affected you, caused genetic distortion. Just like the rest of the females here."

I have felt the change. Now even Sion's instruments can detect it.

"The Institute will want you destroyed along with the rest, but I may be able to convince them to sterilize you instead. Then you'll be able to leave when this is over."

"That's not an option," Joren says, his jaw tight.

"It's not up to you, to me, to any of us. This system can't be fixed at this level. The Institute will need to be sent for."

They all start talking over each other, getting louder as they argue. But a curious feeling of calm settles over me, I know what I have to do.

"Wait," I yell. The others fall silent in surprise. "The Institute won't come if they believe the problem has been fixed, so what if they believed that it was?"

Sion erupts in a bark of shocked laughter. "You expect me to lie for you? And what happens when the readings continue?"

I shake my head. "They won't."

Kya looks curious, a line between her brows. "And how will you manage that?"

I'm asking them to risk their careers, their lives. I owe them the truth.

"Something… *happened* during the ceremony. More than just communication. She transferred something to me… some of her power."

Kya looks at me, considering. But she believes me. I can tell.

"I can help her to change things, change the way the readings appear." I hadn't even known that I could do that until I said it. "Then they'll never know. You could go home, Sion. Leave Hestia alone. She can heal herself."

The offer hangs there a moment. But I can see it in his face—the pity, the conviction.

"Let's say that your plan works," Kya says. "There's still the problem of Darla. I'm worried that she still hasn't arrived. She might have warned them already."

"We'll deal with that if it happens," Joren says. "Kya, what do you say?"

She grins. "I say, let's do this!"

Joren pins Sion in a searching gaze. "Sion?"

Sion shakes his head. "I can't condone something like this. It's reckless."

Joren runs his hand through his hair, cursing. "Then the Legion will come. You know what that means for Hestia. They'll never let this get out."

"Ha!" We turn to see who called out. Lahne is walking toward us, the herdsmen who slipped away earlier following behind her. He must have come to get her when we arrived. When she reaches the tent, she settles herself on the stool as regal as always. "Don't you be so worried about those soldiers and their big ships."

"We have a reason to be worried," Joren says, his tone deferential. "The GRIP will send ships, weapons, soldiers."

"They're going to try. But that doesn't mean they're going to win." She reaches up to pat my arm. "We've got our daughter here to help us do Her work." She grins at Joren, her eyes soft. "And now She has you as her champion, our solider of the Far Away.'"

We haven't told anyone yet, what Joren and I promised in the tent. And yet somehow, Lahne knows. Sion will take this acknowledgement as an admission of treason. As for Kya... Lahne includes her too. "You have learned our music. You are part of Her story too, my daughter."

Kya nods, tears standing out in her eyes.

Sion's is perspiring, his face pale. "You won't win this. The Republic is stronger that you know."

"The Far Away men, they may be strong. But the mountain, She's been here a long time." She grins wide, showing her missing tooth. "And Hestia, She's a tough old bitch!"

CHAPTER THIRTY

Lahne knows the mountain. She has walked most of it, over the years.

Today she leads me to a sheltered valley hidden between jagged peaks. A stream flows from an opening in the rock, a bush of lehua flowers on its banks. This place feels enchanted, an oasis away from the rest of the world. We settle down next to the bush of lehua flowers at the edge of the stream. I trail my fingers in the water, waiting for her to speak.

She reaches over to pluck flowers from the lehua bush, laying them carefully at her feet. "The lehua flower is a gift from the mountain. It is said that the blossoms are born from her fire, from her blood." She begins twisting the stems together, weaving them into a chain of scarlet flowers. Her nimble fingers work quickly, and soon she has joined the flowers into a garland, like the one she wore when I first met her. "The Mother, She told me to make this for you." She sets the wreath in her lap, fixing her keen green eyes on me. "She has called you. But it must be your choice to answer. If you take it, then you're one of her daughters for real. It's not a costume that you put on for play."

I had already agreed to accept this duty when I accepted the power from Her in the ceremony. This is just an acknowledgement, the final step. I nod solemnly, bow my head. "I accept this honor."

Lahne places the wreath of red flowers on my head. When I look up, she's smiling, her green eyes shining in her lined face. "You brought the gift?"

I reach behind me, opening up the wrapping to uncover the urn of glazed clay. It holds the coal from the sacred fire of the city. I didn't know at the time why I had felt compelled to take that coal. "Why does She want this, Lahne? There must be a reason."

"Reason? There may not be a reason, but there is a purpose." She rises to her feet. "Come. We must bring it to Her."

I scramble to my feet, following Lahne up a steep path to the mountain peak, holding the urn close to my body. She walks steadily over the rocky terrain as I struggle to keep up.

The air gets hotter as we climb, the path steeper and rougher, until finally we arrive back at the cusp of caldera. We are once again looking down into the pool of fire, watching the mesmerizing flow of magma within.

Lahne stares down into the caldera, her eyes lit by flame. "What you carry with you in that jar is your inheritance. It is what was given by your father and your mother, by your people... your duty as a woman... your hearth."

I feel a curious tenderness for the urn I am holding, for all it represents. It was not hearth and home that I rejected when I left Hestia, only the limits of who I was allowed to be.

"The hearth is a sacred duty," she continues, echoing my thoughts. "But it is not all that a woman is given to create. She is meant to be a partner in the creation of the world. She must take back her rightful power to renew the balance of life." She looks up at me, her gaze fierce. "Are you willing to join your hearth with her cookfire, to give it into Her keeping?"

Her cookfire is the place where the world is made. This is not a destruction of my hearth, but an enlargement of it.

I hold the urn aloft over the rim of the caldera. "I am willing."

"Then She is ready to receive your gift."

I tip it over.

The coal falls into the lake of fire below, sinking into the molten lava, absorbing with a hiss. A jolt of energy flashes from the lava and moves through my body as quick and powerful as lightning. Something flashes in my mind, gone before I can fully see it. An image of Hestia, but different. How it will look when it has been transformed. I try to remember what I saw, but it's gone.

"She has accepted your gift."

I just stand there for a moment, absorbing the energy, taking it all in.

"What happens now?" I ask.

She turns away from the caldera, beckoning for me to follow.

"Now," she says, "we begin."

*   *   *

On the eastern side of the mountain, all I can see are grasslands stretching out to the horizon. The wind moves through the grass in undulating patterns, like currents in a stream. In the distance, a herd of wildebeests are grazing.

Lahne is perched on a large rock, her feet gripping as agilely as a mountain goat. "The power that She has given you, it does not belong to you. You must know this. It was borrowed. You must only use it for the purpose it was intended for. If you try to benefit yourself, to cause harm to anyone, it will hurt you."

"I wouldn't do that, Lahne," I assure her.

"That is easy to say now. But this power can be seductive. It can confuse you. Make you think it's for the good when it's really for selfish means. That's why it must be used in the right spirit."

"But how do I know, then, that I am in the right spirit?"

"Do you remember how it felt when you were with Her?" she asks. "When you were on the journey?"

During the trance of the ceremony, I'd felt endless, uncontained, launched beyond myself. "I wasn't a 'me,'" I answer haltingly. "I was part of everything."

"Yes." She nods, as if she knows how it was. "You are part of everything. It is from that awareness that your power must be used. Only to benefit all the creatures of Hestia. Otherwise, you cause harm."

This cause of harm is making me nervous. "But what if I don't use it right? If I don't remember?"

She ponders my question for a moment. "What is one thing, one detail, to remind you? Something from when you were on your journey?"

I close my eyes, try to remember. The songs of the mountain people. I heard them singing when I was lost. *Joren hovering over me, calling me back*. And I saw the streams of light weaving through the world. They were what connected me.

"Do I tell you?" I ask.

"You keep it yourself, to remind you when you need it." She bends down and picks up a large red rock, hefting it in both hands. "Now... what is this?"

There must be a trick to her question. "It's a rock."

"From the outside, yes." She smiles. "But I am asking, what is it's true nature?"

I am at a loss.

"To discover this, you must use the power She has given you. She is part of everything that is of the mountains. Now, you practice."

"Practice? Now?" I don't know what she expects me to do.

"Just remember how it was in the ceremony, how you entered into the communion with Her."

I try to remember what it was like. Everything got fuzzy, and then I just dropped down into it. Or with Joren, when I could sense what he felt. It was the same.

I look off into the distance at the endless plains, letting my eyes unfocus. I feel the rocky soil under my sandals; the warm breeze on my skin, gently moving the tendrils of my hair; the drifting of the clouds above; the subtle, silent drumbeat of Hestia and Her rhythms.

I can feel a pulsing now, beneath my feet, from the flow of lava under the ground as it slithers through the rock. I can feel my awareness expanding, but slowly, like gently rising water. There is a humming, almost inaudible, like a vibration, like the sounds of the priestesses and their chanting lulls.

My awareness moves outward, farther from the mountains. I sense a disharmony. Something is out of tune.

The beasts here, they are wrong somehow. No, not wrong, just different from the song, out of balance. Another song has made this creature. "This is the life that was made from the Far Away." I realize.

She nods. "It will tell you its nature. It will tell you what it needs to be."

I hum inwardly, connecting with the beasts.

"You don't force the change. You just remind them of their original nature. Then the change happens naturally."

Something changes in them. The song is changing them from the inside. They are in tune with the song now, with the mountain.

"That is enough, my daughter." Lahne says.

I gradually withdraw my attention until I am back to where I am standing, exhilarated. "I did it, Lahne!"

"Yes, you have begun." She peers at me, an emotion on her face that I can't name. "You may need to be ready soon, my daughter."

Before I can ask her what she means, she gets up and starts walking back down the trail to the village. "Now, let us get back for a meal. And maybe you can share it with your soldier?"

She chuckles as I follow her down the mountain.

CHAPTER
THIRTY-ONE

Outside my tent, the low chirping of birdsong wakens me from sleep.

Thrk-thrk. I raise myself up on my elbow, listening carefully. I know that call. And it's not from any Northern bird. Simon and I used to signal each other with that call back when we planned to sneak out after dark.

Thrk-thrk. The call is coming from just below us.

Joren is asleep, his arm thrown across my stomach. I carefully extricate myself from his embrace, then slip out of the tent.

The moon, bright and full, illuminates the mountain, a stark landscape of light and shadow. In the darkness just down the ridge, a row of bushes provides the only likely shelter. I clamber down the mountain toward where I last heard the call, pitching my voice to a low whisper. "Simon?"

He emerges cautiously from the bushes, his eyes wary, keeping himself in the shadows of the hedge.

"What are you doing here?" I whisper.

He inches out into the moonlight. "I came to tell you something—" His voice trails off as he looks behind me.

I follow his gaze to where the drape of the tent has been pulled open. Joren steps out. His chest is bare, carved starkly by the moonlight. He is barefoot.

Simon's face tightens as he takes in Joren's state of undress, realizing what that means. I tense, expecting him to say something, but he only shakes his head.

Joren pulls on his shirt and his shoes and clambers down to us. He joins me at my side, sliding his arm around my waist.

Simon nods, acknowledging the unspoken communication. "I can tell you both, then. Maybe your commander can help."

"What do you know?" Joren demands.

"The Patriarchs, they're heading here now," Simon answers. "I'm just ahead of them."

Suddenly, I feel it. An energy disruption coming up the mountain toward the village.

"They're here!" I scream. It's too late. The warning came too late. "They're coming up the mountain."

*   *   *

The Southerners charge up the hill, a moving wall of young men, their white clothing bright against the dark landscape of stone and brush. A handful of older men hang back, protected by the wall of young men grappling with the herdsmen.

The herdsmen brandish their spears, but then one of the Patriarchs pulls out a stunner. He fires, felling several of the herdsmen. The young men push through the hole in the herdsmen's defense, advancing brutally upward.

"Let them come," Lahne stands proudly at the front of the village. "They think they can conquer Her, wipe out Her fire. They're wrong."

"Lahne, get back," I yell, running to her.

Lahne allows me to tug her into retreat as the Patriarchs crest the hill, gathering in an angry mob on the plateau before us. The wall of young men parts as a senior Patriarch pushes his way forward, his face contorted with rage.

I know that face.

Lucas, my eldest brother, has aged since I last saw him. His strong body has thickened with age, his black hair and beard colored with touches of silver, like Papa.

"How..." he sputters, his eyes widening in recognition as he scans my face, "What... what are you doing here?"

The last time we saw each other was when I was being marched away by the Patriarchs, bound for the Capitol and the Vestals. He and Papa had decided my fate together. He must have known that I wasn't dead. I'm sure that Papa must have told Lucas, at least, the truth.

Simon steps out from behind the crowd of herdsmen gathered around us, facing Lucas in challenge. Lucas's face twists in rage. "Traitor! You brought her here! You warned them!"

But the men behind Lucas have no patience for talk. They're pushing forward, restless for action. "The witches! Burn the witches!" one of them yells, and the others rally the cry.

Lucas tuns his back on us to face the army of young men, raising his voice over the tumult of the crowd. "This world has a poison in it." The men's cries settle down, listening intently. "It's been here always, from the very beginning. And now we know why. It lives in these evil mountains." He turns, his arms stretching out to encompass the village. "It comes from these witches and their dark powers. They corrupt good women, make them do unnatural things." He's looking at me now, his eyes accusing. "They leave their hearths. They abandon their duties. They act like men. Our ancestors, the first Patriarchs, they had to put an end to it."

The crowd of men are yelling things, ugly things, priming for an attack.

"You're wrong," I yell, stepping forward. "The herdsfolk are saving us."

Lucas's lip curls in disgust. "You're one of them!" He points directly at Lahne. "This woman is a witch! She's raised this unholy fire to destroy us all. She must be stopped. Take her to the fire! Destroy her!" Lucas surges toward Lahne, men massing behind him.

"No!" I stand in front of her, protecting her with my body. Lucas lunges at me, and I quickly pin him to the ground. He may outweigh me, but he's no match for my Legion training.

The crowd of men surge forward.

Joren pulls Lucas to his feet, his blaster held to his temple. "Keep coming and he's dead."

The men stop, looking uncertainly between us.

"Traitor," Lucas hisses. "You made your choice a long time ago when you betrayed your family, abandoned your hearth."

The hearth. The hearth fires. That was it! That was what I saw in the vision!

The realization hits me like lightning, rattling me to my core.

They've been lying to us. All this time, the Patriarchs have been lying to us.

"You knew." My voice quavers, shaking with rage. I clear my throat, projecting my voice across the crowd. "All of you, you've always known."

I point, accusing, at Lucas.

"I saw it. In the ceremony." I look to Joren, to the others. "There were blockages in the South. Little isolated sparks, where the women's hearths are... Don't you see, they've known since the beginning! The first Patriarchs, they knew about the power in the North since we first settled on Hestia."

Secrets. So many secrets. From the beginning, they have hidden these lies. They knew. They knew about women's power.

"That's why you kept all of us women at our hearths. You were keeping us away from this, from the power that the herdsfolk know about. You've kept the herdswomen up north where no one sees them." The men are restless, angry. But so am I. "You controlled us, Lucas. You made us small."

"We gave you what you could handle!" he spits. "We kept you safe."

"You kept us tending to our little hearths, when all this time, we were part of something so much greater." I raise my arms, the fire flaring around me. "This, the source of creation."

"You're one of them! The witches!" The cry rises from the crowd, echoed by angry grumbles. The men try to push forward again.

Joren fires a warning shot into the air. "Stop! In the name of Republic!"

The men stop dead.

"The GRIP is here!" Lucas yells. "You have called them in, just as we feared." His eyes squint, his mouth twisting in rage. "She's a witch. She must be burned!"

But the men gathered around him are frozen in place. They know what Joren represents, the power of the GRIP. They won't fight him, won't risk bringing down the wrath of the GRIP on Hestia.

A standstill. Neither of us know what to do next.

A roar fills the air. A terrible, familiar sound.

A TX freight lander. The GRIP is here.

"They've brought the GRIP down upon us," Lucas screams. "Run!"

CHAPTER THIRTY-TWO

The Patriarchs had turned and fled at once, a frantic rush of bodies, falling and trampling down the mountain like a landslide. The herdsfolk retreated, moving swiftly to take shelter in the caves. The rest of us are still standing here in the open, watching as the TRX lander circles the village.

"Go!" Joren yells, gripping Simon shoulder. "I'll stay with her."

I push him toward the stream of mountain people seeking shelter in the caves.

"I'll come back for you," Simon yells to me as he joins them.

Sion looks hopefully up at the Legion vessel, Kya by his side.

"They may attack first," Joren yells at Sion and Kya. "Take shelter in the caves. That's an order."

Sion and Kya reluctantly agree, fleeing with the villagers.

Lahne is still behind me. "I must stay," she says calmly. I'm fine with that. I don't know how I can do this without her.

The compact Legion ship circles over the narrow mesa, seeking a landing spot on the uneven volcanic rock. We huddle together, watching the ship's descent. The craft lowers down, a hiss of exhaust marking its landing. Its exterior weapons swivel to focus on us as the landing ramp unfurls and the capsule door whisks open.

"Nice to see you again, commander." I recognize that gruff voice. Darla saunters down the ramp, a blaster on her hip and a smirk on her face. Her eyes move to me, hard with malice. "And I see the little traitor is with you."

I want to get revenge, just one solid hit, but Joren grabs my elbow, jerks his chin toward the gangplank. Five more armed guards stand at the ramp, their weapons ready. "I wouldn't say that *I'm* the traitor," I spit. "You must have gone right for the Legion the minute you hit that relay station."

"What do you want, lieutenant?" Joren asks, wary.

"It's not me, commander. It's Admiral Sennon." Her sneer is pure poison. "He wants you taken in. I told him that you've been lying about this mission from the start."

Joren's eyes dart to the turrets mounted on the ship. "Fine. Take me in. The rest of them can go. They're not important."

"I don't think so. He's going to want to punish this one too." Darla grabs me by the neck and pins me against her body, her blaster pressed to my temple. It's embarrassing how quickly she does it. I can feel Joren's rage, but all he shows outwardly is a cold composure. "I know you'll follow orders if you don't want your precious little witch getting hurt." Darla's attention moves to Lahne. "And who is this, one of the natives?"

Lahne looks to Darla and then at us, a look of stupefied confusion on her face. "No understand," she says, playing dumb.

"Can't hurt to have another hostage," Darla says, tightening her hold. "I'll follow you, commander."

The troopers at the ramp focus their weapons on us as we walk single file up into the craft, Joren in front. They shove us into a large freight lift, and the armed troopers encircle us. Darla spins me around and shoves me into Joren so he is pressed up against my back and Lahne is squeezed to my left. I can't see Joren's face. No way to even try to plan what to do. Lahne meets my eyes, curiously calm.

The lift rises smoothly to the next level. The doors open, and two of the guards grab Lahne by the arms and push her ahead of them out of the lift.

"Where are you taking her?" I demand, pushing against the restraining hands of the guards, trying to reach her. But the lift door closes in my face.

"Relax, she's just a prisoner," Darla grins, malicious. "She'll get out when we're done with you."

I twist around, looking back at Joren, but he warns me with a glance, *Don't make trouble.*

The lift continues upward.

"And you, commander," Darla sneers, "You're about to meet someone who'll put you in your place." Joren glares at her, cold and contemptuous. That seems to make her even more angry. "You had everything: the Academy, the rank, and you threw it away for these outworlders."

Joren says nothing, his eyes flickering to me, but I can't get a read of what he's thinking.

The door to the lift opens. Darla shoves me in front of her. Joren walks out before the soldiers can nudge him forward onto the bridge.

A man is standing at the helm, watching us approach. He wears an immaculate Legion uniform, his muscled arms crossed over a powerful chest. He looks like he's about the same age as Joren. His blond hair is cut close to his head, Legion-style. He looks handsome but in a brutal way, like a predatory animal. His eyes are focused on Joren as prowls toward us, an ugly grin on his mouth.

"Bruin." Joren spits out the man's name. "I should have known."

I remember that name. Bruin was the boy that Joren mentioned, his rival at the Academy. It looks like Bruin's animosity toward Joren is still alive and well.

"It's been a long time, Conrad." White teeth flash against a tanned face.

Joren nods tightly. "Since the Conflict."

"And look at you now. The great Conrad Joren, chosen son of Patria, battalion commander of the Twelfth Fleet…" He prowls closer. I see something frightening in his glacial blue eyes, something cold and pitiless. "I've got orders to take you back to the Core. The admiral's not too happy with you."

Joren shifts, moving his arms in front of him, subtly shifting his weight. "I'm sure you had something to do with that."

Another gloating grin. "Lieutenant Darla had some interesting things to tell me. You did know the Admiral hired her to keep tabs on you?"

So it was no accident that we had the bad luck of having Darla. She had been Admiral Sennon's minion all along.

"Is this the outworlder?" Bruin asks, shifting his focus to me. "The one who's been causing all this trouble? The admiral wants her back at Central Command for punishment." Bruin reaches over to grab my arm, but Joren knocks it away. "Oh." Bruin grins wider, looking me over in a way that combines a leer and contempt. "So that's how it is! I didn't believe the lieutenant when she reported it. I always thought you were too 'honorable' to break the code against fraternization. But it's true, isn't it? You're fucking the little witch priestess."

"Shut up!" Joren growls.

"You were always trying to help the weaklings, Conrad. You never had the strength for the kill."

A flash of memory hits me, from Joren.

A younger Bruin, holding a boy's head underwater. Young Joren races down the hall and knocks Bruin to the ground. The boy sputters, gasps for air. Bruin and Joren grapple and Joren pins him down. Bruin grabs a metal chair leg, bashing Joren on the side of his head. Joren falls, bleeding. The boy jumps on Bruin, defending Joren. Together they pin Bruin to the ground, pummeling him until he surrenders.

I can feel both of their emotions…Joren's, of nauseated horror. And Bruin's, of hatred and humiliation.

"A solider only kills when he has to, Bruin. Not for fun. That's what you never understood."

Bruin shoves his face at Joren's. "And whose side are you on? It better not be these frigging savages." Bruin stalks over to the control console. "We're going to teach the natives a lesson, about what happens when you lie to the Republic." He pulls up the weapons array, a look of barbaric joy on his face.

"Stop it!" I scream. "You can't do this!"

"It'll be just like Thea." His eyes are fixed on Joren, hungry for his reaction. "Thea was the best, wasn't it?" Joren frowns, confused. And then his jaw drops open, his eyes wide. Bruin smiles at Joren's reaction. "Didn't it feel good when you gave the order and those stupid colonists got blown to dust?"

Bruin. He was the traitor, the one who ruined Joren's career, his future, his conscience.

"I always wondered who turned me in. It had to be someone in the chain of command."

"You were going to let them humiliate us! A bunch of outworlders!" He snorts in disgust, turns back to the weapons console. The missile array is primed. Bruin lifts a finger, ready to launch the first volley.

Joren lunges at him, but the guards wrestle him to ground before he can reach him—five against one. I run to him, but they pin me to the floor too. I'm crushed by the weight of the guards on my back. A hand grabs my hair in a painful grip, yanking my head up, just as Bruin releases the first volley of missiles.

Within moments, the missiles hit their targets. Pieces of the mountain are blown apart, people fleeing from the caverns like ants. Structures are burning, people running and screaming for cover. I can feel their fear, their pain. Not just of the people this time, but the pain of the planet itself. I can't let this happen again. I won't.

A surge of rage explodes out from my body like a shock wave. My blood burns like lava. My breath is poison.

The weight of the guards' bodies is gone. The guards are backing away, their faces terrified, incredulous. I stand up, unsteady. Joren is on his feet too. He's backing away, palms up. He looks terrified. "Vesta, you're burning up!"

I can see my reflection in the mirrored wall of the bridge. My black hair is glowing red. My eyes shine like they're on fire. I look like the goddess Herself, the one I saw in my dream.

"She really is a witch!" someone yells.

Bruin is crouched by the weapons console, horrified.

He fears me, I rejoice. *He knows that he will pay for what they did. But the fire... It burns! It burns!*

Beneath us, the planet seethes in revolt, the crust breaking up with founts of lava and steam, the lands collapsing all around the village. Deep crevasses open in the firmament, devouring the trees and the grass, hungry and insatiable.

My rage was supposed to turn on Bruin. But it's out of control. The power is hurting the mountain people instead.

The planet is burning, breaking apart, and so am I.

And the destruction is spreading. It's traveling south now, spreading its chaos, opening fissures in the ground, tearing up the landscape. It's reaching the grasslands, the farmlands. Soon it will reach the Capitol itself.

"Save them!" I scream. "Make it stop!"

In a blur of movement, Joren runs toward Bruin, tackling him to the ground. At the edge of my vision, I can see them grappling, struggling for control. The ship is shaking too, the deck shifting beneath us, the guards struggling to stay on their feet.

The missiles may have stopped, but the destruction has not. The planet is being ripped apart. But now it's my fault, my doing. I can't stop it on my own.

Lahne, I need you!

I search for her, following her energy trail through the ship, but she is no longer in the brig. Somehow, she has escaped the guards. And she's fled to... the engine room?

This shouldn't be possible. No human could withstand the temperatures and radiation inside the engine room. But neither should a human be able to stand at the center of a volcano, to breathe its heat and fumes. And Lahne has withstood all of that. It seems that an engine room can't kill her either.

She stands before long columns of glass, glowing inside with blue energy. Her arms are raised in the same way she stood at the caldera. She holds a ceramic container in her hands, like the urn that held the sacred fire from the city. I know what it contains—a burning ember from the fire of the volcano itself, from the Mother's cookfire.

Lahne, I cry. *Help me.*

She turns. Her face is lit electric blue from the columns of energy. *I can't help you, my daughter. You have your work to do, as I have mine.*

A wave of terror moves through me. I don't know what to do.

She turns back to face the energy columns. Then she opens the lid of the urn.

Jagged bursts of energy shoot from the columns, striking the ember in Lahne's hands. The energy flashes through her like a lightning strike. Her muscles seize, then go rigid. But she holds steady.

She's a conduit, I realize, between the ship's engines and the energy from the mountains. Somehow she is connecting Her power and the power of the ship.

The lights in the columns shift from blue to purple. As the colors shift, the energies of the engine room begin to shift, the vibrations moving through my body like music, like rhythm and harmony.

The engines of the ship are singing! The tones that I heard on Hestia, when Lahne taught me how to listen, are in harmony now with the ship engines. The ship is now carrying the song of Hestia mixed with its own frequencies. The tones of the Far Away are still there but subdued. The voice of Hestia, of the original song, can now be heard, felt.

I open myself to its frequencies, allowing my body to be filled with its energies, to be attuned to its blended harmonies. The anger is fading away. I am cooling down.

I make myself translucent inside, so that the song can travel through me. I am a conduit now too, like Lahne, and the energies are traveling through me like a live wire, like an instrument of song... down, down to the surface of Hestia, to the priestesses, to the mountain, to the firmament, to the myriad creatures below. The priestesses receive the song, amplify it. Their voices, their drums, their flutes, are all joining in. Their voices are chanting, singing now. And the energies are not just music but a song, a story. The song is telling a story that I could never hear before. But now I can discern its meaning.

They are saying... this is the story of our world, of us. This the story that was interrupted so long ago, back on the homeworld. This where we left off, went astray, and now the original story is restored, can be sung, lived, finished.

The energy of the song is like thread, a ribbon of golden light that weaves everything together. It's like stiches, sewing the seams together again. The song is mending the tears in the web of life, healing the cracks in the world, making them whole and in harmony again. The animals, the grass, the trees, the insects, all of life joins in. All the tones together, balancing each other. It's grounded and safe and contained, like a lute in perfect harmony.

This is what we are bringing, it says. We are bringing the balance back from a song that has been out of tune. It needed all of us together, to have our separate notes in harmony. I couldn't have ever done it myself. We are all part of this, together.

Lahne, can you hear?

I reach out to Lahne to share this joy.

The engines are singing the same song as Hestia. But Lahne is not singing. She is burning up. Like I was burning, but her burning is not stopping.

She needs to cool down, like I did.

I try to channel the music to her, to balance the fire. But it can't reach her. She is burning all the way into ashes, her energy being consumed into the Far Away.

Lahne, no, you can't go. I can't lose you too.

I scream, but there is no answer. There is no Lahne to call to, not anymore. The conduit that was Lahne has been consumed.

All that remains is Her, the energy from the mountain, blended with that of the ship.

I can see where She is going. She will travel to wherever the ships travel. She will go to wherever humans live to bring them back into balance. Hestia is just the beginning.

This was Lahne's purpose on this ship, to bring Her energy to all the human worlds. She meant to sacrifice herself. She knew what she was doing.

The song is fading now. I can't see the engine room or hear the music. I am losing touch with the planet's surface, with the priestesses there.

I am on the bridge of the ship again. My body is so cold.

Warm arms wrap around me, bringing heat, comfort.

"What happened?" My voice is rough, sore.

Joren leans back, scanning me. "You were burning up. I couldn't get near you."

I look around. The bridge is empty except for us. "Where's Bruin?"

His face tightens. "He's dead. I had to kill him."

I feel halfway there myself. "And the guards?"

"They'll be in the landing bay trying to get off the ship."

That rouses me from this stupor. "We can't let them do that!"

"Why not?" he asks, frowning.

"Because this ship needs to go back to Republic space. There's something that Lahne put into this ship. It needs to reach the Core worlds, and it can't do that without a full crew."

He doesn't ask me any more questions, just goes to the navigation console and sets a course. I follow him to the landing bay, moving slower than I'd like. The other crew members are already gathered there, ready to flee, but they back away when they see us.

"Get out of the pods," Joren yells with authority. They scramble out, but they're looking at me, not Joren. We don't need a weapon to make them comply, not after what they saw. "This ship is functional again," Joren announces, his voice carrying across the small landing bay. "I've set a course for this vessel to leave Hestia immediately and to rendezvous with Legion forces when it exits this district." The crew looks at each other, surprised but relieved. They must have expected to be executed. "You have seen what happened to your commander. I would advise you not to make trouble." From the terrified looks on their faces, none of them look likely to disobey.

Joren leads us to a vacant escape pod and opens the cockpit. I pause before I follow him in. They're all still watching me. I turn to face them, raising my voice. "Go tell them what you have seen." It's my voice saying the words, but it feels like the message comes from beyond me. "Hestia is a free world now."

We close the cockpit door, and then launch from Hestia's surface.

I hope this is the last time that I will ever leave it.

CHAPTER THIRTY-THREE

"I could have killed them."

The damage to the village is on full display from where Joren and I are standing, high above where the weapons struck. Most of the dwellings have survived the upheaval. The tents, with their flexible frames of leather hide and poles lashed together, were able to sway and bend with the movements of the earth. But the fresh gashes in the ground show clearly where the lava flows and tremors broke the land apart. Those were my fault.

"But you didn't."

Joren's reassurance doesn't ameliorate the guilt about what could have happened, what almost did.

"Only because Lahne helped me, by what she did in the engine room. Because the priestesses were able to help direct the energy. If they hadn't done that, I would have…" My voice trails off. Lahne told me that the power from the mountain was only to be used for the good of all, or it would cause great harm.

"Lahne saved us." I choke back a sob. "And I couldn't save her."

The dam breaks. Ugly, racking sobs pouring out from inside of me. With a muffled oath, Joren gathers me in his arms.

"She's gone," I keep saying as I'm ripped apart, each wave stronger and deeper than the last. And Joren's warm, strong body is all around my pain, helping to hold me together, making it safe to feel. He doesn't back away, just holds me until it passes.

I lean against his warm strong chest, inhaling his scent, my arms wrapped loosely around him. I'm so tired, emptied out. I take a step back, and he loosens his hold.

I look up into his face to find his brown eyes searching mine. "I know what it's like, Vesta. Questioning your judgement. Wondering what could have been different." His forehead is creased with concern, with a pain he knows well—from Thea, his own battlefield. "Every choice has a cost. Lahne made her choice. And you did too." He gives me a gentle shake. "Whether you can see it or not, we made it because of you."

It may not be absolution, but it helps. It will take a long time, maybe forever, to get over what happened here today, but we won't have that much time. Because the GRIP will be coming back, eventually.

"What happened up there?" I ask him. "You said Bruin was dead."

"I knocked him down. You saw that," he says. I nod. "He ran to the landing bay. Tried to get a small ship so he could escape. I got him before he could get in the craft. We fought." His jaw tightens. "He fell."

I don't regret what happened to Bruin, but I do regret that Joren was the one who had to do it. He has paid a price too. "I'm sorry about all of this," I say. "That you can't go home again."

He shakes his head. "I was never going back." He cups my face with his palm. "Now I have a reason to stay."

I've been lucky. I never thought I would say that, but I have. Because everything I've done has taken me to this moment. And I can't imagine not having all this—Joren, Hestia, Kya, the mountain people... home.

We stand like that for a while, just holding each other. I know we'll have to go down into the village soon. But I just want this moment.

I hear someone calling out. As they get closer, I recognize my name.

Kya is running toward us. In the tumult of the last few hours, I haven't even had time to think about whether she and Sion were all right.

She barrels into me, enveloping me in a hug.

"Thank the goddess you survived!" I say when she lets me go.

Sion trails along behind her, his clothes covered in streaks of dust. He looks older and frailer than before, his already pale face ashen.

"Commander." He nods to Joren, but he doesn't even acknowledge me.

"We took shelter in the caves," Kya says, looking askance at Sion, "but they started shaking. Sion got hit by a few loose rocks, but he's fine."

That only leaves Simon unaccounted for. "Have you seen my brother? Simon, the younger one?"

"No, we didn't see him. But that doesn't mean anything. There were so many people in there. And so many caverns. He could be anywhere."

She's right. He's probably just lost in the crowd. But I won't be able to relax until I know he's safe.

Sion walks over to the edge of the mesa, looking down on the devastation below. The scar of a recently sealed crevasse cuts through the edge of the village.

"This is more damage that I would expect from a few weapons," he says, shaking his head. "It looks like lava flowed through here."

"It did," Joren answers.

Sion's eyes widen in shock. "It's true then. The volcanism process has restarted itself." His eyes shift back and forth frantically, as if he's searching for an answer.

Sion may not believe me, but Kya needs to know, so I say, "It's not random, Sion. It wasn't an accident. It was me. Well, the power of the mountain, but I was channeling it."

The look he gives me is a mixture of pity and contempt. "You really believe that don't you?"

I can't blame him for not believing me. What I'm telling him goes against everything he believes to be true.

He turns to Joren and Kya. "The whole planetary system is in danger of collapse. We need to get off this planet... now!"

I need to explain, whether he believes me or not. "It's not collapsing, Sion. It's being remade. Hestia is stable again. She's taking her new form."

"Stable?! You can say that, after all this?" He waves his hand, indicating the damage.

Even now, I can sense the subtle humming all around me, the symphony of energy that is Hestia. But Sion can't sense it. He can only believe in what his devices and his thoughts tell him. He only knows one half of the whole.

"The mission is over," Joren says, putting his hand on Sion's shoulder. "You should take the wagon to the Capitol. Get the next ship off-world."

"Finally, someone is making sense." But then he frowns as he realizes what Joren just said. "Commander, aren't you coming?"

Joren's hand grasps mine, our fingers intertwining. "I think you know that I'm not."

Sion looks me up and down, his eyes catching on the embroidered herdsfolk leggings and tunic I'm wearing. Joren wears a similar pair, a farmer's tunic. Sion must think I've corrupted Joren, turned him into a traitor. He shakes his head, then turns to Kya. "Come on. Let's go." It takes a moment for him to realize she isn't following.

"Sion, I'm staying."

He looks shocked. "No, you can't do this! You're throwing away your whole career, your life, and for what?"

"You're wrong." Her eyes are alive, excited. "I've experienced something here that I've never felt before. That's what I'm here to learn."

His shoulders collapse. "But… what about your family?"

She takes a shaky breath, as if holding back tears. "I'm going to miss them, but they don't need me. They still have each other." She clenches her elegant fingers into fists. "Anyway, I'm doing this for them. What's happening here is what's going to save them on Cava, and all the other worlds. I'm not sure how, but I know it's true. Maybe I'll even get to see them again someday."

My heart is breaking for her. She must know how unlikely that is. The GRIP will never let her go back.

"Go back, Sion," she says gently. "Cara is waiting for you. Your kids."

"I hope you know what you're doing," he says finally.

He climbs into the wagon, then closes the door. The wagon powers up, then starts moving down the mountain.

"Do you think he'll make it off Hestia?" I ask, watching the wagon move away. The GRIP will be monitoring the space port closely. No one will be allowed to leave Hestian airspace without their consent.

"He will," Joren answers. "He'll be a valuable source of intel for Command."

Kya snorts. "Not that they'll believe anything he tells them."

It's true. What's happening on Hestia is outside of their ideas of what is possible. They'll be looking for any other explanations.

"What happened up there, Vesta?" Kya asks, her voice gentle.

"Lahne, she gave herself up. To the energy of the mountain." It hurts to say her name, but it helps too. I have to honor her sacrifice. "She brought the mountain with her onto the ship, and then she transmitted it onto the ship so that what is happening here on Hestia can be brought to the other worlds. So the Mother can save their systems too, prevent them from failing."

The Legion doesn't yet realize what they are carrying. They are bringing the seeds of change, spreading it to all the worlds, bringing not destruction, but renewal.

"It's funny, really," Kya says after a moment. "All this time we thought we were fixing things, making them work again. But it was just the opposite. What we thought were problems were actually the solution."

Joren nods tightly. "Well, the Patriarchs certainly don't see it that way. The GRIP will want to track down the Patriarchs to interrogate them about us, if any of them survived."

The last thing I saw of the Patriarchs was them fleeing downhill during the attack, Lucas among them. I hope that Lucas made it. Even if he betrayed me, he's still my brother. And I need to find Simon too. The last I saw of him, he was fleeing to the caves.

We walk down the hill and back into the village. The mountain people—*my* people now—are putting their tents back up, digging through the rubble for their possessions.

A man dressed in Northern clothing is crouching by the village hearth, his dark hair mussed and covered in ash.

Simon. We rush together, embracing. I pat him all over, checking that he's real.

"I took refuge in the caves," he tells me when we finally break apart.

"And Lucas?"

Simon looks down for a long moment, then shakes his head. "I haven't seen him. He was with the Patriarchs when they all rushed down the hill. That's where the landslide hit. The whole mountainside came down on them."

He couldn't have survived that. None of them could.

Was it my rage that made it happen, I wonder? Was it the spinning, out-of-control power that made the mountainside crumble? Or was it the missile launched by Bruin? I have no way of knowing. I'm not sure if that makes it better or worse.

"Simon, this isn't going to end here. The GRIP will be back."

He nods, solemn. "I know. And I'll help you if I can. But I need to get home and check on Rachel and the kids."

"Go home, then. We'll be back there soon. Maybe a week. Once we get things settled here." I smile. "I can finally meet your kids."

"Yeah." He grins shakily. "I'd like that."

He looks over at Kya and Joren, his eyes narrowing at Joren, standing at my side. "And you're staying too?"

Joren nods, a slight incline of his chin. "I think I can make myself useful. For what I know about the Legion's battle tactics, if nothing else."

Simon looks at him suspiciously. "So it doesn't have anything to do with my sister?"

"I wouldn't say that," Joren answers evenly. "Although I'd say that's up to her."

"Hmm," Simon responds. "I guess that's true. I never could tell you what to do, could I, sis?" He gathers me in for a hug, holding on tight. "I'll see you back home." Then he extends his hand to Joren, offering it for a handshake. "Both of you, I guess." That's about as much of an acknowledgement that I'm likely to get from my brother that Joren has been accepted into the family.

"Bye, sis." Simon mounts up on his gray mare and heads slowly down the mountain.

*   *   *

We find Raina in the village helping the people to sift through the rubble, pulling out remnants of shelters and supplies that were felled by the earthquake. She stops when she sees us coming, greeting us with a weary smile.

"You have decided to join us," she says to Kya.

"Can I help?" Kya asks. "I'm good at fixing things."

"The main lodge needs some repair," Raina accepts gratefully.

Kya heads back to get her tools.

"Come with me," she summons. "I have something for you."

Joren stands there as I start to follow her.

"You too," she says to Joren.

We follow her a short distance to a cave, its entrance covered by an animal hide. Inside the small cavern, the area is lit by lamps. Raina digs around in a basket by the wall.

"Lahne wanted you to have this." She offers me an embroidered bundle of fine cloth.

I gasp as I unfold it to reveal the ceremonial robes of a priestess. "These belonged to Lahne. This was her gift to you."

"But how did she know?" She would have had to set these aside, tell Raina before we were taken prisoner on the ship, before the GRIP ever arrived.

"She knew enough to bring a piece of Grandmother with her onto the ship. So the Mother can bring life back to other worlds, bring back what they lost."

"Lahne said to me that we were one people, once. The farmers and the mountain people. That means the Southerners are a part of this too."

"Not just them. It's going to be all of us, all the worlds, together."

It's hard to believe that all the worlds of the Republic could transform so completely. But what I've experienced so far has been miracle enough.

"And you." She holds out a small object wrapped in soft hide, offering it Joren.

He opens it carefully. Inside is a small dagger, inlaid with polished stones, the blade carved from obsidian. The hilt has a design of the lehua flower inlayed.

"Joren, you are a now warrior of the mountain people. This is your gift from Grandmother mountain."

He takes it by the hilt, turning it to feel the weight of it in his hand. "It's a precious gift, but I don't know how I would use it when the GRIP comes back."

"Your courage will be useful to Her, soldier of the Far Away," she answers. "Now, you will be a warrior for peace."

He nods his acceptance, tucking the dagger into his belt.

"We have our solider of the Far Away and our priestess of the mountain." Raina has a gleam in her eyes as she looks between us. "A very auspicious mating." She leans into me, presses her hands to my belly. "The Mother, she's got one more gift for you."

She can't mean—

"You have a baby inside."

"But that's impossible! The implant…" The implant should have prevented pregnancy. I've never heard of it failing at that task.

I place my hand on my flat stomach.

"She is part of both of you," Raina says.

"It's a girl?" Joren asks. He looks shocked, shaken.

She nods, smiling. "A daughter of a daughter of Hestia, and of a son of the Far Away. A granddaughter of the mountain."

Joren places his warm hand over mine, on my stomach. His eyes meet mine, a look of wonder on his face.

I should be scared by this. But I'm not.

"What do you think?" I ask him.

"It's a hell of a time for a child to be born," he says slowly. He's blinking, tears standing out in his eyes. "*Our* child."

I think I have my answer.

Raina withdraws quietly, leaving us alone.

"Are you really OK with this?" I press.

He takes a moment to answer. "It's sooner than I thought."

"Wait, you thought about this?" We can't have met each other more than a week ago.

He chuckles uncertainly. "As soon as I realized how I felt about you… yeah, I did. Although I didn't think we'd live long enough to make it real."

Something could happen to this baby. That would be so much worse than anything happening to me or Joren.

"Don't worry." He squeezes my hand in his. "We'll protect her. Both of us."

"And we have everyone here." The villagers, and the priestesses, would never let anything happen to this baby. Nor would Grandmother, from her place in the mountain. Although she won't be contained to the mountain for long. Already, she is spreading her energies south. And, in the Legion ship, beyond Hestia.

"Yeah, we do."

We're not in exile anymore. Either of us. We have a home. Together.

And we have a world to help build, a better world than what came before it. A world in which I can be who I was meant to be. A world in which everyone can play a part.

"We should go out and help."

He nods his agreement. "As long as we get to share a tent tonight."

I grin wickedly. "I don't think that will be a problem." As tired as I am, I miss being with him, our bodies intertwined in the dark.

He draws the drape aside, and I walk through. We stand together at the cave entrance, watching the work of the villagers as they rebuild. Kya is among them with her bag of tools, helping to rebuild the frame of the main tent.

We are all part of this work, I realize, *all part of the change that is coming.*

It started with the mountain people. But it will expand to the farmers and the Capitol in the South, to the outer worlds, to the freeworkers, to the rebels, and to the center of the Core Worlds. We will all be part of this transformation, this renewal, despite our apparent differences.

All this time, ever since I left Hestia, I thought that my life was out there. I thought I had to get away from my destiny as a woman, that I had to be strong, independent, and alone to prove my worth. And maybe I did, for a time. But I had to come back home to find who I really was, what I was meant to do.

And now I've found it. With Joren and the mountain people, and all the others on Hestia. And now, for our daughter. For the world she will inherit.

We are all here for a reason. That's what She taught me. We all have something essential to offer this world. No matter who we are.

And it's going to take every single one of us—the farmers and the mountain people, the outworlders and the privileged, the cherished and the forgotten—to make this world complete.

CHAPTER
THIRTY-FOUR

I am growing strongly now within my mother.

Grandmother brought them together, called them to weave themselves into a strand, with me as one of the knots. I can feel the presence of Grandmother in my veins, my lungs, my heart. I can see my father looking into my mother's eyes in love, holding her. I can see her trusting him, them standing together.

I know that the others are coming, my father's people. They are coming in their big ships with their clever minds. They are coming to make my Grandmother, my whole family, all of us, prisoners.

But they aren't as clever as they think they are. They have clever minds, but they are only half-grown. My father's people didn't love him like my mother does. And my mother's people, they have kept away the power of Grandmother, of women's power. They don't know that Grandmother is everywhere, not just on this world, but she is becoming part of all their worlds, all of my father's people's worlds.

We will go out to meet Grandfather. He is the ruler of my father's people. He does not know Grandmother—he denies her. I have the knowledge of all that my father knows in my cells—all he knows of the human history from old Earth. Grandfather thinks that he can make life all by himself, from his cool mind. But Grandmother is coming out to meet him, to change things.

I am her inheritor. And we will make life grow again, in love.

Look at that tree, that branch, with its ripe red fruit. That is the true tree of knowledge. It has been waiting for us, to return us to where we came from. We are going home.

ACKNOWLEDGMENTS

This book would not be published without the help of Rachel Carter, writing coach extraordinaire, who shepherded me through the process of writing and publishing this novel. In a twist of fate, we also share the same birthday.

I also want to thank my husband, Daniel Bixler. When I told him I could write a book, he encouraged me to go for it.

Also, thank you to all the authors whose books are in the Sacramento public library, where I first learned to love reading.

ABOUT THE AUTHOR

Marcella Strang Bixler grew up reading science fiction paperbacks and borrowing her mom's romance novels. Her first love was Han Solo, and she wanted to be Princess Leia. As a result, all of the books she reads (and writes) have to include a fantastic adventure and a good love story.

Marcella now lives with her husband and two daughters in Arcata, California, where she serves her community as a psychotherapist in private practice.

Daughters of Hestia is her first novel.